THE END TIMES

OF

MARKUSZ ZIELINSKI

THE END TIMES OF MARKUSZ ZIELINSKI

KEITH STEVENSON

First published in paperback in Australia in 2025

by coeur de lion publishing

www.coeurdelion.com.au

© Keith Stevenson 2025

www.keithstevenson.com

cover artwork and design by coeur de lion

Print ISBN 978-0-6457466-5-5

Ebook ISBN 978-0-6457466-6-2

A catalogue record for this book is available from the National Library of Australia

TO SCIENCE.

THE ONLY WAY WE'RE
GETTING OUT OF THIS MESS.

Prologue

Helena was worried. She was worried about the region of space their ship was approaching. She was more worried about the ongoing destruction of the universe. But the thing that worried her most was Markusz. His relationship with the rest of the team had hit rock bottom. Or maybe somewhere beneath rock bottom.

Case in point: the latest in a long line of arguments with Teel, the project leader. Although Helena was – in no small part – to blame for this one.

"What do you mean we're doing another drone test?" Markusz said in that tone he'd perfected that not only implied the subject of his enquiry was an idiot but that it was a fact carved in stone. "There's no more useful data to be gained from a drone. We need onsite calibration of the annulus, fine-tuned to direct readings inside the Effect area. We're due on Redout in a month with a cast-iron solution and this won't get us it."

Teel glanced Helena's way and she concentrated on her augment window. He'd promised and she was determined to hold him to that promise. Thankfully, Teel was as good as his word.

"I hear you," he told Markusz. "But I've decided. I want one more drone test before we commit a team. There's another Effect due in a week within range. We can calibrate onsite then."

"It's probably a better option," Rachik – second in Markusz's team – offered, and Helena appreciated him going in to bat for her. "It'll be sm—"

"If I want your opinion, I'll ask for it," Markusz snapped.

Helena cringed. Time to cut this short.

"Okay," she said, placing a hand on Markusz's shoulder. She could feel the tension there; he wasn't such an arsehole under normal circumstances. "If it's a drone shot, you don't need us. Come on, Markusz. You've been working around the clock. Get some rest and the data will be waiting for us in the morning."

"Much use it'll be," Markusz grumbled. But he let her turn him towards the door.

Teel nodded at Helena as they left. She felt like a traitor.

Out in the corridor, the ship was in night cycle. Gold cherubs looked down at them from the shadows – somewhat reprovingly, Helena fancied – as they walked to their stateroom.

"Markusz …" she said.

"I know. I know." He at least sounded regretful for his outburst. "It's just –"

"*I* know," she said, taking his arm in hers and pulling him close. "You take on too much. You haven't been to bed the last two nights. Forget about all this for one evening and get some *rest*."

She palmed the door open and led him to the bed. He sank down to sit on the mattress edge. Poor thing was dead on his feet.

He kicked off his shoes, and she helped him with his cravat and blouse, and he lay on top of the bedcovers and sighed deeply. She pulled a blanket over him and leant down to kiss him on the lips. A normal kiss, like any of the dozens they shared in a day. She didn't dare anything more.

His eyes opened sleepily. "You're not coming to bed?"

"I've just got a couple of things to switch off in the workshop," she said. "I won't be long."

She waited in the doorway until his breathing settled into a steady rhythm. Then she left and took the elevator to the shuttle bay.

Teel and Rachik were waiting for her. Teel's glare was particularly reproachful.

"I'm really, *really* sorry," she said. "Thank you for keeping your promise, Teel. And thank *you*, Rachik. I'm sorry he spoke to you that way."

"*You* have nothing to apologise for," Rachik said.

"But he is *insufferable*," Teel said.

She nodded. "He is. He's the insufferable genius that created the annulus. Something that none of us could have achieved without him."

Teel raised an eyebrow. "You're so sure of that?"

"I've worked closest with him and I am. Just as I'm sure we can't risk him on a calibration mission. If we lost him now, none of us could finish the work."

"And he wouldn't let you go without him," Teel said. "I understand, but –"

"But in the meantime, he *is* insufferable, yes. But when this is over and he allows himself a breath, he'll realise how badly he's treated you. Both of you." She smiled. "We'll save the universe together. Then we'll look back on all of this and we'll laugh. But first …" She looked towards the shuttle.

"The calibration mission," Teel said. "The ship is prepped."

"Five hours there, two hours onsite at maximum, five hours back. And still thirty hours before the Effect hits," Helena said.

"He won't be happy when he finds out you went without him," Teel said.

"I know. But by then I'll be on my way back to *Endeavour*. Get him to call me when he wakes. I'll take the brunt of it."

"Be safe," Rachik said.

She kissed him on the cheek and he drew back a little, shocked. But what the hell. They'd been colleagues for eleven years.

"See you in twelve hours," she said.

Keats turned in the pilot's seat as she entered the shuttle. Originally from Alba, he was the same age as Helena but a dusting of freckles across his nose and cheeks made him look like a pubescent youth.

His lips twisted in a wicked smirk. "Have you charmed the dragon to sleep with your feminine wiles?"

"Don't make me laugh about it. I feel bad enough." She strapped into the seat beside him.

"I don't know if all this subterfuge is worth how pissed off he'll be when he wakes up," Keats said. "We're going to be perfectly safe."

"He's too important to the project to lose."

"Aye." Keats's smile was kinder now. "And he's too important to you."

Keats piloted them through the atmosphere envelope and set them on course for Hesione, the outermost moon of the Deucalion System settled by the Thousand Worlds only a century before.

"Best speed," he said. "Just time for a decent nap."

"If only."

Helena opened an augment window and read the sensor feeds from *Endeavour*, rearranging and tweaking the outputs to her liking.

Deucalion was the eleventh collapse she'd observed directly and so far it looked textbook, though on the smaller end of the scale. The area of space involved was twenty-three light years wide and fluctuations in quantum particle creation and destruction were elevated everywhere. The uptick had commenced simultaneously right across the region in a non-local way. Everything about the Effect was non-local. Markusz believed that was due to a remnant of entanglement across the Effect area from the earliest inflation period of the universe. Not that it really helped them work out how to stop it. But he was a completionist. He liked to have an answer for every aspect of a thing.

She sifted more data, looking for something atypical in the readings, but everything was steady and by the numbers – if those terms could be applied to something that annihilated space in a way that broke every physical law established by science over two and a half millennia of gradual progress towards understanding the cosmos.

Two hours in and nothing on comms. Markusz was sleeping soundly.

Even though Helena couldn't sleep, she did feel at rest.

Thoughts came and went and she let them, not really engaging.

Deucalion System was laid out before her. Four planets. The outer two gas giants, both haloed with orbital mining rings supporting massive extraction needles that thrust down into the cloudy atmospheres even as far as the molten centres to sup up precious elements. The inner two worlds were completely settled; though the millions of inhabitants had been evacuated on two highliners a month before and were well on their way to Redout. Even so, the twinkling lights of continent-spanning cities showed on the night sides. Cities of ghosts now. Nothing there but the memories of the people that had called them home.

"Coming in on the moon," Keats said.

She shook herself. Maybe she *had* fallen asleep.

She opened a window to *Endeavour*. Rachik appeared, looking as tired as she felt.

"We're about to land," she said.

"Everything checks out here," he said. "I'll let you know the moment that changes."

It was clear from Rachik's demeanour that Markusz still hadn't surfaced. Good. He deserved the rest. And maybe he'd be a bit more forgiving of the others when he did wake.

The moon was a declared wildlife sanctuary for the indigenous flora and fauna. Even though its atmosphere and mild climate made it entirely liveable, it had been deemed too small for a colony world. Keats brought them down to a cleared and fenced area that had been used by a rotating team of botanists and zoologists. The windows and doors of the main structure and ancillary buildings were all shuttered, the facility mothballed for a return that would never occur.

As the lock opened, Helena smelled rich, loamy soil and a jumble of animalish scents.

The ramp to the hold at the rear of the shuttle extended and Keats trundled a case – half as tall again as he was – onto the landing apron and clear of the ship.

An alien whooping echoed from the pine tree analogues past the fence line. They were safe enough behind the fence, but Helena activated the annulus cradle's protective field out of an abundance of caution and the world beyond the force wall took on a bluish, hazy cast.

Keats undogged the latches and the casing fell away. The annulus floated free above the cradle, a colourful spectrum extruded like toffee and twisted around itself into a mobius strip. This was the visible projection of the mathematical transforms Markusz had wrought. There was far more to the annulus, reaching deep into the magnetic, strong and weak nuclear forces, gravitational wave forms and down to the quantum level. A unifying synthesis that achieved the impossible. Or would do when it was perfected.

Helena and Keats stood opposite each other with the annulus between them. She raised an augment window, linked it to Keats's and opened a channel to *Endeavour*.

"We're starting now," she said on comms.

She nodded to Keats and he keyed the initiation sequence while she monitored the substrate. The annulus rotated slowly counterclockwise then backtracked before reversing again, zeroing in on the key resonance driving the quantum particle uptick. It stopped turning as it locked on and Keats brought the annulus up to full operation.

That's when the readings in Helena's window uniformly trended into the red.

"Keats," she said.

"I see it. Shutting down."

"What's happening?" Teel asked.

The readings were getting worse. She flipped to Keats's window. The annulus wasn't shutting down. She looked up but the sky above was a cloudy daytime, hazed by the shield.

A window opened from *Endeavour*. A view from beyond the edge of the Effect.

Space was melting.

"Get out of there," Teel said.

Then she heard Markusz. "What's happening?"

He sounded as bewildered as she felt.

Then he shouted. "Teel! What the *fuck* have you done?"

1

Sylfe Cachand stood at the penthouse's windowwall and stared out at Redout. This apartment – much like her own in the adjacent tower – sat atop one of the older buildings in the Palisades, a suburb named for the barrier the early settlers built against the high UV and borderline poisonous atmosphere of this world when it had been known as Garia. But, she reflected, there wasn't much of *that* world left now.

The view was completely urbanised. Buildings crowded against each other like rival trees jostling for space and sunlight, covering the river valley her building overlooked and burying the far-off coastline beneath pontoons. There were underwater dwellings too. Since the establishment of the Redout Project, there wasn't much of the planet's 1.6 billion square kilometre surface that wasn't being actively developed – not to mention the network of tunnels and underground cities the Corps d'Ingénieurs had built under the direction of Ernes Fontaneau's Destruction sur Commande SA, the biggest terraforming company in the Paradisan Combine.

The atmosphere had, of course, been reprocessed long ago, but as for the high UV – well, that was something SolEng SA, Sylfe's own family's business, was working on, along with a few other tweaks to the local sun.

Redout was the biggest humanitarian effort in history. And for the last three years Sylfe had served as a member of the project's governing council while directing solar operations. Fontaneau was council head, and both he and Hugo Denantes – the only other Paradisan council member – kept apartments in the Council Tower.

She'd been offered one when she'd first arrived and promptly refused. She could think of nothing worse than bumping into either of them in the corridors.

Sylfe took a final look around the salon to check everything was in order and gestured a comm window open. The edges buzzed with static and echoes of exotic energy. That wasn't normal, and she couldn't help thinking it was some portent of the Effect closing in on them. It deepened the anxiety she'd been feeling ever since the evacuation of Paradis had been scheduled. She just wanted it over with. She wanted her family here. Safe.

The interface cleared and Adele Cachand – her mother and Matri of the Great Family of Cachand – and Sylfe's sister, Yvette, appeared, both sitting in the summerhouse judging by the view of the family vineyards behind. The setting sun picked out the red highlights in Yvette's hair. She looked like a slightly younger twin of Sylfe. Just as Sylfe looked like a much younger twin of their mother. Both sisters had been born by parthenogenesis. It was their mother's thing. She'd never found a partner she considered her equal.

"Sylfe!" Yvette's smile was as sunny as usual, and Sylfe stifled the surge of relief that threatened to overwhelm her. She didn't want them to know how much she missed them.

"Sister. Maman," she said. "Is this how you spend your days when I'm away?"

Yvette raised a glass of wine to her. "We eat, drink and are merry while you slave at thankless tasks for the common good."

"And is Suzanne carousing with you?"

Yvette's smile dimmed. "No, she's more like you. She's still at the hospital getting patients ready for evacuation. I've barely seen her all week."

Sylfe's augment threw the data up in her field of view. The GH highliner was en route and on schedule to arrive at Paradis in eight days. That gave them a full month for evacuation to Redout, and another month's safety margin before the Effect was predicted to hit Paradis.

"Where exactly *are* you?" Adele asked, peering into their shared comm window.

Sylfe smiled. "You recognise …?"

"I recognise my own salon in the main house, but … You're not here. Are you?"

"I wish I were. I've had the furnishings fabricated to exactly match your rooms. The bed chamber and en suite too. Everything as you are familiar with it. Smaller of course, but I want you to feel settled when you get here."

"That's very thoughtful, my dear," Adele said.

"And what about me?" Yvette asked.

"You, dear sister, have an apartment beneath mine in the next building. But it's a blank canvas. I thought you and Suzanne would want to furnish your first home together."

"You're looking after yourself?" Adele asked. "Eating regularly?"

Sylfe gave the rote "Yes, Maman" monotone response she and Yvette had developed for such maternal inquiries, which Adele ignored.

"*And* keeping out of trouble? I don't like to think of you at the mercy of Fontaneau."

"I'm hardly at his mercy," Sylfe said. "If anything, he's at mine."

She'd been spying on the Patri of the Great Fontaneau Family from the moment she'd arrived on Redout. Unlike the other Great Families, who had sent their ablest – or in Denantes's case most embarrassing – children to aid the Redout effort, the Patri had chosen to come in person. That alone was enough to make Adele Cachand – and Sylfe – suspicious, even without Fontaneau's long record of shrewd and devious business dealings.

"Though," Sylfe continued, "it's worse having to be in the same room as Denantes."

Yvette shuddered and refilled her glass. "That mental image demands another drink."

"They're both terrible people," Adele said. "But at least Denantes wears his ugliness on the outside."

"It will be a relief when M-Gov arrives to take over," Sylfe said. "In the meantime, the *Endeavour* group are nearly here."

"That's good," Yvette said.

"Maybe, but Fontaneau has been in regular communication with the project head, Teel. More so than you'd expect from even the council chair. He's *really* turning on the charm."

"He's up to something," Adele said.

Sylfe agreed. "I've stepped up my surveillance."

"Good. I'll see what other intel we can discover from this end," Adele said. "Fontaneau doesn't suspect you're spying on him, does he?"

Sylfe shook her head. "Not in the slightest."

"Well, be careful. It sounds like you're in more danger than we are."

"I'm not going to do anything stupid."

A voice called out and Yvette put down her glass and half-rose. "That's Suzanne. Do you want to say hello?"

"No," Sylfe said. "I'll talk to you later. Enjoy your evening. Love you both."

"Love you," Adele and Yvette said together and the connection ended.

Sylfe went to the bureau and poured herself a glass of wine, silently toasting her mother and sister. They were safe and they'd be here soon. And together they would face whatever came next.

2

"You're thinking too much."

"Hmmm?" Markusz focused past the image of his face in the mirror – he'd acquired far too many wrinkles around the eyes and mouth for his liking.

Helena was in bed, her black hair and pale skin a strong contrast to the faded gold of the brocade headboard. Faded and pretty threadbare too actually. This was one of the lesser accommodations on the Cooperative Sciences and Technology Organisation Task Force ship *Endeavour*. They'd had a far more sumptuous room on the upper decks, all giltwood and marble, with big picture windows out to the infinite. But that was before ... Before.

"*Thinking* too much," Helena repeated.

"There's nothing to think about." He concentrated on tying his cravat again. "This is the culmination of everything we've worked for. Now – *finally* – we start." He gestured and an augment window opened beside the mirror showing Redout's sun clearly visible now, the brightest star in this remarkably unremarkable part of space. "Our new home. Or ... it would have been."

"Don't." She was behind him now, her face clear over his shoulder. A broad, open face, green eyes alive and liquid, her dark brows drawn together.

"Don't worry," he said. "I'll be fine."

She smiled. "You really won't. And you have to watch Teel. Don't piss him off."

"Huh. He should worry about pissing *me* off."

"You said it yourself – this is where it all starts. Teel joined the

Task Force right at the beginning twenty years ago, and he's led it for the past sixteen. He may not be as brilliant a scientist as you – "

Markusz snorted gently. "There's no 'may' about it."

"But he has political nous. He's a survivor. He has to be to still be project lead after everything that's happened."

Markusz felt the hot flush of anger again. "A lot of which *he* caused."

"I'm as much to blame for that as he is," Helena said.

She was right. But he didn't like to think about that.

He finished his cravat as best he could and pulled on his justacorps, adjusting the collar and turning up the cuffs. He wanted to make the best impression possible. Show Teel everything was fine.

"How do I look?"

"Like the man I married?"

He grimaced.

"Too painful?"

"You know it is."

The engine tone – heard and ignored for so long on this voyage – shouldered into his consciousness as it shifted pitch. The ship was decelerating, but they couldn't be there already.

He still had passive access to the bridge feed. The augment window shifted to show a much closer view of Redout space with multiple views. Central was an "over-the-shoulder" image from the Master's seat, looking past the navigation stations to the main display, which was flanked by external views forward and aft.

The *Endeavour* was slowing up behind a ship that would dwarf something fifty times its size – one of the Galactische Handelsonderneming highliners pressed into refugee service. To either side and behind them, the volume around Redout space was overwhelmed with vessels of all designs and sizes, stretching as far as Markusz could see.

Helena, Markusz and the others had been on the *Endeavour* for years, chasing the Effect and running their experiments, all under the constant pressure of news reports from those parts of the

Thousand Worlds that were being evacuated ahead of a predicted collapse. But this was the first time Markusz had seen the human impact of that unfolding in real time before his eyes. Redout was the final destination for so many whose homes no longer existed.

The rough armada of vessels was ranged along some invisible barrier, perhaps simply a stipulated distance from Redout's sun. As the highliner moved past this dividing line and into the clear space beyond, Markusz saw what was holding the other ships back: M-Def battleships. Massive elongated spearheads, studded with weapons pods and emplacements along their central spines, with singleship ports and booster strips open along the sides. Markusz had no idea how many were deployed, but enough to hold back the sea of refugee ships and maintain some kind of order. For the time being at least.

The Master ordered *Endeavour* forward but, as they picked up speed, the ship began to heel over. Bottles tumbled from Markusz's dressing table as artificial gravity strained to catch up. A klaxon shrieked in the corridor and the bridge view blanked, replaced by a "transmission paused" card, but the external views were still live.

Markusz saw something streaking towards *Endeavour* from behind, like a silver fish through water. Beneath the klaxon's steadily rising whine, the ship groaned as its engines struggled to push it onto a new course away from the incoming missile. There was no way they could move fast enough. It was going to hit.

Then two "somethings" streaked in from the left of the window and the missile blossomed into fire. Markusz shut his eyes against the glare. When he opened them again a singleship shot past from the direction of the M-Def picket line, through the expanding flames, swerved with course-correction, then fired a single burst from its nose cannon.

Its target – a nondescript mining ship – was clear because the ships around it must have started distancing themselves as soon as the missile was fired. There was a brief flash near the ship's engines and then it began to drift. There was nothing to indicate why it might have fired on them, though Markusz suspected frustration or desperation may have played a part.

Then the bridge view was back and the Master was speaking to the ship.

"Apologies for the sudden manoeuvres. I trust nothing has been damaged," he said. "M-Def assure me there will be no further trouble and we will dock at Redout in a little over a day."

The long gallery on the very top deck of *Endeavour* was all fluted columns topped with chubby infant statuettes. It was much better lit than below. Cleaner too. The ship had been a pleasure cruiser before the Task Force acquired it, which somehow made it far easier to plot Markusz's descent: from first class to somewhere just above steerage.

Teel had explained it as a temporary move. Time for Markusz to take a step back. Process what had happened. So he'd processed. As far as he could, anyway. But, beyond that, Markusz couldn't help feeling that Teel was behind every little slight and indignity he'd endured since the mathematical paper he wrote ten years ago brought him to the Task Force's attention. Helena was right. Teel never stopped playing politics.

The intricately moulded gilt doors to the drawing room opened at Markusz's approach. Teel stood in front of the large picture windows that looked back along their direction of travel. Much of the visible sky was missing, replaced with the spectral red blossoms of Teel-Attar radiation. The universe was dying. They'd watched that death play out across space for over twenty years — though it may have been going on for much longer than that. Now it was time to do something about it.

Teel had his back to Markusz. He was a tall, thin old man with a pronounced dowager's hump obvious from this angle. He dressed in the same style as Markusz — they'd both been raised on Respaxon, though Markusz had been brought there as a child, and their upbringings had been very different. The cut of Teel's justacorps was far more severe, accentuating his thinness like a stick insect.

He didn't turn when Markusz entered. Instead he said, "We've achieved much together, Zielinski."

The obvious retort was, *I've achieved much while you took the credit*, but Markusz bit down on that. This was the moment he took back control. Teel could administrate to his heart's content, but the real work lay in Markusz's hands.

Then he noticed there was someone else in the room with them. Rachik, lounging on a chaise along the back wall. He smirked at Markusz.

Teel turned, finally, and indicated a chair at the long table. "Please."

Markusz didn't feel like sitting. So they both remained standing while Teel observed him.

"How are you feeling today?"

The faux concern was calculated to rankle him, Markusz knew that. Again he avoided the obvious reply. "Ready. The annulus is primed. Once we've made our presentation to the Redout Confederation Council, I'll oversee installation and make the final adjustments to bring it up to full operation. There'll be a settling-in phase, but with the data we got last time," he chose his words carefully, edging around the pain, "and the additions I made to the theorem as a result, the dimensional harmonics are better than they've ever been."

"I agree," Teel said. "Rachik does too."

Why the hell should he care what Rachik thought?

"Your work has been brilliant," Teel went on. "After the last test, the changes you made were nothing short of inspired. You have given us – all of us – a real chance. But that work is done now."

Markusz snorted. "Done? Who the fuck's going to run the thing?"

"Rachik and his team are more than able."

If Teel had slapped him, Markusz would've felt no different. "No, no, no, no, no," he said and slipped the leash on the anger he'd been holding back. "You don't get to make that decision."

"The fact is, I have," Teel said. "You're erratic. Which means you're unfit to control our only means of survival."

They couldn't take the annulus away from him. It was all he had left. Markusz looked to Rachik but saw no help there.

The door opened and two M-Def officers entered. Security to lead him away.

"Apologies, Ind Zielinski," the officer who took his arm said.

Markusz felt numb.

"You know," Teel said, "I'd intended to send *you* on that test. It was Helena who convinced me otherwise."

"That's a lie," Markusz said. But even to his own ears, he didn't sound convinced.

The M-Def officers deposited Markusz back in his room, bowed and left.

"That could have gone better," Helena said.

Markusz sank onto the bed. The sound he made was somewhere between a laugh and a sob.

"What Teel said. Is it true?"

"How could I tell you? I'm just your memory of me."

Helena sat beside him, her hand resting on the tapestry bedcover a finger-width from his own. For the thousandth time he wished he could lift her fingers to his lips.

He looked into her eyes and thought about their last kiss. Was there something in it that should have alerted him? Had it been longer? More passionate? Charged with an emotion he didn't understand? If it was, he'd missed it completely.

Instead, he'd woken to an empty bed and the news that something had gone badly wrong. As soon as the annulus was activated, it had triggered the collapse. Accelerated it even. Helena was dead and … His memories didn't make sense after that. Not for some time. But he knew there'd been a blazing row with Teel and he'd had to be restrained. Sedated.

After that, a period of intense work. He'd forced himself to read the data from the test. Every detail of Helena's death. And he saw it. He *knew* what had gone wrong. And he knew how to make the annulus work this time. Helena's sacrifice would not be for nothing.

He'd perfected the device. It was their crowning glory. But she was still dead. And he had to learn to live with that, even though he didn't understand it. If what Teel said was true, why had she done that?

The chime of an incoming message sounded. He gestured and an augment window opened. Message from *Endeavour*'s Master, but it was Teel's handiwork.

"This is to confirm you are to be confined to quarters until journey's end," Helena read over his shoulder. *"Your lab privileges are revoked and all other accesses are set to minimum."*

"When we reach Redout, I'm off the ship *and* off the project." What the fuck would life be like with his patronage revoked?

"They can't do that," Helena said. "They need you."

"Teel doesn't see that. But others might."

3

Markusz imagined some kind of scuffle. Security would have to drag him kicking and screaming from the ship and everyone would know how he'd been wronged. But in the end it was all very quiet. The two M-Def soldiers unlocked his room, one picked up his bag, the other nodded amiably to him, and they walked together out to the promenade and down the gangway to the dock. The first soldier deposited Markusz's bag at his feet, then both saluted and walked back onto the ship.

Markusz stood for a while, looking up at the vessel that had been his home for the last ten years. The only home he and Helena had shared together. Far back towards the stern, gantries and cranes slid into position along the dock and began to cut and pry at the superstructure. Massive pincers peeled back the skin of the ship and lasers cut into the subframe. This would be the last voyage of the *Endeavour.* There was nowhere else to go.

Markusz sat on his bag and felt the full weight of a world of injustice settle on his shoulders. Or to be more precise, 119 per cent of that weight since Redout was almost four times the mass of ancient Earth, if only just over half as dense. To add insult to injury, his augment – which had failed to keep up with the reality of his dismissal – reminded him he had thirty minutes before he was due to present the annulus to the Redout Council. Imagining Teel smugly taking the credit for his and Helena's work was enough to make his blood boil.

The *Endeavour's* gangway became crowded as more and more crew and support staff debarked for the final time. Markusz recognised some of the technicians and cleaners, but he didn't know their names, their histories, their hopes. The project had been like a pressure cooker. Everyone focused on their jobs with one, shared goal in mind: find the cause of the Effect and stop it. Nothing else had mattered. There wasn't time for small talk, making friends. At least that's how Markusz had felt. Though somehow he'd found the time to fall in love with Helena.

The steady stream of people reached the prow end of the dock and queued at three large cargo elevators. A sign above them read *To the Refugee Centre*. Markusz knew what was expected of him: follow everyone else deemed surplus to requirements and disappear. Live what life was left to him quietly. Survive as best he could on whatever Refugee Management provided. They'd been taking in refugees here for over a decade. And still more waited at the heliopause or were on the way. How many more could Redout take? And how would they feed them when supplies from other parts of the Thousand Worlds dried up?

Seeking distraction, he stood, turned away from the ship and leaned on the handrail at the edge of the dock. At this elevation, he looked across the tops of towers and skyscrapers. Smaller and clearly older buildings were in the minority, dwarfed by newer and far taller constructions, many bearing the lustre of hull-metal cannibalised from earlier ship arrivals. Looking down, he couldn't see the bottom of the buildings. If there were streets at surface level they were lost in the gloom.

"Grim place," Helena said, leaning on the rail beside him. "You don't belong down there."

Markusz wondered why he still imagined she was here. Perhaps he didn't have a choice.

"Of course you have a choice," Helena said. "I'm here because you want me here. Even if you don't understand the reason."

"It's because I love you. I miss you."

She looked at him. "Is it? Maybe you're just lonely. You were lonely when I met you."

"I was always alone."

"You were always *lonely*. It's a different thing."

"I know." But now he was truly alone. Cast out on an unfamiliar planet with no money, no job, no idea of what to do next. Teel had engineered this. Markusz felt his anger flare again, but in truth he had played a role in his own fall.

"You're not easy to get along with at the best of times," Helena agreed.

On *Endeavour* Teel had the final say, but here on Redout others held the ultimate authority. Markusz wasn't meant to be a refugee. He was meant to be a saviour.

Far off to the left a blocky peoplemover flew parallel to the dock. His augment flagged it as for essential personnel only. He linked to the Confederation database. His privileges had been cancelled on the ship, but here he was still listed as a senior in the CSTO – for the time being at least. He sent a flag and the vehicle's repulsors flared as it turned towards him. He stepped aboard and registered his destination, then sat quickly on the plastic bench, placing his bag on the floor, as the mover took to the air again.

There were others on board. Two severely dressed men sat together on the opposite side near the front. Each wore his hair short at the sides but long on top, oiled and combed back with a precision part above the middle of the left eyebrow. The differences in their clothing were far outweighed by the similarities, so the overall effect was that they wore a uniform. Highly polished black shoes, charcoal-grey suiting (one had a faint pinstripe), starched white collars sitting above conservatively thin lapels. Each wore a small bronze badge on his breast pocket, a cursive "F". Fordana then: bureaucrats in the mighty organisational machine that enabled most of the business ventures in the Thousand Worlds. Here to apply their planning and resource management prowess to the refugee effort.

And where there were Fordana ... Yes. Sitting on Markusz's side of the vehicle and easy to miss, as the folklore went, because they held themselves so preternaturally still: Haibeu. Ascetic was the word that came to Markusz's mind when he thought of Haibeu, and these two were no different. They looked sexless. Both perfectly hairless, their faces were a study in relaxed expressionlessness, gazing out at the passing scenery. Or perhaps they were oblivious to the outside, focused instead on some internal landscape.

The mover dipped and landed on a pad near the top of one of the newer towers and two men and a woman embarked. All three wore sidearms and body armour, but they weren't M-Def. That organisation would never have allowed soldiers with full face tattoos. These were Opitauans: mercenaries who traditionally supplied security for the "Great Paradisan Families".

They sat and Markusz noticed the younger of the two men glared at the Haibeu. The tattoos made him look fierce – which was obviously the intent – but this was more than that.

"Fucking Hivers," the man said and spat on the floor.

The Haibeu gave no indication anyone had spoken.

The older Opitauan reached past the woman and slapped his younger comrade on the side of the head. "Mind your manners or I'll put you on report," he said.

The younger man didn't acknowledge him, but concentrated just as fiercely on the floor.

There were bound to be tensions with so many people from different worlds living on top of one another, Markusz thought. But he knew there was a special and widespread disaffection for Haibeu. They were quiet, polite and subservient. Or – if you preferred – uncommunicative, secretive and just plain weird. The fact, only discovered by accident, that their augments went far beyond the standard allowed by most of the Thousand Worlds deepened the distrust felt by many. The derogatory term Hivers was coined, indicating they functioned as brain-linked drones: worker bees serving some cybernetic governing module. It was uneducated bullshit. Originally the Haibeu were named the Fukei after the system they'd colonised. The Fukei government hadn't offered an explanation for the extent of their citizenry's implants. Neither did they confirm or deny the rumours and conspiracy theories that had sprung up around them. They did, however, change their trading name on the Consource from Fukei to Haibeu, which meant "hive" in their language. Perhaps they'd held on to a sense of humour despite all the changes they'd wrought on their physiology.

The mover climbed and Markusz saw they were heading for a broad landing skirt surrounding a pavilion of glass and metal that sat even higher than the dock he'd left behind. His augment tagged the main entrance and labelled the structure: *Redout Confederation Council Chamber.*

4

Inside the council chamber, Sylfe watched Fontaneau pompously introducing her fellow council members and other notable personnel to Kelan Teel, the CSTO's chief scientist, who had just arrived off his ship. Fontaneau's charm offensive indicated he obviously had some plan in mind, but Sylfe had as yet been unable to determine what it was.

Fontaneau introduced Teel to the stuffy Torhild Rask, commander of the M-Def garrison on Redout, then the innocuous Jan Pieter Leeuwin, Galactische Handelsonderneming's sector governor-general, and finally the bloodless Evan Beltran, consummate chief bureaucrat for Fordana Management Services. The CSTO scientist looked like he was having trouble keeping track of everyone's names and roles.

And then it was her turn.

"Ind Sylfe Cachand is our solar expert," Fontaneau gushed, "and an invaluable member of our little team."

Teel extended a limp hand.

Since before she'd entered finishing school, Sylfe had made a study of handshakes. Teel's spoke of a man who clearly lacked moral fibre. She resolved to watch him as closely as she watched Fontaneau.

Teel was next introduced to Hugo Denantes, who looked completely bored – social niceties were not on his list of peccadilloes – and finally to Mayor Marthe Firmin, the only native Garian on the council and leader of the planet before Redout was initiated. The mayor contributed very little to council debates and had politely but firmly rebuffed any attempts at friendliness on Sylfe's part. Consequently she remained an enigma.

Introductions over, Sylfe retired to her seat at the curved council table while Fontaneau, Rask and Teel converged at the centre of the chamber.

They spoke softly together, but Sylfe had ways of augmenting sound, particularly around Fontaneau.

"… M-Def came swiftly to our aid, but it was indeed touch and go for a few seconds," Teel was saying.

"Shocking," Fontaneau said. "The situation with the refugee ships at the heliopause is becoming worrisome. Too many new arrivals and those who have been stuck there for much longer."

Fontaneau made all the right sounds, Sylfe thought. He could be charming, conciliatory, cajoling. He could be whatever the moment required. But it was all just playacting. The real Fontaneau wouldn't experience a real emotion if it bit him. He was cold, calculating, and more than a little dead inside.

Sylfe became aware that Denantes was staring at her from across the room. His chubby features twisted into a greasy smile when he saw her notice him. He was a different type of sociopath to Fontaneau, she thought. Entirely focused on experiencing pleasure in its most insalubrious forms.

"It's regrettable we had to disable the ship," Commander Rask said, drawing Sylfe's attention back to the trio. "But we need to maintain order out there otherwise the situation will quickly dissolve into chaos."

"As above: so below," Fontaneau agreed.

God, he was so pompous. Sylfe let her gaze drift up to the sun shining through the clerestory windows. She opened a private augment feed to her SolEng sunbarques in coronal orbit. The sun, or HD68745, was an F5 V main sequence star of 1.4 standard masses. It burned hot, hence the yellow-white hue and the unhealthy amount of UV. The early settlers of Garia had erected orbital UV barriers — an inelegant but cheap solution. Sylfe's solar engineers were engaged in something far more precise on the star itself, though this was a minor element of their work. The Thousand Worlds Congress could not ignore the absolute worst-case scenario. If HD68745 did become the last sun, F5 V stars had a far shorter lifespan than the G-type stars preferred for stable system colonisation. That too could be changed. And it was why her company had been engaged.

Data proliferated across her field of view: visible light, extreme ultraviolet, infrared, seismic, magnetic, elemental and gravitational variances and flows mapped in real time from the deep core of the star to its chromosphere. Matter and energy in a constantly shifting, continually balanced dance. It was a beautiful thing, soothing the untameable.

"Thirteen years ago, the first collapse occurred inside Thousand Worlds space in the Ambergis Sector."

Sylfe blinked her private window away and concentrated on the shared data space rotating around the man now standing alone at the centre of the chamber. It seemed Teel had chosen to begin his presentation with a dip into ancient history that everyone already knew. Still, his simulations and imagery were topnotch. The main volume above him depicted local galactic space containing the entire region colonised by the Thousand Worlds – or eight hundred and sixty-seven worlds to be exact, but why quibble – and a graph beneath it showed the rising incidences of the Effect, a moving line ticking off the months and years as Effect impacts played out across the star map.

Sylfe muted her augments and the projected images vanished. She had no desire to relive a timelapse of destruction, but she knew why Teel was showing them this. He wanted to remind them how bad things were so he could demonstrate how valuable he was to everyone in this room.

She studied the others as Teel ticked down the years and events to the present day. Fontaneau looked calm as always but she knew he'd be calculating. Everything was a lever to him. Denantes looked bored. Rask and Leeuwin sat in rapt attention. Both were, in their way, totally committed to their work: Rask to maintaining order in what may become humanity's final refuge; and Leeuwin to ensuring GH ships met their schedules to evacuate threatened worlds.

Beltran had the look of a man whose attention was a thousand light years away – no doubt concentrating on some private data space of columns and numbers and completely ignoring everything else. Firmin looked more equivocal. While Sylfe had no evidence to suggest this, she imagined the mayor considered Teel just one more incomer selling something that would ultimately benefit others more than the original settlers who came here to find peace and freedom.

From her seat in the alcove nearest the door, Asymptote Eleven – Beltran's most regular factotum – looked on as impassive as ever. She was another closed book to Sylfe, like Firmin, and it was easy to forget the Haibeu was even in the room.

There was one more person in the chamber: Tane, the Opitauan chief of security. Like Asymptote Eleven and Commander Rask, Tane wasn't a member of the council, though he was much harder to miss than the Haibeu. He wasn't watching the presentation; he was watching everyone else. "Keeping you all safe" as he liked to remind them. As if any of them were really safe in the face of this destruction.

"At this point, observed collapses in the light cone totalled four and a half thousand," Teel was saying. "And all of them indicated that either time was running at an accelerated rate within the Effect's boundaries, or some aspect of it permitted super-luminal movement within standard spacetime. But it wasn't until eight years ago that we discovered the field that we believe is a significant contributor to these uncontrolled contractions of spacetime."

Significant contributor, Sylfe thought. They were still guessing at the true cause.

"By then all of our night skies were noticeably different. But we were making solid progress in understanding the fine scale workings of the Effect, which suggested a way to intervene at the substrate level of four-dimensional space."

Teel raised a hand, ever-so dramatically Sylfe thought, and all eyes focused on him. The shared data space must have closed, leaving the scientist standing beside a small table topped with a privacy shield.

"And now we have perfected that method and created a device that will save us all," he said. "The annulus."

Teel swept away the shield and floating just above the table was the most radiantly beautiful sight Sylfe had ever seen. It was as if a rainbow had been pulled from the sky, intensified and twisted into a mobius strip.

5

Markusz was the only person to debark at the council tower. He made quickly for the entrance, left his bag with the concierge and crossed the light-filled foyer towards the inner core of the building, where his augments showed the council chamber was located. Council was in session according to the data space, and he knew this was where Teel would be.

As he approached the chamber door the M-Def officer there came towards him, arm raised to slow his progress.

"Sorry," Markusz said, "I am *dreadfully* late. Ind Teel must have started by now and I'm meant to be in there to assist with the presentation."

The officer paused and Markusz saw he was reading whatever information his augment was throwing up about this newcomer. It must have checked out because he stepped aside.

Markusz graced him with a quick smile then entered the chamber. "I'm most sorry I'm late, Ind Teel and ladies and gentlemen of the council. But I see we've arrived at the good bit. The annulus. It is *magnificent*, isn't it?"

Teel, standing beside the annulus, gaped at Markusz like a dying fish.

Markusz pressed on. "Ladies and gentlemen of the council, allow me to introduce myself. I am Markusz Zielinski, your most humble servant, senior mathematician of the Cooperative Science and Technology Organisation and chief architect of the device you see here before you. A device that, with careful and precise operation, creates a null field to ensure the space within it cannot fall prey to the impacts of the Effect. A holding measure to be sure, but a necessary one, as we fortify a beachhead from which we can turn our attention to negating the Effect on a larger scale."

Teel finally found his voice. "This man is *not* meant to be here."

"Indeed, none of us are," Markusz said. "But we are more fortunate than many others. My work continues on ways to extend and augment the annulus and, with your continued support, ladies and gentlemen, I am confident the progress you see here will only be the springboard to greater things. In the face of hopelessness, we bring you hope. Now, I am eager to install the annulus and prime it for full operation. Where –"

"This man is not meant to be here!" Teel repeated.

Markusz could see he was almost apoplectic with rage.

"He no longer works for CSTO," Teel hissed. "And he has no business here."

"That's not what the records indicate."

The speaker was a woman at the far end of the curved council table. The augments told Markusz she was Sylfe Cachand, a director of SolEng SA.

"And his published work on the Effect is … impressive," Cachand added.

Markusz understood that pause. She was fast scanning his biography, assimilating his papers into her knowledge base. It was nice to have a fan.

"That's as may be," Teel said, "but I fired him recently. It was in the best interests of the project to do so. Our team is more than capable of operating the annulus and continuing his work."

"But you admit it's *his* work," Cachand said. "We don't have time to fuck around with second best."

"I misspoke," Teel said. "I meant *the* work of the CSTO, of which Ind Zielinski was an important but not irreplaceable part."

"If I might interject," said an older, rather grim-looking man.

Markusz learned he was Ernes Fontaneau, council chair, head of the Paradisan terraforming company Destruction sur

Commande, and Patri of the Great Family of Fontaneau.

"It is not for the council to interfere in the internal affairs of CSTO. Chief Scientist Teel has the full backing of the Congress of the Thousand Worlds to lead his task force as he sees fit. I suggest to the council that we let them get on with their work."

Markusz cursed inwardly but struggled to maintain an outward calm. "But that's the pro—"

"Tane," Fontaneau said softly.

Suddenly Markusz was held in the powerful grip of a large Opitauan with a particularly scary tattooed face. And just as suddenly he was through the council chamber doors and back outside.

The man — Tane — relaxed his grip and smoothed the lapels of Markusz's justacorps. He grinned. At least Markusz thought it was a grin, but Tane's expression was hard to read through the tattoos.

"Relax now, young mathematician," the Opitauan said. "You gave it your best shot. Now they," he indicated two M-Def soldiers who had appeared behind him, "will take you safely to where you really belong."

"But my bag," Markusz began, desperately trying to think of a stalling tactic.

"We'll have your bag sent along," Tane said and stepped back.

The M-Def soldiers clasped Markusz's upper arms and not-quite-frogmarched him out of the building.

As soon as the council meeting broke up, Sylfe returned to her apartment and linked to a system that was completely separate from her SolEng network and encrypted beyond the commercial security her company employed. It had to be: many of the cybernetic tools it employed were illegal.

She moved through the shells of Fontaneau's systems, turning AI-hardened countermeasures into something as tenuous as mist until she connected to Fontaneau's own surveillance network. The Patri recorded everything because he was paranoid about everything. Sylfe liked to think she supplied the unknown justification to that paranoia.

This particular file was timestamped as occurring ten minutes after the council meeting broke up. Fontaneau sat at his hideous desk – a gilt and mahogany abomination with ormolu lions and medusa heads he'd had transported from Paradis at outrageous expense. Teel entered with another man, younger, with dark skin and pale amber eyes, but just as po-faced. They were both dressed in those ridiculous long coats with wide turned-back cuffs and brocade on the collar and front. Sylfe's own scientists didn't dress like that. It must be some shared cultural thing.

"That could have gone better," Fontaneau said.

"The interruption was regrettable, but the demonstration was well-received by the council, I think," Teel replied stuffily.

Fontaneau grunted and settled his attention on Teel's companion.

"This is Rachik," Teel said belatedly. "My senior mathematician."

"Zielinski's replacement. I thought I told you to get rid of that man and then he turns up and causes a scene."

Teel looked blank. "I fired him."

"Yes, you said that." Fontaneau didn't bother to conceal the contempt he felt. Sylfe knew how he viewed those who didn't carry out his wishes to the letter.

"In any case," Teel said, rallying against Fontaneau's opprobrium, "Rachik will oversee the installation and activation of the annulus. He's my best man."

Rachik gave a short bow. "I won't let you down," he said, but it wasn't clear to Sylfe whether he was reassuring Teel or Fontaneau.

"And once it's installed, what else will it do?" Fontaneau said.

"Else?" Teel glanced at Rachik, who looked equally nonplussed.

Fontaneau let the silence grow to Teel's obvious discomfort, then he smiled. "Come now, it's a poor tool that only serves one purpose. Your former employee indicated more was possible. He spoke of 'ways to extend and augment the annulus'. A shield is all very well, but there may come a time when we have need of a sword. For our own protection, of course."

Teel again looked blank. Sylfe knew there was the reason Fontaneau gave for a thing and then there was the real reason he had for that thing. The two were rarely the same.

"Have I backed the wrong man?" Fontaneau prodded.

Seconds ticked by and it was clear Teel was suffering for lack of an answer to please his new master. His eyes shuttled back and forth between Fontaneau and his assistant.

Rachik, for his part, was beginning to realise his boss was counting on him for a way forward. His forehead glistened with sweat. Finally he licked his lips and said, "I suppose ..." But whatever he supposed was stillborn on exit.

He looked at Teel, whose eyebrows were now threatening to push into his receding hairline, and tried again. "I suppose ..."

"Yes?" Teel urged, appearing close to apoplexy.

"I ... I ... suppose the formulae which support the annulus's function do suggest certain ... novel applications that may be developed," Rachik said finally, then looked rather ill.

Teel by comparison looked triumphant.

Sylfe's augments informed her that "Rachik" meant "one who is on the right path". Well, scrub one for nominative determinism, because this poor fool was out of his depth.

"Something to keep us safer?" Fontaneau pressed.

"That and possibly other things," Teel agreed, exuding a sudden confidence that was clearly unfounded. "A number of avenues may be fruitful."

Fontaneau relaxed back into his bureau chair. "Then I suggest you get to work."

Teel and Rachik made to leave, but turned back as Fontaneau spoke again.

"And since you haven't been able to deal effectively with Zielinski, I'll have my people fix that loose end."

Sylfe closed the window. Even if she showed this recording to the others in the council – something she'd rather not do – some might agree Fontaneau was being prudent, investigating other options to stay safe. Even if he was doing it without the council's knowledge.

Regardless, it looked like Markusz Zielinski was not long for this world. Sylfe thought that was a pity.

6

The walls of another station blurred past the submover's windows. The M-Def soldier opposite Markusz swayed a little as the vehicle began a long, slow turn. She seemed to be staring straight through him but she was probably just watching something on her augments. After all, both of his escorts carried sidearms and the threat level of an unarmed mathematician had to be somewhere south of zero.

"You're in luck," the other M-Def soldier said. "The latest highliner will have cleared through processing. No queues."

"I'm overwhelmed by my good fortune," Markusz said.

Helena, sitting on his other side, said, "Don't antagonise them. They're just doing their job."

He reached for inner calm, but he was fucked if he could find any.

"I warned you not to underestimate Teel," Helena said.

"Not helping," Markusz snapped.

Across the aisle, the soldier's eyes cleared and focused on him, her hand moving ever so slightly towards her weapon.

"Pardon," Markusz said. "Just thinking aloud."

Yes, Teel had well and truly cooked him. There'd been a moment at the annulus presentation when Markusz felt he might just be going to pull it off. The SolEng director had been onside, but that older man – Fontaneau – had shut him down. It was clear now that Teel had laid his groundwork before they arrived. A political animal for sure.

The mover slowed and the female soldier stood and grasped a ceiling handhold. "Our stop," she said.

"So, you're dropping me off at processing?" Markusz said, standing also. "I don't want to take up your time, but I'd like to make a call just before that. It won't take long and it's very important to me."

The woman glanced at her partner who shrugged.

"Sure. Let's just get off the mover first."

They disembarked together and Markusz walked off a few steps for privacy. He'd tried to brazen it out and failed. Now came the grovelling, much as it sickened him even to try.

"It won't work," Helena said. She looked sad.

His augments connected with the Redout registry and he input the ident string. *Calling* flashed across his field of vision. Seconds ticked by. He threw an embarrassed smile at the waiting M-Def soldiers. They didn't seem too perturbed.

Finally a window opened and Rachik was there.

"I wasn't sure you were going to answer," Markusz said.

"What do you want?"

Not a great start, but he rallied his brightest smile. "Look, this is crazy. You know how much I've contributed to the project."

Rachik was silent, but Markusz could see that sneer he loathed hovering at the corner of his mouth. He bit down on an angry retort.

"There's still a great deal I can do," he said. "I want to continue. The safety of everyone demands it."

"Jesus, you really are insufferable," Rachik said. "Teel wanted to sack your arse when you first came aboard, and lots of times after that. But Helena always talked him out of it. She spoke up for you with all of us, and look how that ended up."

"What do you mean?"

"You were never a team player."

Team player? Massaging the egos of lesser intellects was a great way to waste time in Markusz's book. What mattered were results. But he remembered lots of occasions when he or Teel or one of the others had stormed off after a disagreement. Later, or the next day, they'd get back to work and nothing more was said. Until the next argument. He'd assumed it was because they felt like him: nothing was more important than the work. Had Helena been soothing troubled waters all along?

He didn't want an argument with Rachik. He needed help.

"Rachik, you're right. If I've wronged you –"

"Oh fucking save it, Markusz. You've burned your bridges with Teel." Rachik paused and, even through the augment window, Markusz could see calculation there. "Look, I can't get you back on the team. But that Fontaneau wants what you said you could do."

"What I… Oh the improvements, you mean," Markusz said. Perhaps he'd been embroidering the facts to make his pitch more attractive. But there was some truth in what he'd said; something he'd been mulling over since the final equations. Fontaneau, it seemed, had bought it and now Rachik needed his help. Markusz grimaced. This wasn't the time to indulge in schadenfreude.

"Yes, those and more," Rachik said, licking his lips.

Markusz realised Rachik was more than a little nervous. "What do you mean 'more'?"

"He's looking for some defensive or possibly offensive properties."

"Offensive?" Markusz wasn't sure he'd heard correctly. "The annulus is a finely balanced instrument."

"I *know* that," Rachik hissed.

Yes, he was clearly worried and now so was Markusz. They couldn't fuck around with this thing.

He glanced at the M-Def soldiers who were now staring at him intently. Time to wrap this up. "I'm just going into Refugee Processing, but with any luck they'll let me make and receive calls. Let's keep a line open."

"Wait. No, *wait.*"

But there was no time. The female soldier was walking towards him. Markusz closed the window. Let Rachik sweat on it, he thought. They couldn't make any changes until the annulus was installed and operational. In the meantime, he had other things to think about.

Markusz expected the strip up out of the station to come out on a street somewhere. Instead, after passing through an exit, he found himself inside a large, enclosed volume at the very bottom of an inverted well that towered above him. Layers of balconies receded all the way up to a distant sky-filled atrium.

"This is where we leave you," the female M-Def soldier said. "Good luck."

Markusz didn't answer. He was too busy looking at the crowds of people on this ground level who were standing still and staring into some infinite nothingness. Then his vision cut off and he was in a small cubicle with white walls, standing in front of a much older man with a welcoming smile.

Markusz blinked. Tried to reset his augments. But the vision persisted.

"Please, the disorientation will pass. There's nothing to fear," the man said. "I'd offer you a seat, but you're still standing exactly where you were a moment ago. This is a private interview space. We won't be overheard."

The man was small and dressed in a light grey business suit. His skin was deeply lined and sagging, and deep wrinkles gathered around his eyes and the corners of his mouth. But his eyes, beneath bushy white eyebrows, were alive with an amalgam of amusement and kindness.

Markusz noticed the cursive "F" badge on his lapel appended with a superscript "i". "You're an artificial intelligence," he said.

"Regulations require that when asked I confirm I am an artificial intelligence currently employed by Refugee Intake." The answer sounded rote and mechanical, but at the end of it the man smiled his sweet smile again and said, "But you can call me Safdi."

"Okay, Safdi, give me back control of my implants. Now."

Again the smile. No doubt this whole persona had been created to make the hapless refugee less fearful, but Markusz just found it irritating.

"Presently," Safdi said. "Please, just a few questions to help get you settled in. Your records …" His eyes lost focus. "You're not part of the latest highliner complement. No record."

Perhaps there was a way out of this. "That's right," Markusz said. "It's a mistake I'm here."

"Hmm, this going to be a real headache."

"Not at all. Just take down your augment control and I'll find my own way out."

"Ah, here it is." Safdi's smile was back. "Priority record from Redout control. Your Refugee Status Determination has been fast-tracked. It's all good."

Someone – possibly Fontaneau or Tane – had made sure he wouldn't fall through the cracks.

"Welcome to Refugee Reception Centre RMCZ7-8U," Safdi said. "Your stay here will be short, I assure you. There are a number of intake assessments for physical and mental health including any mandatory therapy and counselling requirements, behavioural classification to determine your best fit for resettlement, and a series of orientation activities. You'll find everything you need here during your brief stay but your augments will be geofenced to this location. I'm afraid you can't go outside unless accompanied by a refugee worker."

"I'm a prisoner?" Markusz said.

"Confinement is for your own safety as much as anyone else's. We don't want you wandering off and getting lost."

"I bet you don't," Markusz said, but Safdi seemed immune to sarcasm. "Look, I want to appeal my refugee status. I'm not a refugee."

Safdi blinked at him. "We don't get many people claiming that."

"But there's a process, isn't there?" Markusz was sure there had to be. The Fordana were consummate bureaucrats. There was a process for everything.

"There is a process. A series of forms. A tribunal and hearing."

"Well, let's get started."

"After intake assessment."

"But intake assessment is superfluous if I'm found not to be a refugee," Markusz said.

But Safdi was firm. "*After*," he replied, his smile slipping an AI-calculated fraction.

The Fordana had a process for everything, but they also had a rigid sequence for how those processes fitted together.

The room and Safdi disappeared, and for a moment Markusz was back on the ground floor with the crowd of others staring into space. Had any of them moved?

Then his vision was hijacked again and he was looking down from the atrium, descending gently in a spiral that afforded him views of the different levels. A disembodied voice accompanied the visuals.

"Welcome to Refugee Reception Centre RMCZ7-8U, your home away from home during your assessment. Redout Refugee Management is dedicated to your safety, comfort and support as you transition into our population, and this centre has everything you need to achieve that under one roof. Soon you'll begin your assessment process, but first this short orientation will tell you everything you need to know about living at the centre. On the levels you see here we have a range of dormitories, family rooms and couples accommodation with everything you need to settle ..."

Markusz tried to ignore the voice, thinking instead about what Rachik had said about Helena. To hear him tell it, the task force had been a cosy little family until Markusz turned up.

"Need to work off some excess energy or simply relax?" the voice continued. "Each level has a gym, and there's easy access to the rooftop arboretum to get back in touch with nature. As well as health and fitness, your nutritional ..."

Markusz's view shifted. Now he was at the end of a long cafeteria with rows of tables. And he knew where this was located in the building.

Helena had been on the team for a couple of years before he joined, but she'd never spoken much about that time. Would they really have gotten rid of him if not for her? And what did it say about their relationship that she'd been talking to the others behind his back? Taking the role of peacemaker when he'd never asked her to.

"You wouldn't have asked," Helena said, standing beside him. "You're too proud."

"No. I just wouldn't have given a shit."

"And the project would have suffered."

"So, what – you *managed* me, managed the others, 'for the greater good'?"

She dipped her head, looked at him through a lock of hair falling across her face. "I don't expect you to understand."

"But it set the pattern, didn't it? It meant you'd always intercede on my behalf. It made you get Teel to lie for you so you could go on the mission instead of me. It made you die."

But Helena was gone.

"Fuck!" It made sense and he resented her for it. But most of all he felt again how much he missed her. How he wished she were still alive. And how she might still be if he hadn't been such a dick to everyone.

"Please enjoy your stay and don't hesitate to contact Centre Administration with any questions or requests."

"Oh fuck off," Markusz said as his vision returned to normal.

He had to get out of here.

7

Markusz moved quickly before his augments were hijacked again, cutting through the crowd still locked in their own little augment heaven or hell.

A row of doors was set into the clear curtain wall at the edge of the building. He could see the narrow street outside and another identical wall beyond that. But as he got close his vision blanked again to be replaced by scarlet words: *Geofence warning. Exit is prohibited unless accompanied by a Refugee Worker or you have another valid reason.*

A clear rectangle pulsed beneath the last two words. Markusz activated it and a form opened up titled *Reason for Exit.* A process for everything.

He scanned down the possible options, none of which applied to him except the last one: *I am not a refugee.*

It couldn't be that easy, and it wasn't.

Another window opened, again multiple choice.

— *I am a free citizen of the former colony of Garia [birth record required]*

— *I am part of the M-Def deployment to Redout [service number, garrison and commanding officer required]*

— *I am a contractor engaged by Refugee Management or the Redout Confederation [contractor ID required]*

— *I am an employee or contractor of the Thousand World Congress [citizen ident required]*

There were no other options. He tried the last one in case his employment with CSTO hadn't been cancelled yet. But it returned a *Not Valid* warning. Then he was looking at the doors again. He may as well have been staring at an impenetrable fence.

He turned back to the floor full of standing dreamers. What now? A nutritionally balanced meal in one of the cafeterias or a peaceful walk in the arboretum?

He could see Congress was doing its best to make a bad situation as comfortable as possible. But this was still a prison on what would soon be a prison world. Even the jailers would be trapped. It could be something very different if they'd just let him do his work.

"Ind Zielinski."

Two M-Def soldiers and an officer were approaching. Perhaps the two that dropped him off had forgotten to deliver a required beating or something.

"Yes," Markusz said.

"There's been a mistake," the officer said. He was tall, dark-skinned and bearded. "We're here to take you back to the CSTO facility and get you settled in."

Finally. Someone had listened. Maybe it was the director of SolEng. She'd certainly spoken up for him at the council.

"If you'll follow us."

Markusz fell in between them but instead of retracing his steps to the underground mover, they paused at another set of doors. The officer satisfied whatever security protocol was necessary for exit, and they walked out onto a different street. A ground vehicle sat at the bottom of a short flight of steps. It was windowless, armoured and the rear sat on a half-track. It seemed an odd vehicle for the city.

Markusz slowed. "Is this —"

"Just a precaution. You're an important person," the officer said.

Sections of articulated armour on the vehicle slid up and back. The officer nodded towards the crash-gelled interior. "After you."

Markusz climbed in the back and pulled the movement restraints tight across his chest. One of the M-Def soldiers got in beside him, and the officer and the other soldier took the front seats. The armour resealed and the vehicle moved off.

The officer turned in his seat. He was holding a handgun. His face flickered. It was the same face, but now it was covered with the intricately tattooed lines and curves of an Opitauan mercenary. The M-Def soldier beside Markusz had transformed too.

"I don't mean to be rude," Markusz said, "but I get the feeling you're *not* taking me back to CSTO."

The officer just smiled.

"Where are we going? Who sent you?"

"Don't concern yourself, Ind. Just sit back and try to relax," the officer said.

"Well, that's the problem, you see. When I don't know what's happening I tend to run off at the mouth. It's a nervous tic, one I don't find easy to co—"

"Soon you won't need to worry about keeping your mouth shut ever again." The Opitauan was still smiling. "You'll be at peace. One of the lucky ones if you ask me."

Peace, Markusz thought. No more decisions to make. No regrets to add to those he already carried. Put that way, it did have a certain allure.

The car jumped, tumbled, and the armour split open. Markusz was rammed against the side wall then thrown up against his restraints. He was weightless for a moment, then the straps jerked him sideways and down as the vehicle crashed into the ground. It spun, metal shrieking as the interior broke apart, then he was sliding on his side, still fastened in the chair.

Another impact in his back and he came to a sudden halt. His ears were ringing and it was hard to focus. He blinked repeatedly, vision doubling. The vehicle was in pieces, scattered across the roadway. Someone groaned nearby.

Markusz blinked again and saw the Opitauan who'd been holding the gun lying a few metres away, also still strapped to his chair. A figure stood above the Opitauan. It wore riot-suppression body armour and a full helmet, but there was something painted crudely on its back: an open hand in a circle. The figure levelled a gun at the Opitauan's head. There was a sharp crack and the body slumped lifeless. Then the figure moved out of sight. Markusz heard two more cracks then nothing.

He slapped at his harness, fell painfully to the roadway and managed to push himself upright. There were two armoured figures now. He blinked but they both persisted. One was a lot larger than the other. Smoke drifted across the roadway.

"Hey," he shouted. "Why don't you finish the job!"

"What are you doing?" Helena was kneeling beside him.

"What do you think I'm doing? We're all going to die anyway. You're dead and this place is a fucking madhouse."

The smaller armoured figure walked back towards him through the smoke.

"I'm with them," he told it. "Shoot me too."

"Markusz, stop." Helena pleaded.

"Just keep out of this," he snarled.

"Who are you talking to?"

The voice startled him. It sounded like a teenage girl.

"My dead wife. Can we get this over with? They were going to kill me. Now you can have the privilege. Here, let me help you."

He grabbed the muzzle of her gun and pulled it against his forehead, but she wrenched the weapon out of his grasp.

"What the fuck," she said.

"Come on," the other armoured figure shouted. "We don't have time to fuck around."

The girl grabbed Markusz's arm and slapped a metallic strap on it, which wrapped tight, then pulled him upright. "You're coming with us."

Markusz felt like he was concussed. He probably *was* concussed, but this was somehow worse. His vision was crowded with glimpses, like constantly moving blindspots that insisted on being seen. Some were there and gone before he could register what they were, but others persisted for a second or two – a circuit diagram, showing pathways in different colours, some kind of race involving flyers looping through the limbs of a giant forest, an alphabetical listing of late 27th Century neoclassical composers, a treatise titled *Asymptotic Burnout and Homeostatic Awakening: a possible solution to the Fermi paradox.* He couldn't mute his augments, which made it fucking hard to see where he was being dragged. He scrambled to keep his feet under him as the armoured girl terrorist pulled him across the roadway.

He managed to raise the arm she was dragging him by. "What the fuck is this thing?"

"Scrambler cufflet. It stops you being tracked by scrambling your ident code. But it means you pick up random augment feeds for the codes the scrambler cycles through."

Markusz lost the battle with his footing and slammed against the road surface. The girl grunted as she wrestled him up again. "Come on!"

Her accomplice was crouched at the edge of the roadway. The girl pulled Markusz towards him, then swung him round by the arm until the man – definitely a man – caught him. Then they dropped him through a hole.

He was falling but he couldn't see a thing, because his vision was suddenly hijacked by a full-sense wraparound experience of skydiving towards jagged mountain peaks. The sun dipped below the cloud deck far beneath the summit and he felt a yawning sensation in his stomach as his body or his mind – or both – told him he was in freefall.

He hit the floor and bounced off something soft, the vision dissolving as he latched onto a wall and vomited the meagre contents of his stomach – mostly bile – against it.

He vaguely registered he was in a kind of access tunnel.

"Is vomiting a side effect of the scrambler too?"

"No," the girl said, pulling him away from the vomit and sitting him down with his head between his legs. "That's probably the concussion."

He closed his eyes but the random augment windows persisted. He tried not to focus on them.

"Where are you taking me?"

"Somewhere safe."

"Really? Your rescue method seems a bit chaotic. You blew up the vehicle I was in."

"Everyone was alive after the crash until they weren't," she said. "Besides, who said anything about rescue?"

Markusz opened his eyes. The girl had shed her armour and was pulling on a red and yellow onepiece with *Fabrika SA Environmental Services* across the chest. She looked barely fifteen years old, though he wasn't good at guessing ages. Her skin was dark and her face was framed by auburn hair, long and curled on one side, shaved to stubble on the other.

He raised his arm to wave away an augmented graph of beet futures and his hand seemed to pixelate and break apart. He clamped his eyes shut again and swallowed. "I can't walk like this."

"You won't have to for the next bit."

"Get in," her accomplice said.

Markusz opened one eye and saw the big man through a topographical map of the Balearic coastline of Montresor III. He was supporting a long cylinder leaning on a handcart. The cylinder, etched on the side with the words *Fabrika SA Environmental Coolant – Corrosive*, was split along its length, the top half cantilevered open. Inside was well-padded and looked blessedly comfortable. Markusz really just wanted to lie down. His head was thumping and a rainbow migraine aura had formed on the left of his vision.

The girl helped him stand and he sank into the padded interior.

"What's your name anyway," he asked.

She stood over him, her face shining in reflected light. "I'm Elly Capalian and this is Brak."

As she pulled a maintenance helmet with a full rebreather mask over her face, the lid of the cylinder snapped shut and it jerked and started moving. Markusz felt like a skewer was working its way between his frontal lobes, and the augment junk kept flashing across his vision whether his eyes were open or closed. But somehow he managed to push all that to one side. He had some thinking to do.

Capalian. It sounded Paradisan.

Wherever they were taking him and for whatever purpose, this whole thing had been meticulously planned out. It wasn't a random attack on the vehicle: the change of clothes, this access way and the fake coolant tank were all evidence of that.

They'd scrambled his augments too, but what about their own? If they had friends in high places who could hide their idents, those same friends could just as easily hide Markusz's. So why the device? Maybe his captors didn't have augments. But augments were nigh on universal except for the odd religious cult or throwback society. Elly didn't seem the type for either.

Had someone on the council sent them? Barely anyone else knew Markusz existed, let alone that he was on Redout. Teel held no love for him, but death squads seemed a bit extreme as an offboarding mechanism. Besides Teel didn't have that kind of clout here. The council member Fontaneau had backed him up though. Did *he* want Markusz dead?

Markusz thought back to the meeting. He had no data to indicate which of them might want to rescue him. Or, if not rescue, then at least stop the Opitauans from killing him. Although Sylfe Cachand had at least seemed sympathetic. Capalian *sounded* Paradisan. But Elly's accent didn't quite fit. Brak hadn't spoken enough but Markusz would wager Elly was native Garian. If Brak was too, then they could be working for Mayor Firmin. His augments had indicated she was the only Garian on the council. But maybe that was too obvious.

He was going round in circles. His migraine had settled into a dull ache and he felt disconnected from his body, which was a good thing considering the punishment it had suffered lately. The aura had subsided too and the augment chatter seemed easier to ignore.

He realised he wasn't in complete darkness. There was a palm-width inspection window just above his shoulder. The plastic was badly scratched and clouded, but one small section was clear. If he twisted his neck a little he could see outside. At first he thought they were passing through a sunlit patch, then realised it was more like the faux sunlight he remembered from *Endeavour*'s promenade deck. Still underground, but they'd emerged from the access tunnel into a narrow street with buildings on either side. Accommodation units, maybe three storeys high – that was as far as he could see without dislocating his neck – with raised walkways running along the building fronts.

He saw people too, walking or sitting in groups. Going by their dress they were predominantly Fordana, with a few of the seemingly ubiquitous onepiece-wearing Fabrika SA service personnel dotted among them. These must be living quarters for the organisational machine that breathed life into Redout. Or at least those not important enough to live above ground.

The cylinder veered left. A handful of children chased each other around a water feature to one side of the narrow street. Poor little shits. What sort of life would they grow up to here? Which led his thoughts back to Rachik.

Markusz had never rated Rachik as being worth much attention but he was reasonably competent. Certainly competent enough to operate the annulus as it was intended. Fontaneau wanted more. But if he wanted what Markusz had promised, why send his goons to kill him? Teel, of course. Teel must have convinced Fontaneau that he and Rachik could do whatever Markusz could. Well, he was sorely mistaken there.

For the first time in a long time Markusz felt a savage glee, until he remembered the worried look on Rachik's face. Messing about with the annulus could get them all killed.

8

The council reconvened at the CSTO tower to witness the annulus being brought up to full operation, but it wasn't quite the control centre Sylfe had imagined. Nothing about the place screamed *ability to bend the eldritch powers of the universe to our will.*

She'd been hoping for something monumental: huge power buses crackling with energy discharges and heroic technicians clad in heavily shielded environment suits – like something ripped from the pages of a science romance. Fuck, if only. Instead of a pale-but-interesting-with-a-secret scientist leaping up to halt the experiment at the last moment and save everyone from a fatal dimensional rupture, she had pinch-faced Teel and his sidekick Rachik fussing over some dull-looking control surface near the annulus. A handful of technicians clad in mundane lab onepieces strolled among the controls, gesturing in the air of their own private data spaces. It was all very anti-climactic.

But at least there *was* the annulus. The twisted rainbow of esoteric energy floated on a clear platform, with banks of monitoring and control stations radiating out from the centre of the room.

The technicians gave it no mind, and most of the council seemed too busy massaging each other's egos to care, but Sylfe did notice one other remarkable thing. Standing off to one side, where she no doubt assumed she was unobserved, was Asymptote Eleven. The Haibeu's eyes were fixed on the annulus and her usually neutral expression had been replaced by a look of pure rapture.

Sylfe didn't want to draw attention to the Haibeu, so returned to her augment windows and the multiple feeds from her SolEng sunbarques. Her role here was to monitor the star's output in case something about operating the annulus didn't agree with it. So far so 'nothing to report', but here came Fontaneau looking more smug than usual, which was no mean feat for him.

"Ind Cachand," he said and attempted a smile. "Everything is in order at your end?"

She returned the smile out of general politeness. "It is."

"It's a momentous day. And a comfort to know those we have toiled to rescue will be all the safer for it."

Sylfe held the smile but felt a gag reflex coming on. Fontaneau cared nothing for the refugees. This was about him positioning himself to take the glory for something that had nothing to do with him.

He leaned closer. His breath didn't smell unpleasant, which surprised her. "I think you and I should work more closely, going forward."

"Oh?" she said, and he nodded gravely, then paused as if struck by a memory. Everything about the man was so contrived.

"You know, your mother and I were close at one time," he said. "*Years* before you were born, of course."

Sylfe doubted that, but could believe that even a fleeting acquaintance with Fontaneau would have contributed to Adele's poor regard for the male gender.

"Marooned as we both are now, so far from polite society, I must admit I feel protective towards you."

Sylfe stiffened. Was this a sexual proposal? But no. This was strictly politics.

"We Paradisans must stick together. I feel things are going to get much worse before they get better."

She agreed. And Fontaneau was going to be the cause of much of that "worse", she was sure.

"This latest terrorist attack is just another indicator of that," he continued.

Sylfe had heard about the murder of M-Def soldiers on the

highway system. It was one of a string of such incidents. "We all need friends in difficult times," she said noncommittally.

Fontaneau nodded and drifted off to talk to one of the other council members.

Most of them were here, with the exception of Mayor Firmin. She was a strange one. Out of all the council members Firmin was the only elected member of Congress – though a minor one, given Garia's standing – but she'd quickly been sidelined when the Redout project was established. Politically it was difficult for her. While native Garians acknowledged how necessary Redout was, many were unhappy with how the project had been rolled out. Their planet – a planet nobody had wanted and which they'd toiled for generations to make liveable – wasn't theirs any more.

Sylfe focused again on her data space, but extended her surveillance capacity as she saw Commander Rask enter and walk purposefully towards Fontaneau, who excused himself from whatever he was trying to do with Leeuwin.

"Your pardon, Patri Fontaneau," Rask said softly. "I thought you would like to know that Congress Deputy Speaker Rao is en route to Redout with a small delegation of Congress members."

"Oh?" Fontaneau said. His expression remained as neutral as if Rask had relayed the weather forecast.

"*Officially* it's a simple inspection visit to report back progress to Congress," Rask said. "But unofficially I've heard that Deputy Speaker Rao and the others will be staying. Indefinitely."

Fontaneau casually looked around to see if anyone was paying them undue attention. Satisfied, his voice dropped to almost a whisper. "So. This is the beginning of the transition of power to Redout." He clapped the M-Def commander lightly on the shoulder and smiled. "Thank you, Rask. Why don't you stay for the operation?"

"Thank you. I will," Rask said with a brief bow.

Was Rask Fontaneau's man, Sylfe wondered. Or was he simply doing his duty as he saw it and advising the leader of the council of Rao's intent?

"Inds!" Teel spoke loudly to gain everyone's attention and the low drone of multiple conversations across the control centre stilled. "We are ready to activate the annulus. There will be a low level of visible radiation, but it is entirely benign. As well as our monitoring technicians, your esteemed colleague Ind Cachand," he spared Sylfe a yellow-toothed, patronising smirk, "will also be assessing any impacts on Redout's stellar environs. Rachik, you may commence when ready."

Rachik nodded and busied himself among the technicians, speaking softly on a private channel. All eyes turned to the annulus but – dazzlingly beautiful as it was – it exhibited no change.

Teel continued to radiate smug confidence, so Sylfe surmised this was expected. On her windows it was a different matter.

A waveform was building in the substrate. Gently at first, introducing itself into local spacetime and causing barely a ripple as it brushed against the stellar corona. Other than that there was no disturbance in the chromosphere, or further in, and no increase in flares or prominences. Her ships on the far side of the star matched her observations.

But when she switched to observing the substrate itself … The manifold was altering in a way she'd never seen. Not gravitational. Possibly quantum, but the series of transformations required would be … She switched to a mathematical depiction of whatever the fuck was happening out there.

"It's beautiful."

Sylfe jerked in surprise at the sudden noise, then tried to stifle her reaction when she realised it was Asymptote Eleven who had spoken. The woman was leaning over her shoulder staring at Sylfe's window.

"I suppose it is," Sylfe said.

Asymptote Eleven was focused on the numbers and accompanying plots scrolling across the data space with that same joyful expression Sylfe had observed before.

"Imperfect, but even more beautiful for that," she said.

"Imperfect?" Sylfe asked.

The joy on Asymptote's face dimmed as she looked from the window to Sylfe. "Your pardon. I should not disturb you." She was gone as suddenly as she'd arrived.

"The glow," Leeuwin said. He was pointing at the shared data space above the annulus.

The main feed was a view of the Redout system from way above the plane of the ecliptic. A faint golden glow covered the system, the only visible effect of the annulus from what Sylfe could determine. It reached as far as the heliopause. She reviewed its appearance in a private window. It hadn't spread in any conventional way from Redout. It had simply appeared all at once, which indicated it was somehow caused by the annulus's operation on the substrate in a non-local way. She'd need to study that in more detail.

"Nothing to worry about, Ind Leeuwin," Teel said. "As I said, there is some low-level visible radiation. To my mind, it makes for a cheerier-looking space."

Sylfe thought Teel was a little giddy with success, but Leeuwin was unimpressed.

"Yes, but it stops at the heliopause," he said. "The undocumented refugee ships are all outside the glow."

"It's not a barrier, if that's what you mean," Teel said. "It's simply an outcome of the annulus's operation on the curvature of local spacetime."

"Do the refugee ships know that?" Leeuwin said, looking around at his fellow council members.

Teel's good humour faltered.

"You're right," Commander Rask said. "I'll have messaging relayed out to the border patrol. Nothing to be alarmed about. That sort of thing."

Rask left, but Leeuwin was not mollified. "We need to move those ships inside the heliopause. They're not going to believe some government comms."

"Now that's not a decision to be taken lightly," Fontaneau

said, stepping onto the annulus platform to gain the high ground oratorically speaking, Sylfe thought. "We can't afford to lose order out there. We need that space between the heliopause and Redout to provide a buffer in case there's a stampede. The M-Def forces could be easily overwhelmed and you know where that leads."

"I'm simply saying move them a few hundred thousand clicks inside," Leeuwin said. "Rumours about this glow could lead to a stampede anyway."

Sylfe was inclined to agree. If the place of safety was inside the glow and you were outside, it was bound to lead to all kinds of conspiracy theories and paranoia.

"We'd need a tactical view on that from Commander Rask," Fontaneau said and smiled again, reaching, Sylfe thought, for kindly father figure and managing ghoulish rictus. "Come, Leeuwin. I think we fully appreciate the dangers you have raised. We'll convene the council as soon as possible to discuss the best way forward."

"I suppose," Leeuwin conceded.

Sylfe settled back into the dataflow of her private feeds. The addition of the annulus's operation on the substrate notwithstanding, it looked like everything was as one might expect. Whether the annulus actually protected Redout space from the Effect was yet to be determined.

Rask entered the control centre again, ashen-faced. "Council members, we're getting reports of an Effect coalescing around Paradis."

"You're mistaken," Teel said. "Our modelling shows Paradis is clear for at least two months."

"That doesn't accord with the reports we're getting from our forces in-system."

Sylfe jerked a hand across her windows, clearing the feeds and linking to her solar observatory in the Paradisan system.

She heard Teel say, "That's not possible." But she could see that he was wrong.

It began with a strange attenuation of form, as if giant fingers were drawing across the face of stars and planets, smearing vacuum and matter, stretching out shapes until they blended and ran together.

She tried to open comms to Yvette and her mother, but all she got was static. Then the feed from her observatory cut off.

"No," she whispered, desperately connecting to an extra-system feed.

The red pall of Teel-Attar radiation was already forming as stellar mass, atomic structure, the fabric of space, all became malleable under the Effect.

Just as Sylfe magnified the view, the entire volume of space leaped inward with insane acceleration. She felt unhinged from reality, caught up in a vertiginous plunge into annihilation. An endless fall that stripped every thought and feeling away because how could she comprehend something so full of awe and so horrific?

Her mother. Her sister. Six billion Paradisans. Gone.

9

The cylinder jerked to a sudden stop and the lid swung open, bringing Markusz back to the here and now and a fresh assault of augment windows plying everything from some very soft porn to a newsfeed report of a terror attack on the highway by "Garian Separatists". This caught his attention, but he'd only just learned that all passengers in the vehicle had been brutally murdered before the window was whisked away and Brak was hauling him to his feet.

"Just what do Garian Separatists want with me?" Markusz asked.

"Don't believe everything you see on the newsfeeds," Elly said.

Perhaps not, but maybe a council member hadn't engineered his kidnap after all. Maybe he was the captive of some crazed local political group. What the hell were they fighting for at the end of the worlds?

He looked around. They were in another tunnel but this one was far less salubrious. It was time to put his foot down.

"Look, I appreciate you got me out of the vehicle. The killings afterwards seemed a bit extreme, but I'm new here so I'm not up on the local etiquette. But I'm going to have to insist you tell me: who do you work for and where are you taking me?"

Brak slammed the lid of the cylinder shut with unnecessary force. It was hard for a fifteen-year-old girl to look menacing, Markusz thought, but Elly gave Brak a run for his money.

"Insist or …" she said.

"I'll struggle every step of the way." It sounded lame but he *was* only a mathematician.

"You'll walk where we tell you to walk," Brak said. "Or I'll start shooting off bits we don't need. You have plenty of fingers for a start."

Same accent as Elly, Markusz thought. Definitely Garian. He started walking in the direction indicated by Brak's drawn weapon. The walls looked like they'd been scoured by giant talons, and the roof was partially collapsed, letting in a steady flow of water that pooled in puddles on the cracked and silt-caked floor.

"What are these tunnels?" he asked, more to keep his mind off the rapidly changing augment junk than with any real expectation of an answer.

"They were excavated by the original Garian settlers so they didn't die from UV exposure," Elly said, moving to take the lead.

She turned on a lumen which pierced the darkness ahead. Markusz saw the tunnel ran downhill and twisted to the left. Groundwater streamed in rivulets ahead of them, following the natural curve.

"They were pressurised too until the atmosphere reprocessors did their job," Elly continued. "Many of them were collapsed by the Corps d'Ingénieurs when they started the Redout earthworks."

The gradient was steeper now and the turn of the tunnel more pronounced. As if they were corkscrewing down to a lower level. A new flurry of augment windows jittered across his field of vision and he had to stop and grab onto the cold, damp wall to keep from falling.

Brak's firm hand clamped onto his shoulder and guided him forward until he could see again, then he shrugged it off and quickened his pace to catch up with Elly, a silhouette against the light of the lumen.

They kept walking down and round. The walls looked naturally formed in places, but mostly showed signs of rough excavation far removed from the smooth tunnelling he'd seen earlier.

Making a planet into a home wasn't easy, even with the full resources of the Thousand Worlds behind the enterprise. Settlers were generally of hardy stock, highly trained and used to privations. They had to be. But Markusz knew something of Garian history. The planet's original settlers had been Paradisan. Or rather the dregs of Paradisan society, led to this unpromising world by the head of one of the Great Paradisan Families in an act of benevolence that was far removed from the status quo for that oligarchy. As a result, settlement of Garia had been tougher than most, because resources were limited, the settlers were mainly unskilled workers, and many of them suffered from chronic ailments or disabilities. But Paradisan society was harsh for those who weren't independently wealthy or born into wealth. A quick death on an inhospitable planet had to be better than a slow one under the boot-heels of the oligarchs.

Elly stopped and he saw the tunnel ahead had straightened and levelled out. A dark, broad trench ran along its length against the right-hand wall.

"This looks like a submover station," Markusz said.

Elly glared at him. "That's because it is. Was. We weren't fucking cavemen before the glorious Redout Project came."

"We?" he said.

"Yes, 'we'," she snapped. "You happy now? You've solved your little puzzle?"

Markusz didn't feel any kind of satisfaction. Quite the opposite. He was neck deep in something he didn't understand.

"We have a long way to go," Elly said, her tone all business again.

Were they going to walk through submover tunnels?

The lumen floated up and increased in intensity so that even the trench – or the submover way – was illuminated. He saw the single rail, as flawless as the day it was laid. And lying on top of it, level with where they were standing, was a flatbed with four seats raked back at a ridiculously obtuse angle.

Brak leaped down from the platform and shifted the flatbed so it sat straight on the underlying rail. He swung a pack from his back, pulled out a fist-sized metal block and kneeled to feel around under one of the seats.

"Do you need the light?" Elly asked but Brak shook his head.

Markusz heard a click, then a rising whine and the flatbed lifted a few centimetres.

A weather report for the southern hemisphere flitted in front of him. Hot with thunderstorms moving in from the east. Markusz shivered. It was cold down here.

"Get on," Elly said.

"Are you seriously proposing we ride on this thing?"

"Not proposing. Telling."

Brak helped Markusz to step onto the flatbed, which shifted a little under his weight, then pulled himself up, strapped Markusz into the back left-hand seat and took the seat next to him.

Elly grabbed the lumen as it descended again, then leaped onto the flatbed and sat up front. "Lie flat and keep your arms by your side," she said. "These tunnels aren't as clear or intact as they used to be."

The lumen winked out and the flatbed accelerated, pushing Markusz back into his seat. They were in total darkness and his stomach tensed against an impact he knew he wouldn't feel. Because if it happened at this speed, he'd be dead in an instant.

Whether Elly and Brak were "Garian Separatists" or some other flavour of local rebel or revolutionary, it seemed he was the pawn in some political machinations. It was the bitterest irony for someone who didn't have a political bone in his body.

He'd hoped to have left all that madness behind when he escaped Wiszenti. Now *there* was a planet consumed by politics. Every week, it seemed, there was another pamphlet, a new group of political evangelists shouting their message from the street corners, gathering supporters to their cause. Grievances were aired, calls for change were made and ignored by those in power, which led to a round of "direct action" with bans, walkouts, strikes, protests and riots escalating to bombings, government crackdowns, then overthrows, then revolutionary tribunals followed by incarcerations and executions until the whole cycle started again. Egalo-fascists, radical elitists, crypto-reversionists, groups splitting, merging, reforming until whatever their message was became meaningless. Office politics and individual powerplays Markusz could understand, but from what he'd seen of political movements they were smoke and fantasies at best or cynical manipulations at worst. And usually the latter.

He'd had a hard upbringing among all that turmoil. Raised by a commune that regularly fragmented, he didn't remember his biological parents. It was maths that saved him. Not only because it showed him a world where meaning was objective and persistent, but also because it was his facility with maths that showed up in the annual M-World screenings that were a prerequisite of Wiszenti's continued membership – and whatever political party was in power that week, they couldn't risk losing the benefits *that* entailed. So Markusz left Wiszenti at thirteen years of age and entered a mathematical seminary on Respaxon. He'd never missed anything or anyone from his old life. But he remembered the lesson he'd learned on his homeworld: that anyone who believed in politics was a fool.

Augment pixels flared in the darkness, but instead of fighting it or trying to ignore it, he let it wash over him, too exhausted to think. Not much of it made sense and that was fine. Nothing in his own life made sense to him any more.

He'd lost track of the passage of time too. They could have been travelling for twenty minutes or three hours. All he knew was darkness and augment bleed – but then the lumen flared, washing everything out, and the flatbed slowed and stopped.

Markusz blinked until his surroundings resolved. The tunnel ran off ahead for maybe ten metres until it was blocked by a pile of rubble. They'd pulled up alongside an emergency siding, really little more than a person-width channel cut into the rock. A tubular metal ladder ran up into darkness above.

"We climb?" he asked, already knowing the answer.

"We climb," Brak said. "You first."

Markusz didn't have the energy to protest. At least his headache was gone. He was about to ask for a lumen, but the shaft lit up, so he moved into the opening and looked up. There were lights at regular intervals, but he still couldn't see the end of the ladder.

Climbing wasn't hard at first. The rungs were evenly spaced and his arms and legs fell into a steady rhythm. It felt good to be moving after sitting immobile for so long. But then his thigh and calf muscle began to ache and pretty soon he had to stop, wrapping his arms around the ladder as his legs shook with fatigue.

Brak grabbed his calf from below and pulled it.

"Don't! I'll fall," Markusz said.

But Brak just pulled again, so Markusz let his arms take the strain and lifted his legs from rung to rung as if they were dead things.

After a while he could climb normally again and when he looked up he saw the top of the ladder. He found a new reserve of energy and pushed on, ignoring the augment junk and focusing on his hands moving up from rung to rung. Left, right, left, right. Until there were no more rungs.

He reached one arm above his head and felt something give. The roof was fabric. He grabbed a handful and pulled it aside and light – this time he could tell it was the real light of a sun – fell on his face.

With one final effort he pushed himself through the opening and onto the floor, lying spreadeagled and tasting the dusty air. Then he rolled onto his hands and knees and took in his surroundings. Rows of storage containers. And above, a fabric roof, a pyramid enclosing the space. Wind blew against the walls, making them ripple.

Brak pulled him to his feet, and Elly brushed him down and pushed his arms into a bulky jacket. She pulled at the shoulders, then dragged a thick cowl over his hair.

"Keep this up and your head down," she said.

She turned and pushed through a break in the fabric wall. Brak took hold of Markusz's left arm above the elbow and steered him out the same opening.

Rows and rows of pyramidal tents – like the one he'd emerged from – were crammed together on a segmented causeway laid on top of sandy soil. The road was about six metres wide and on the other side, a queue of people slowly shuffled along the nearest row of tents. Markusz couldn't see the front of the queue – or its end – but it looked to be headed towards a taller more permanent structure in the hazy distance.

On his side of the causeway, people – refugees, he expected – sat huddled on battered metal chairs or stood in groups in front of their open tents. Their clothes were worn and uniformly dusty. Some looked like they may have been affluent at one time and not used to living in such makeshift accommodation, but all seemed resigned. None of them even registered the appearance of Markusz and his two captors.

"This is one of the holding camps," Elly said.

"Holding for what?"

"Holding until better accommodation is ready. The people here have been waiting for four years now. But it's one of the better ones."

"When do they get better accommodation?" Markusz asked.

"Hmm. Not for a while."

Elly gestured at a gap between the row of tents and Markusz caught a glimpse of some sort of half-formed tower structures. But they were far off on the horizon.

They started walking in the opposite direction. Markusz could see he was in the middle of a barren slum. Even the tents had seen better days. Most were patched and lashed in places. Some had been joined together or otherwise extended; some had ratty canopies to keep the sun off. This place was the endpoint of a desperate flight from the destruction of everything these people knew. They had food, a place to rest, but did they still have hope? He couldn't believe that they did. Not after waiting so long for their lives to restart.

Still, he didn't have another option. He wrenched his arm free and ran towards the nearest man sitting on a bent chair. "Help," he said. "You have to help me – I'm being kidnapped."

Brak was closing on him, so Markusz ran again, stopping in front of a skinny young man with sun-bleached hair.

"Help me!"

The man just stared at him, so Markusz grabbed his thin arm and shook it. "Help me," he repeated.

But the man turned away, pulling his arm free, and Brak had firm hold of Markusz's arm again.

"He can't see you and he can't hear you," Elly said. "And he certainly doesn't need you reminding him he's not where he believes he is."

"What?"

She gestured at the sad collection of refugees. "Their augments are running the refugee program. It keeps them pacified. What they experience is a purpose-built facility with every comfort and entertainment they need."

Markusz was horrified. "That's monstrous."

"It's humane," Elly said. "At least they're not fretting about rotting in a sand-blown slum."

As Brak propelled him along the causeway at a brisk pace, with Elly striding along in front, Markusz struggled to parse what he'd seen since leaving the intake centre. He supposed the Redout Council were doing their best, but they seemed to be falling well short of expectations. And the mismatch between the living conditions at the Fordana underground habitat and this place didn't sit well with him. Sure, the success of Redout depended on the support staff and it was important they were properly housed. But one might also surmise that those in power were diverting the best resources to them and theirs to the detriment of genuine refugees.

Suddenly Elly struck right and disappeared into another tent, and the next instant he and Brak were inside with her. More storage containers were stacked against an outsized cargo pod that brushed the tent roof.

"Now what?" Markusz asked.

Elly said, "We don't need you conscious for this part."

He was about to protest but Brak punched him in the side of the head and he lost interest in everything.

•

Finally safe back at their base, Brak dropped the unconscious Markusz on the cot and straightened up. "Fucking incomers."

"Yeah, I don't know what the big deal is with him," Elly said. "He seems kind of weak."

Brak grunted and slapped her on the back. "You did good out there. But you could have saved one of them for me."

Elly smiled up at the big man. "You taught me too well. Come on, let's eat."

Her stomach rumbled as soon as she mentioned food. She'd skipped breakfast so she could go with Brak. But when they re-entered the corridor, she saw that mealtime was going to have to wait. Her grandmother stood there with hands on hips and a particularly grim expression on her face.

"Mayor Firmin," Brak said, oblivious to the sudden tension in the enclosed space. "I was just telling Elly –"

"Save it, Brak. I'll talk to *you* later. First, I want Elly to explain why she went outside without permission."

"Without …" The big man's brow furrowed then cleared with sudden comprehension. "Ah … See you later," he said and made good his exit.

Elly's expression matched her grandmother's. This had been a long time coming.

"I'm not sorry, Mamie," she said. "I did what had to be done. Brak –"

"You lied to Brak. You put him and yourself at risk."

"I didn't –"

"And you disobeyed me and broke security. What would have happened if you were captured?"

Elly knew how this argument was meant to go. She was meant to capitulate. But she was done with that.

"If I was captured, I would have done what any of us would do," she said.

Her grandmother's lips drew together more tightly. "You're not ready."

"The dead Opitauans would disagree with you. Or are you angry because I killed them?"

Her grandmother grunted. "God, no. They deserved it. And more."

"Then why? The fact is I *am* ready. I've been ready for months. And every time I ask you to use me there's some excuse. I'm sick of it."

Elly waited for an explosion. For more excuses.

But her grandmother's shoulders slumped and – unexpectedly – she smiled. "I'm having a hard time letting go of my granddaughter."

Was this another kind of excuse, Elly wondered. Appeal to their relationship?

"But … you're right. Brak says you're the best fighter he's ever seen. I'm proud of you, but I'm scared for you too. I'll make a deal with you. You agree I'm in charge, and you follow *my* orders to the letter. And if you want to go on an operation, you ask me."

"And you'll say no," Elly countered.

"If I say no, I promise it'll be because it's not operationally wise, not because I'm scared you're going to get killed. Deal?"

Elly considered. This was progress. Her grandmother was a woman of her word. Still, she wanted more. "And if it's a no, we can discuss the reason?"

Her grandmother grunted again. But this time she looked amused. "Yes, we'll discuss it. But no more lying to me or Brak."

"Yes, Mamie."

Her grandmother held an arm out. "Come on. You look hungry."

Together they walked to the elevator. Inside, Elly pressed for the mess level.

"This guy we picked up is cracked," she said. "He wanted me to kill him. He talks to his dead wife. Why's he so important?"

"He may not be," her grandmother said. "And if that's the case, I'll want you to dispose of him."

10

After the disaster at the control centre, Sylfe's journey to her mother's apartment – the apartment Adele would never live in now – was a blur. But as soon as the entry door sealed behind her, she sank to the floor and gave herself over to grief.

An indeterminate time later, she found her way to the lounge and sat. Her throat and chest ached. Her thoughts came sluggishly. Her family were dead. It was too enormous a concept. And the method of their death … it denied understanding. It could *not* have happened.

The racking sobs took hold again and an overwhelming despair dragged her down into hopelessness.

Eventually, exhausted and emotionally wrung out, she slept. And woke to the apartment announcing an entry request.

Sylfe rolled over on the lounge – momentarily confused to wake up in her mother's salon – and remembered her family were gone. There was pain attached to that thought but exhaustion numbed it.

The windowwall was tuned to a view of the Paradisan estates, but her augments showed it was mid-afternoon. As if time had any meaning. Clearly it didn't. It had judder-leaped ahead in the space around her home planet. Processes that should have taken years or centuries wound together in an eye-blink.

There is an entry request, the apartment patiently announced again.

Sylfe opened a window and stared at the puffy face craning to look up. She recognised it but rejected the recognition because what in hell would *he* be doing here? It didn't make sense. Nevertheless it *was* Hugo Denantes.

She must have been more off-kilter than she realised because a moment later Denantes was in the entry hall though she didn't remember admitting him. She pushed herself off the lounge and stood groggily. She was still wearing yesterday's clothes. She pushed helplessly at her tangled hair.

Denantes stood in the doorway with his head cocked to one side and his mouth half open, as if shocked by her appearance.

Well, fuck you, Sylfe thought. "What are you doing here? How did you even find me?"

"Tracking anyone on Redout isn't that hard. I'm sorry to intrude," he said. "I … was concerned. After you left the facility so quickly. I wanted to check in on you."

He sank onto the lounge, hands clasped and body hunched forward, the picture of solicitude. It was bullshit and Sylfe relished the anger that surged in her. Relished the opportunity to lash out and hurt someone. But she didn't. Denantes didn't give a fuck about how she felt. Which meant he was here for an altogether different reason. Her brain fog was quickly dissipating. She knew what Maman would say: *focus*.

She sat on the other end of the lounge. "You must have lost family as well," she said.

He looked away, grimaced, then turned back to her with a sad smile. "I hadn't quite imagined them dying this way."

But he'd imagined it in *some* way, she thought. Probably brutally and by his own hand. After all, his family had sent him here when his excesses became too public to ignore.

"Do we have any idea how it happened?" she asked. Now she'd turned her attention to it, her augments were full of the *news* of Paradis but none carried an explanation.

Denantes shook his head. "Chief Scientist Teel is very close-mouthed at the moment. It would be fair to say the council is not happy. This doesn't breed confidence in the general population. And there's been more trouble with the ships at the heliopause. It's a bad situation all around."

A bad situation. The understatement of the millennium. But she was sure things could still get worse.

"Fontaneau is taking control, of course," Denantes continued. "He's made it clear to Teel in no uncertain terms that the annulus's performance must be flawless from here on in."

Sylfe was aware that Denantes was watching her more intently now. Perhaps he thought she'd be too stunned by her family's death to notice.

"It's the least we can expect," she said. "Would you like some coffee?"

She may as well play hospitable since Denantes was playing at being a friend. But he raised a chubby short-fingered hand and shook his head briefly. "Please don't trouble yourself."

He sat back against the overstuffed cushions. "Of course, the Congress representative will be here soon to take control."

The words hung between them with an odd kind of pressure.

"That was always the plan," Sylfe said.

"It was always *a* plan," Denantes said.

He sighed in what Sylfe thought of as a very mannered way. The man was all artifice. How exhausting it must be to maintain. It was exhausting enough for her just to pierce through to whatever truth he was labouring to both hide and reveal at the same time. And she knew the "revelation" would be simply another manipulation, truthfulness being only one factor and far from the most important.

"Fontaneau thinks very highly of you," he continued, pushing his wet bottom lip out in a pout.

"Should I be flattered?"

The pout turned into a toothy grin. "Well …" He shrugged.

She could smell him now through his expensive cologne with a top note of stale sweat. He exuded an amalgam of fear and desire, the twin drivers of everything he did. Which one was Fontaneau leveraging, she wondered. Because clearly Denantes was here at *his* bidding, at least nominally so.

Time to cut through the mannered artifice. "And what is

Fontaneau's plan?"

"Nothing so provocative as a plan," he said. "But there are other 'options', you might say, to an orderly transfer of authority. Whether one of these scenarios gains sufficient weight to play out depends on so many moving parts."

"Of which I am one," Sylfe acknowledged.

"Just so, and I am another."

He paused and regarded her for a moment. The hesitation, Sylfe knew, was meant to impart some sense of deliberation about whether he should confide in her. But she knew there was no decision. Everything he said had already been worked out to the finest degree.

"I'm no friend of Fontaneau," he said. "I think you know that. And neither are you. I'm wondering what you think we should do about the situation?"

Denantes was hoping honesty would be met with honesty. But there was no way in hell she'd tell him what she really thought. Denantes would sell her out to Fontaneau for advantage even while plotting against him.

"There is no 'we'," she said. "But there is an old saying: a rising tide lifts all boats."

The toothy grin flashed again. "True enough. I'm glad we had this conversation. I will leave you to your mourning. But I hope to see you at the next council session."

He left, no doubt to scurry back to Fontaneau to report that Sylfe Cachand would not stand in his way if and when he made his move. It bought her time while committing her to nothing.

Sylfe sank back on the lounge, exhausted by the exchange. Part of her wanted to ignore all this politicking and sit with her grief. But she knew her mother would not be impressed. Adele had despised Fontaneau, and the prospect of him scheming his way to a position of power over all Redout would have sickened her. The fact that Sylfe also would be subject to Fontaneau's whims if that were to happen was equally worthy of consideration.

There was also the question of why Paradis had been destroyed. Sylfe was unimpressed with Ind Teel, but CSTO was the pre-eminent scientific organisation in the Thousand Worlds. "Accidents" such as what occurred to Paradis didn't just happen.

She was going to find out. And she was going to make damned sure that things did not go Patri Ernes Fontaneau's way.

11

Markusz's face hurt. He touched at his cheek gingerly. The skin was rough and tender but the bones underneath felt intact. And he was lying on a particularly comfortable cot.

The light was soft and diffuse but enough to see by. He was in a room with no windows and a single ellipse-shaped door. The threshold was curved and not flush with the floor. It reminded him of an ocean-going vessel. He could hear a low kind of rumbling. Like machinery but not. Less rhythmic, more like an ocean maybe. The movement of currents. Ebbs and flows. It made him think about the door design again, but he was sure the room wasn't moving. Why build doors like that anyway? They seemed designed to be tripped over.

He sat up. The augment spam was gone, as was the cufflet on his wrist when he looked. But when he tried to connect to the network, there was nothing. No signal.

His justacorps and breeches – shredded in the crash, and soiled on the journey to wherever the hell he was – were gone and he was dressed in a utilitarian but comfortable shirt and trousers.

He stood and crossed to the door. It remained resolutely shut. A prisoner then. But things could be a lot worse.

He hunkered down to inspect the wall. It was warm to the touch and gave slightly, like it was covered in felt. Or made of felt. There was a faint pattern in it, and he studied it more closely. It looked grown. He could see veins running through it. Primary veins branching off into secondary and tertiary and so on. Like a leaf.

He moved his hand down the wall to where it met the floor.

This surface was harder and more polished; less like felt, more like plastic. But he could see the same vein patterns running through it. They were too faint to be decorative. Who grew walls and floors and rooms? Even the elliptical door looked organic to him now. The way the rim of the frame rolled back on itself.

"How are you feeling?" Helena sat on the bed looking at him.

"I thought you'd gone," he said.

"You were busy enough getting kidnapped without having to worry about me."

He sat beside her. "*Worry* about you? You're dead. How much worse could things get?"

She scowled, but he could tell she wasn't really angry with him. This was that faux sparring that couples did with each other.

"I didn't want you distracted is what I meant."

"Talking to your dead wife again?"

Elly stood in the curved doorway with a tray of food in hand. She looked less the terrorist and more the girl she was, wearing a bulky asymmetric jumper and patterned leggings.

"Her name's Helena," Markusz said.

Elly stared at empty space a little to his right. "Nice to meet you, Helena."

Helena was sitting to his left. It was nice to know this wasn't a shared delusion.

"I'm not mad," he said. "You don't need to play along with me. It's just a habit I've adopted to work through problems."

"Thanks a bunch," Helena said.

Elly put the tray on a side table. Some kind of stew and a cup of coffee. It smelled good. Markusz picked it up and ate, suddenly hungry.

The girl remained standing. Markusz swallowed and said, "Thank you."

She nodded but didn't seem inclined to leave.

After a few more mouthfuls and a sip of coffee, he said, "What is this place?"

Elly paused, then pulled a spindly metal chair over to sit opposite him. "You're not allowed to know yet."

Markusz considered whether the "yet" made what Elly said more or less ominous.

"Why did you want to die?" she asked.

"What?" Markusz felt disoriented.

"You put my gun against your head. You said we were all going to die anyway."

Markusz glanced at Helena then smiled ruefully at Elly. "We all have our dark moments. But you have to admit, the future's not exactly rosy right now."

Elly grunted, then said, "Your friends activated the machine you brought."

She had an annoying habit of keeping him off balance.

"That's teenagers for you," Helena said but Markusz ignored her. Just how much did his abductors know about him and his work?

"I think we've established they're not my friends," he said. "Is it working?"

Instead of answering, Elly opened a shared window between them. At least his augments still functioned, even if he couldn't connect on his own. He was looking at a region of space bisected by the warm glow of the annulus field. But this space looked familiar.

He reached into the window and pulled the image out into three dimensions, throwing his arms wide to expand it and zoom in, then swept one hand up to orient the view as seen from above.

"This is the heliopause," he said.

The annulus glow stopped at the border he'd crossed on the way here. The place where unregulated refugee vessels huddled together, held back by the blockade of M-Def warships. Now, searchlights played across broken hulls. Bots with long actuator arms moved on puffs of gas, gathering broken pieces of ship into bulbous nets. Smaller craft moved between them, darting in and out of dark chasms of twisted metal. Debris and bodies drifted through it all. A chaotic mass of destruction.

"What happened?"

"Your annulus started up, the refugee ships discovered they were on the wrong side of its border and everybody panicked, trying to break the blockade. M-Def stopped them."

Killed them, she meant. But why here?

"The annulus is designed to operate within a light year of the star," he said. "The heliopause is seventeen light hours away. Why the fuck is the border there?"

"Rachik was worried about Fontaneau —" Helena began.

"Changing the operating parameters," Markusz finished. "He's already fiddled with it. And this is the result."

He screwed the image into a ball and threw it back into the window, which winked out.

"Do you think the others know?" Helena asked.

Were the council complicit in this stupidity, Markusz wondered. Maybe. Or maybe Fontaneau was playing his own game. Maybe no-one outside Teel and Rachik was any the wiser.

"What do you mean?" Elly asked, breaking into his thoughts.

"Someone's screwing with my machine. It's not meant to work like this."

"It's not working at all from what I've seen," she said.

Markusz's eyes narrowed. "What have you seen?"

Elly's chair scraped on the floor as she stood. "Okay."

"Okay what?"

"You stay here and someone else will come and talk to you."

"And then?"

"Then we'll see," she said.

"Look, you couldn't be a bit more reassuring, could you? I have no idea what the fuck is going on here."

"You're safe. As safe as any of us are. That's as reassuring as I can be."

Elly left, and Markusz stared at the closed door for a long time. What the hell did she mean the annulus wasn't working?

"I think we're stuck here," Helena said.

The room was feeling more like a prison cell now. He sat on the floor, leaning against the wall. Helena joined him.

"What was all that stuff about killing yourself or getting that young girl to do it?" she asked. "And don't trot out that hopelessness bullshit you told her. We've lived with failure and the threat of failure for years."

Markusz sighed. "I just wonder if you –"

"No," she interrupted. "It's got nothing to do with me going behind your back to keep the peace with Teel either. Our love was real. You know that."

Fuck, it was impossible to lie to a figment of your own imagination. He sighed again, but this time it was long and ragged.

"I'm tired, Helena. I'm tired of waking up and remembering you're not here any more. I'm tired of feeling this hole inside me that I know is never going away."

"It's grief," she said. "It fades. But, you know, there are other things in life that are important to you. You should start focusing on those."

He wiped the heel of his hand across his eyes, pushing away tears. "What if I don't want to?" he asked.

But she was gone again.

12

Markusz lay on the cot and drifted, not quite sleeping, listening to that sound of ocean currents that lay beneath everything else.

When the door opened again, he was immediately awake, sitting upright and swinging his legs off the cot. He didn't stand though. That didn't seem wise.

The woman in the doorway was flanked by two guards wearing the same type of armour Elly and Brak had worn. Their faces were covered by full helmets, but he recognised the woman. She was dark-skinned, stockily built, oldish – perhaps a hundred and twenty or so – with greying long hair plaited and tied back. She wore a green cloak open at the front over a utilitarian tunic, breeches and boots.

"You're Mayor Firmin," Markusz said. Even without augment access he remembered her from his brief visit to the council chamber. "I wondered if you might be involved in this, but it seemed too obvious."

"Marthe will do," she said, unsmiling.

Studying the lines of her face, Markusz could believe she seldom smiled. Careworn. That was the word that came to mind.

He said, "I don't understand why I'm here."

"You've made some powerful enemies who want you dead."

"Fontaneau?"

She nodded. "I have to decide whether you're worth keeping alive."

Then she did smile, but Markusz didn't feel buoyed by the change. It felt apologetic rather than humorous.

"You could just let me go," he said. "I can take my own chances."

"No. Because you could possibly be of some use to me." Marthe sat in the chair Elly had used. "Do you know much about Garia?"

"Only what most people know. How it was settled by Paradisan refugees."

"A nicer word than the Paradisans use. And what about Redout?"

"Again, only what most people know."

"But you've seen more than most who haven't come here yet. They've seen the shining towers of Redout Central, the pristine tunnels and worker habitats and refugee-intake centres. But they haven't seen the holding camps like you have. The camps, the orbital rings and other places far less welcoming, less comfortable."

"You're saying the system isn't working?" he asked.

"I'm saying it's doing its best for the most part but it will never keep up with demand. And people will be people, especially when resources aren't plentiful. There's graft, there are flare-ups of lawlessness that are put down by varying degrees of violent authority. And there are those who want to run the whole thing for their own ends."

Markusz knew Congress had no other option than what it was doing. But, humanity being what it was, did they really expect it would work?

"But you're part of the Confederation council and a member of Congress," he said.

Marthe nodded. "That means precisely nothing when faced with a humanitarian crisis that spans the entire Thousand Worlds. As soon as Redout was founded here, the native Garians lost control. First came the Paradisan Corps d'Ingénieurs, which was a slap in the face to every Garian alive. They ripped up the surface of the planet and tunnelled deep into it to create living space for the billions of refugees to come. Garia supported the Redout project – how could we not? – but our buildings and our history were being torn apart. Our culture was being ploughed into the ground. We wanted to preserve what we were alongside what had to be done to make Redout possible. But peaceful protests were met with violent suppression from the Opitauan security the Corps had brought with them. We no longer had a voice. I no longer had a voice."

Markusz believed her. The Congress was "mainly benevolent", which meant as benevolent as possible when balancing the needs of so many constituent governments: oligarchies, hegemonies, technocracies, democracies, military dictatorships and cyberocracies. The key to peace was profit. Each member government was far better off cooperating than not. The highliners of the Galactische Handelsonderneming and the goods they bought and sold and transported were the glue that held everything together. But beneath that blanket of benevolence there was the day-to-day expediency of local circumstance. And what happened on Redout had to be the very model of expediency. The stakes were that high.

"After the Paradisans came M-Def, then the Fordana and Haibeu and GH," Marthe continued. "They all have their part to play in Redout's success. And as soon as they were here, they made sure to resettle as many of their own people as they could ahead of the refugees. All 'necessary personnel' for the Redout effort. Garians have been effectively squeezed out of any decision-making."

"So – what – you run the 'Garian Separatists' instead?" Markusz said. "How do you think you can resist what's coming?"

"We're not stupid. But there's payback necessary for what the Paradisans and Opitauans have done to us. And the Resistance has other uses." Marthe stood. "Come. Let me show you around."

Markusz followed her out into a long, gently curving corridor. The elliptical door of his cell was just one of many that stretched as far as he could see on both sides. The floor and walls of the corridor were made of the same stuff as his cell. The light was muted with no obvious source.

"What is this place?" he asked.

Marthe started walking and Markusz followed alongside, the guards bringing up the rear.

"Garia wasn't empty when we found it," she said. "There were remnants of an alien civilisation. Long dead."

Which was unusual, but not unique, Markusz thought. During its expansion the Thousand Worlds had encountered several planets that showed signs of previous habitation. But whatever civilisations had flourished there were long dead by the time humanity first set out into space. Barely anything remained for scholars to study.

"The first Garians lived underground for two generations. During that time we came across alien excavations. They didn't look promising, but some explorers persisted and eventually found tunnels and shafts. And finally, this place. When Redout was commissioned, we worried the Corps d'Ingénieurs would find what we had discovered. But we were lucky. They uncovered a few collapsed tunnels and filled them in to ensure the integrity of their own digs. Which means that – even now – they're unaware of this."

Marthe touched a door panel and Markusz's hair was blown back in a sudden rush of air. The low sound he'd heard became louder.

He followed Marthe through the door onto an open gallery overlooking a wide chasm studded with lights. The void was easily five hundred metres across, and the gallery ran right around the space and connected to lower galleries – he counted twenty beneath the one they stood on. A couple were lined with elliptical doorways, but the others were open areas, some holding what he recognised from *Endeavour* as hydroponic units and others packed with rows of empty bunk beds, sometimes both. The impression was of an underground settlement. Markusz realised the lights he observed had a greenish caste to them because the chasm walls were covered in plant life.

In the ceiling above, a rotor – almost as wide as the entire space – turned slowly. Leaning over the railing he could see another turning rotor set into the floor below.

"What is this place? Where are we?"

"The aliens lived here. Perhaps the surface was uninhabitable for them. Perhaps whatever ground dwellings they had were worn away with the passage of time. But this place endures."

She clasped the railing in both hands and leaned forward, looking up to the ceiling. Markusz looked up too. He'd thought perhaps the low tidal sound he'd become aware of was the rotors turning, but he could hear those separately now and they were too regular. That deeper sound below everything else was still there when he listened for it.

"As for where," Marthe said, "we're about three hundred kilometres below the surface, inside a stable magma chamber in the planet's asthenosphere."

Which meant they were beneath the solid lithosphere. Finally, he realised the source of the sound, like waves or a tide. They were surrounded by magma.

"But you can't build something like this here. The rock flows – it's too malleable."

"And yet here we are," Marthe said. "The instrumentality that preserves this space also makes us invisible to sensors. It's almost as if the builders anticipated our needs. Or perhaps they were hiding from something too."

Hiding, Markusz thought. Marthe was watching him as his mind followed that particular path and she slowly nodded as he realised what she meant.

"You've seen what it's like up there," she said. "Redout is doing what it can to feed and house the incomers, but soon it will be at capacity." She grunted a soft laugh. "Such a misleading word. Even at 'capacity' the system is not a closed loop. Food, water, air. Even if they use everything, even if they recycle the dead, there will eventually be shortages. And when they start to bite there will be chaos, no matter who's in charge. I can't help *them*. I can't even save every Garian. There's not enough room here for that. But I can make sure we survive. When the time comes, those selected will move here, close the doors and let whatever happens on the surface happen."

"You're consigning a lot of innocent people to death," Markusz said.

Marthe's face twisted in sudden anger. "We've given over our entire planet to incomers. We have a right to survive." She turned away and looked into the depths of the chasm.

Markusz could understand. If things got as bad as they might, everyone would be out to save themselves and fuck anyone else. Marthe was only trying to save the people she cared about. He thought about the augment-locked refugees trapped in that sun-blasted camp, and all the other refugees who had placed their hope in Redout. *He* might not want to live, but others – too many others – were desperate to. He had to put his own pain aside.

"I get it," he said. "Closed systems will always fail. But it doesn't have to be like this. I know the annulus better than anyone. I can push back against the destruction."

"And *that's* the reason you're here," Marthe said, still hunched over the railing. "Even if we survive in this place, we need a functioning annulus."

"Elly showed me what happened at the heliopause."

Marthe spared him a sideways glance. "You haven't heard the rest. Paradis is gone. As soon as they initiated your annulus the Paradisan system started to collapse."

Markusz sank to his haunches as he struggled to make sense of her words. He thought about Helena activating the annulus and the system collapsing around her. But he'd fixed that. He'd run it backwards and forwards a thousand times.

"Fuck!" he shouted. He needed to *be* with the annulus. He needed to see the raw data. He hadn't missed anything; he was sure of it. This was down to Rachik's and Teel's tinkering.

"I can fix this," he said. "You have to help me. You have to let me help all of us."

Marthe placed a hand under his elbow and pulled him up to standing. "You may be worth keeping alive after all," she said.

13

Sylfe entered the council chamber still feeling "out of body"– a combination of grief and bad sleep. But she needed to be here. If she was going to stop Fontaneau she needed to find out exactly what his plans were. Which might also help her penetrate the mystery surrounding what had really happened to Paradis.

The fact that Fontaneau had sent Denantes to sound her out meant he viewed her as a potential ally or a threat. Or maybe both. Sylfe wanted to be seen as indispensable and someone whose support could not be taken for granted. She needed an edge and it was clear to her what that was. Even with a well-behaved annulus, Redout needed a functioning sun and SolEng's work couldn't continue without her. She'd made sure of that. Even after the resequencing, ongoing adjustments would be required. Solar engineering was like that: suns couldn't be tamed, only constantly nudged along the right path.

Denantes nodded at her from across the room, then glanced meaningfully at Fontaneau who appeared to be in tense discussion with Rask – or at least Rask looked tense. Fontaneau looked implacable. When he looked Sylfe's way his lips spread in a slow smile which he no doubt felt was a credible approximation of a friendly greeting. Sylfe gave it a four out of ten.

She accessed her scopes and ran the conversation back a few seconds.

"You never said anything about a presentation," Rask hissed.

Fontaneau's words matched his expression. "I suggest if you *don't* want undue attention, you moderate your tone."

Distracted, Sylfe almost walked into Evan Beltran. The Fordana's dark suiting and pasty expression gave him the demeanour of a funeral director, as did the words that — if she were being charitable — he probably hoped would comfort her.

"My condolences to you, Ind Cachand, on the death of your mother, your sister and her partner, and indeed your entire extended family. It's hard to … to …"

He ground to a halt, perhaps having expended whatever wellspring of emotion he hid so well behind his tables and figures. His eyes bulged and Sylfe wondered how long she'd have to wait for his emotional circuit breakers to reset.

She laid a hand on his arm and he flinched, but it gave her the opportunity to take control. "Thank you," she said and walked past him. She didn't want his sympathy or his pity.

Fontaneau's voice rang out. "Gentle Inds, I believe we have a quorum. Our esteemed mayor is *incommunicado* so we will have to muddle on as best we can without her."

Someone gave a high-pitched laugh. Probably Denantes.

The council members claimed their seats. Sylfe noted Tane was by the door as usual, and Asymptote Eleven sat in her customary chair pushed into an alcove beneath the clerestory windows. Her expression hinted she was a thousand light years away.

"This extraordinary meeting has been called at the request of Ind Leeuwin," Fontaneau continued, "but before we hear from him, I think it wise to apprise ourselves of the investigation into the unfortunate incident at the heliopause. Commander?"

Rask almost leaped to his feet, his chair scraping on the floor. His pale blue eyes were fixed on Fontaneau. He tore his gaze away and looked around the room with the air of a man whose last meal had not agreed with him.

Something was going on. Clearly Fontaneau had a motive beyond ensuring his fellow council members were up to date on the fatalities. Sylfe knew she should care, but what she really wanted was an explanation for the destruction of Paradis. She felt like a wire twisted to breaking point.

"My office has compiled this report on the action," Rask said, his words barely above a whisper.

Sylfe's augment took receipt of the file and she flashed the whole thing instantly. What a fiasco. It wasn't as if no-one had seen this coming. There had been incidents before. So many ships packed with desperate people stuck out there in the void, many of them for years while their entry petitions were assessed with grinding slowness. Waiting while highliners carrying millions passed effortlessly into a region of space that was interdicted to them.

But the lives lost in previous squabbles were barely a tenth of those that had died when an arbitrary glowing line appeared out of nowhere and all the refugees realised they were on the wrong side of it. Ships started moving with scant regard for the proximity of others. Warnings were issued and ignored. Collisions created confusion and cover for other ships to attempt a dash for what broad comms between the vessels had agreed by consensus was now "safe space".

M-Def had issued more warnings, but here was the point: M-Def was many things but it was not crowd control. Its officers didn't have the training or the finesse to evaluate a situation and respond outside the very limited set of levers M-Def traditionally used to impose order on chaos. One of the M-Def pickets had finally lost patience and started shooting. And more than one ship on the civilian side had decided things were desperate enough to shoot back. Fifteen seconds later, twenty-five refugee ships had been destroyed and three hundred thousand people were breathing vacuum.

The report noted the picket captain had been demoted under military conduct principles, with a sidebar that the Redout Charter did not permit the council to impose additional penalties in matters that had been determined under said principles.

"The action was regrettable," Rask mumbled, "but the outcome … I feel the report makes it clear that I …"

He trailed off, clearly uncomfortable and just as clearly pissed off, but Sylfe didn't feel it had anything to do with the loss of life.

She flashed the report again. Really the wordsmithing was second to none. She'd missed it first time around but every sentence was perfectly balanced to ensure any blame was apportioned as far away from Rask as humanly possible. There were multiple failures that had led to the tragedy but none of them belonged to the commanding officer. Rather it was a combination of the service's intake methods, training regime, the operational status of the M-Def vessels around Redout and the impact of such a long deployment, the cultural upbringing of the picket captain – that was a low blow – and even the threat software on the picket was called into question. If Rask had ordered the entire M-Def contingent to fly at full speed into the sun, this report would maintain his unquestionable innocence of any wrongdoing.

Honestly, such brazen manipulation was worthy of one of Paradis's Great Families – which suggested Rask's staff had *not* drafted the report, rather that it was drafted for him by one of Fontaneau's people. But to what end?

"We appreciate your … views on the matter, Commander," said Fontaneau, saving them all from more of Rask's dithering.

Rask sat again, much subdued. And, Sylfe thought, much diminished.

The atmosphere around the council table indicated she wasn't the only one to see the commander's report as a reprehensible attempt to avoid blame. Denantes looked like he'd just smelled something odious that had dripped out of an antiquated environment sluice; and Leeuwin seemed even more startled than normal, as if the scales had fallen from his eyes in relation to Rask. All of which indicated the report seemed to have had the effect Fontaneau intended, though not the effect he'd convinced Rask it would have.

Fontaneau's rich baritone sounded again. "I thank you for your indulgence, Ind Leeuwin. Please, you have the floor."

Leeuwin stood, opened his mouth to speak, then closed it again. He looked once more at Rask, who reddened and avoided his gaze, busying himself with some private augment window.

Finally, Leeuwin found his voice. "Thank you, Ernes, and thank you, Inds, for your indulgence. We are all painfully aware of the humanitarian crisis we have been charged with alleviating, and I know we all take our duties very seriously indeed. Everyone is doing their best, but I feel we must do more."

Leeuwin was one of the most sincere people Sylfe had ever met. Sector governor-general for GH, he didn't come across as soullessly driven by profit as one might expect from his exalted status in the company. He genuinely cared about the Redout project. One might even say he felt it was his calling, like some sinner who'd undergone a religious epiphany. He had a wife and child, Sylfe knew, but they were still to arrive. Anyone else on the council would have pulled strings to fast-track the arrival of their loved ones ahead of the orderly refugee intake mandated by M-Worlds, and most had, but not Leeuwin, precisely because it wouldn't be fair. It seemed those same sentiments were driving him now.

"The annulus has the power to keep us safe, and that is a blessing. But those on our borders are still at risk, being outside its influence. While I understand the necessity to keep them from landing on Redout, surely there is no harm in letting them move within the annulus's border. It would not make our situation any worse, and it would make theirs infinitely better."

"You would have us move them all closer regardless of the risk?" Denantes asked.

"There is no risk, or a negligible one. And it would calm the panic that led to –" Leeuwin glanced at Rask, who was still absorbed in his private window – "to the deaths out there. It's the humanitarian thing to do."

"The fact is," Fontaneau said, "that as we've seen, there is a very *real* risk to all of us. M-Def can no longer guarantee our safety. I don't think they ever really could."

Sylfe saw Rask's cheek twitch despite his apparent concentration on his window. But there was no point in him objecting. What might have been questioned before was now unquestionable.

"An orderly migration of so many ships *is* beyond M-Def's capability," Fontaneau continued. "But to be fair to the good commander, it is likely beyond anyone's. Too many variables. Too much desperation in the air." He smiled and Sylfe was reminded of a dead thing.

"I too have a report to table," Fontaneau went on, gesturing.

Sylfe again received a file. As did the rest of the council. It made for grim reading.

"I am grateful to Ind Beltran and his staff for crunching the numbers. The data they have gathered, collated and analysed is a monumental undertaking. Ind Leeuwin asks us to do the humanitarian thing. I know the Ind well and I know his heart is in the right place. But we cannot afford to be soft-hearted. The projections you see are precise and flawless. Redout is full, though it pains me to say it. If we admitted those at the heliopause, we would be obligated to supply them. But the mass of humanity they represent would tip the balance. The total system population would be unsustainable. Our act of humanitarianism would sentence everyone on and around Redout to slow, inevitable starvation."

So he's putting the walls up, Sylfe thought. A king needs to define an "us" and a "them" if he is to rally his people to his cause.

"If the highliner from Paradis had arrived in a month's time as expected, would you have turned it away as you would these people?" Leeuwin asked. He was shaking as he spoke. Sylfe had never seen him upset before, let alone this obviously angry.

But Fontaneau was not to be cowed. "I do not deal in hypotheticals," he said. "Just as I would not hypothesise that your laudable motivation is bolstered by the fact your wife and daughter are not yet arrived."

Leeuwin jerked as if he'd been physically slapped. But he remained silent.

"The facts are incontrovertible," Fontaneau continued. "The Fordana have proved it."

"It is not within your power to challenge M-World policy,

Fontaneau. Redout remains open until Congress says otherwise." Rask had finally found his voice and a strategic position he clearly felt was well-enough defended to take a pot shot at his betrayer. Sylfe wasn't so sure.

"I am not challenging policy, Commander," Fontaneau said. "The Redout Charter requires the council to ensure Redout is viable. I am simply saying we must do all we can to discharge our duty."

"You say Redout is full," Sylfe cut in. "But the facts in the report indicate there is a margin."

She could almost feel the shifting lines of power concentrated in this room fold into a new configuration around her – in the same way the fluid surface of the sun twisted magnetic field lines into tighter and tighter concentrations until they snapped back, releasing an intense burst of electromagnetic radiation. Something like that would inevitably happen with the council. She wondered who would survive and who would perish.

Fontaneau nodded, a facsimile of amiability. "There is a margin," he agreed. "But given what we are dealing with, I think it prudent that we do not push our luck."

"That's lazy thinking," Sylfe said. From the corner of her eye she saw Denantes fold his hands over his belly, sit back in his seat and smirk. "Even if the margin were crossed and a collapse became inevitable, the time to that endpoint is more than a century. If we add more and more people, it precipitates the collapse sooner, but even with double our current population that collapse is still a decade off."

"A decade filled with many harsh privations," Fontaneau said.

"No-one promised it would be easy," Sylfe countered.

Fontaneau blinked with reptilian slowness but still appeared benevolent, affecting the air of someone enjoying the mental stimulation.

"Your collapse also presupposes that nothing else happens to change the applicable parameters," Sylfe said.

"Such as?"

"Oh, I don't know. *Anything* would be better than the prospect of a stable population trapped on a single planet for the remainder of eternity. That's not survival. We'll wither in place no matter how sustainable our lifestyle. So why not save as many as we can and trust that one of us will come up with a way to get us out of this mess before we run out of food and air? That man Zielinski seemed to think there was a way out."

"A maverick discredited by CSTO," Fontaneau said. "Would you have us place our fate in the hands of a man like that?"

Well, why not, Sylfe thought. But she held her tongue. She wondered if Fontaneau had had Zielinski killed yet.

"I agree with Ind Cachand," Leeuwin piped up. "And I have more faith in human ingenuity and the will to survive than you obviously do, Fontaneau."

"And I maintain that closing Redout is *not* within this council's purview," Rask added with an almost gleeful satisfaction. Blunted only by the fact he didn't have a vote on the council.

"I must side with Patri Fontaneau," Beltran said.

Well, you would, Sylfe thought. They're your figures. She doubted the Fordana ever included the human spirit in their calculations. Possibly because their bureaucratic machine had bred it out of them. She wondered if that was why they got on so well with the Haibeu and vice versa. But perhaps she was being uncharitable. To the Haibeu at least.

"I fear I must abstain at this time," Denantes said, though he didn't look unhappy about it.

Just stirring shit for the sake of it, Sylfe thought. Though she was doing her own fair share of that.

"Then we must leave the question unresolved at present," Fontaneau said. "My apologies, Ind Leeuwin. The status quo prevails until we can reconvene, perhaps with Mayor Firmin to settle the matter conclusively."

Leeuwin was obviously unhappy, but Fontaneau didn't look particularly put out that things hadn't gone his way either. The council meeting ground to an inconclusive halt and Sylfe left without another word. She had other things to think about now. They needed fresh solutions, not old justifications for control.

On the way home she watched Paradis die again out of some still unsated masochistic urge. It was desperate to think she could somehow come up with a solution that had evaded the best minds in M-Worlds. But desperation was for desperate times. And she was sure to fail if she didn't even try.

If she *could* fix this, then Fontaneau's machinations would be for nothing. She could avoid whatever hellscape he was planning and get on with what was left of her life. Added bonus: everyone else could do the same.

14

Sylfe felt as if a fever had overtaken her. She emptied the remains of the bottle into her glass. A '62 Pinot Grigio from her family's southern estates. A lost vintage from a lost planet.

It was close to dawn and she'd been working alone in her apartment for hours but she'd had enough of sleep. Of remorse. Of the weight of loss bearing down on her. Augment windows cluttered her vision, some running sims or realtime streams or simply scrolling text. She was reviewing everything and bringing her own particular expertise to bear on the problem.

The feeds from Paradis hadn't been the best, mainly because the event was so unexpected. There had been many far better documented collapses, particularly after CSTO perfected its predictive modelling. And she'd kept up with the research papers that intersected her own interests.

The Effect impacted time, as did stars and remnants of stars such as black holes. The Effect bent and contracted space; again something stars did just by existing. The Effect turned matter into something else: that was a star's raison d'être.

Admittedly no-one knew what happened to the matter the Effect destroyed. The remnant Teel-Attar radiation wasn't sufficiently energetic to account for the annihilation of entire planetary systems. What happened to the rest of the energy released? Did it vanish into the substrate?

Suns were intimately connected with the space beneath space and could be used as a sounding board to infer what was happening there. Admittedly the correlation wasn't perfect, but she felt sure something like the energy released by the Effect would not go unnoticed if the substrate were indeed its destination. Unless it was a type of energy they'd never encountered before.

Maybe, instead of the substrate, it was tunnelling into some other non-substrate dimension. But that was another dead end. Such places had been theorised for centuries but no-one had ever detected one.

Perhaps energy wasn't conserved in this case. If theories didn't fit facts, one needed new theories.

What about time then? Did the Effect use it to accelerate the collapse? Or did it flip the arrow of time locally, winding everything backwards so the collapse was simply a byproduct? She needed more research on that.

She realised she was personifying the Effect, trying to guess its motives. Forces of nature didn't need motives. They just were. Was this the way the universe was always going to end and all the theorists had simply missed it in their list of scenarios? Serve them right if it was. But thinking like this wasn't helping either because it negated the chance to fix things. It was impossible to change the nature of the universe, wasn't it?

Maybe she was deluded. Or maybe – a small voice in the back of her mind suggested – she was focusing on a problem that couldn't be solved in preference to acknowledging and working through her grief. And yet … Markusz Zielinski had been hopeful. Maybe he was deluded too. But still. He *had* been a senior on the CSTO team. If he was still alive, he may have an answer.

She finished her wine in a single gulp, wiping away the windows with her free hand. It should be a simple matter to find this man and see what he knew.

The refugee registry opened at a gesture and she entered his name. Lists blurred with dizzying speed. Maybe it was the wine or the late hour or both.

Two words blinked in an otherwise empty window: *Not Found.*

Even a corpse would leave *some* record. She set up a series of data sifters and watched as not much happened very slowly. Her eyes were heavy and she rested her chin on her hand, but pretty soon her arms were folded on her bureau and her head was nestled against them.

She woke, stiff and muzzy-headed, still at her bureau. She groaned and pushed herself to standing so she could cover the few steps to her bed. But one of her scopes was persistent in its efforts for her attention. She sat on the divan instead and opened the scope's window.

Fontaneau sat behind his ghastly ormolu desk while Teel and his subordinate, Rachik, sat on uncomfortable-looking and decidedly low visitors chairs. Studying their faces, Sylfe thought the chairs were the least of their problems.

"I take it you have some findings," Fontaneau said.

"Indeed, Ind!" Teel almost jumped from his chair, like a puppy eager to please his new master. "I apologise for the delay. As you can understand, our review required significant analysis and cross-checking given the ... gravity of the situation."

Fontaneau's face darkened. "Is that supposed to be a joke?"

Sylfe watched Teel pause to review his last few words then look even more stricken. "Oh, no, please forgive –"

"Get on with it."

"The good news is that the annulus perimeter was successfully constrained to the heliopause," Teel said.

Constrained, Sylfe thought. Now that *was* interesting. The appearance of the border had caused chaos. Had that all been part of Fontaneau's plan?

"But once full operation was established there was some non-local feedback," the scientist continued. "It's something we've seen before in earlier versions of the annulus, but ..." His explanation petered out. Clearly he was worried how his news would be received.

"And this non-local feedback?" Fontaneau pressed.

Teel looked at Rachik. Yes, the buck stopped with the boss, but sometimes the boss required his underlings to fall on their swords too.

Rachik swallowed hard, then said, "The feedback could have been managed with standard settings. But the parameters you … ah … requested meant … uh… Paradis was destroyed."

Sylfe paused the playback, all her thoughts rushing together to a terrible conclusion. Fontaneau had killed Paradis.

Her mind scrabbled to comprehend. He'd killed Maman. Killed Yvette, Suzanne, billions of Paradisans. His meddling had … Her hands twisted into claws. She wished he were here now, in the flesh. She'd strangle him, gouge his eyeballs from their sockets, scream into his sightless face. This … *monster.*

Sick to her core, she sank back on the divan, her mind consumed with the enormity of what he'd done. She knew now exactly what had happened, but even so … the import of it kept skittering away from her understanding.

She took a breath. She couldn't give in to rage. She had to be smarter than Fontaneau. That was the only way to gain the upper hand.

The augment window was still frozen in front of her. She waved the playback forward.

Fontaneau gave a short laugh. "You're blaming me for this?"

Yes, Sylfe thought coldly. Yes, I am.

Teel rallied. "Not in the slightest, Patri. I take full responsibility. It was up to me and my team to ensure those 'suggestions' would be assimilated into the annulus smoothly. I think it best the review findings remain *in camera.* I can provide a technical overview to the council that shows the fault lay in transferring operations from a testbed environment — albeit one that had been subjected to the most rigorous trials — to final deployment. We do our best, but we cannot guarantee complete success in such circumstances."

"And the annulus is performing within expected parameters now," Rachik added, jumping on the making-the-best-of-a-dire-situation bandwagon.

Teel could put whatever spin he liked on it, Sylfe thought, but Fontaneau *was* responsible. Without him, there would have been no adjustments. Aside from hushing things up, however, it seemed he didn't really give a damn about what he'd done.

"It's a misstep, Ind Teel," Fontaneau said, his stern visage softening. "The bottom line, however, is that the people of Redout are safe. And for that we all owe you a debt of gratitude."

Teel looked instantly more relaxed. Rachik still looked haunted. Perhaps he took the loss of Paradis more seriously. Or maybe he was just terrified of Fontaneau, which was also a laudable mindset.

"What we have here is a precious seed of humanity," Fontaneau continued. "And it is incumbent on us to do everything we can to ensure its survival."

Teel blinked. "Yes, of course."

"But there is another danger beyond the Effect, Kelan. I *can* call you Kelan, can't I?"

"Of course, Patri. But what danger do you speak of?"

Sylfe noticed Fontaneau didn't ask Teel to call him Ernes. They weren't going to be *that* chummy. Master and servant more like.

"The refugee ships at the heliopause are only the first intimations of a tidal wave that threatens to sweep away our good work on Redout. The Fordana have already calculated the tipping point, which is precariously near."

Teel and Rachik both looked blank for an instant, and Sylfe could tell Fontaneau had dropped Beltran's report into their augments.

"I … I had no idea," Teel said.

"This type of information is not for general consumption, Kelan. The populace must not know how much danger they are in. But the simple fact is we can accept no more refugees. It's devastating, I know. But that is exactly why we are so grateful for your project."

"We?" Teel said weakly.

"The council. We need to act now to secure our borders. M-Def have demonstrated they cannot guarantee our safety. We are balanced on a knife edge, Kelan. You have helped us so much already, but you will recall I said at our first meeting that we might have need of a sword as well as a shield? It has not come to that yet. But we certainly need a stronger shield if we are to keep the rising tide at bay."

"You want the annulus border to be impermeable," Teel said.

The scientist caught on fast. Sylfe suspected that was the reason for his success in CSTO: find your political master and give them what they want.

"Umm …" Rachik began.

Sylfe didn't think he was aware he'd made a sound but she suspected his train of thought was running along the same lines as her own. Fontaneau's first set of changes to the annulus had destroyed Paradis. Now he wanted *more* changes.

Fontaneau and Teel both stared at Rachik.

Fontaneau's expression was mildly interested. Like a sated snake might look mildly interested in a mouse that had fallen into its lair, wondering whether it could manage another bite so soon.

"Is there a problem, Ind Rachik?" Fontaneau said.

Rachik glanced at his boss, who, having only just extricated them from one sticky situation, was now manifesting naked hostility. Still, Fontaneau had asked a question so Rachik no doubt felt he had to go on.

"It's as Ind Teel said. We have only just commenced actual deployment and we're already pushing the boundaries of new technology. There's a very real danger of catastrophic failure, just as we warn–"

"My *assistant* is cautious," Teel interrupted. "As we all are, especially now. We take our duties and the trust the council has placed in us very seriously. But I can see a way that this can be done. In a controlled manner."

Rachik looked about to speak again, but Teel shut him down. "We'll discuss this back at the facility, Rachik. We don't need to waste the council chair's time with technical detail."

"Thank you both," Fontaneau said, standing. "You understand the urgency of this matter and the council expects you to act on it as soon as humanly possible."

"I'll keep you apprised, Patri," Teel said, also standing.

Rachik got to his feet too, looking decidedly ill.

"One other thing," Fontaneau said, as if the thought had just occurred to him. "The M-Def picket line should be *outside* the new boundary. That way they can continue to police the other vessels. We can let them back in later."

Oh no, Sylfe thought. Fontaneau was making his move. And the timestamp on the meeting was seven hours ago.

She had to get to the other council members. Warn Rask.

15

Firmin had given Markusz a lab. It was roomy and pretty well-appointed, though he was still confined to it, so was it really much different to a cell? Still, he'd set up a workstation and arranged a second one, just the way they'd configured it back on *Endeavour* when he and Helena had worked together into the small hours, or sometimes around the clock. He'd realised he wasn't ready to let her go, but he wasn't sure if creating a space for her would bring her back. Perhaps his subconscious had decided it was time to focus on "other important things in his life". Tough self-love and all that.

What he really needed was something to work on. There were only so many times you could arrange and rearrange equipment, check firmware and connections. Firmin had promised him a raw feed of annulus data but he didn't have it yet. He imagined it wasn't an easy thing to procure under the circumstances, but he was itching to do some analysis.

The clock was ticking.

Garia – or Redout – would eventually be all there was. M-Worlds could pour in limitless resources to make it the best, most viable cradle for what was left of humanity in the history of history itself and it would never be enough. It was doomed to fail because: one, any ordered system must inevitably give way to disorder; and, two, GH had been too successful in making sure everything was available to those who could pay for it. The Garians and other hardy settler types were in the minority. Most citizens of M-Worlds – and hence the majority of refugees on Redout – had lived on fully developed planets that provided for all their needs and wants. It wasn't that they couldn't conceptualise scarcity. But it wasn't something that happened to *them*. So when they were eventually confronted with the real thing, they'd do what any intelligent person would do: scheme, fight or steal to get what they believed they had a god-given right to possess and fuck anyone who got in their way.

Those people he'd seen in the camps, they'd been anaesthetised by the perception of living in simulated luxury. But they would only remain compliant for as long as their actual needs were met and the augmented reality held up. At the very first shortage or augment glitch, there'd be a riot.

Markusz wasn't sure what he could do about it. Creating the annulus had been an impossibility right up until the moment it wasn't. They hadn't even contemplated asking "what do we do after we succeed?" Someone else would have to work that out.

The door opened and Elly entered.

"I'm still here, if that's what you've come to check on," Markusz said.

"No need," Elly said. "This is the most heavily surveilled space in the facility. But watching you build your little lab isn't all that entertaining."

Markusz considered her. It could be useful if he made an ally. Though she was bound to see through any gambit he might employ to manipulate her. Apart from being a trained killer, she was a teenager. Still, she was here rather than watching him remotely, which meant she was bored, interested, a bit of both?

"I'm at a loose end myself," he said. "I can't actually do anything until I get some data. And my augments are still in passive mode." He looked at her hopefully, but she shook her head.

"Which reminds me," he said. "That scrambler. How come I needed it and you and Brak didn't?"

Elly pushed up her sleeve to reveal a metal torque twisted halfway up her forearm. "We keep our tech on the outside. The first settlers had only the most basic input implants and nothing like the tech to grow augments in newborns. So they fabricated the next best thing." She rolled her sleeve down again. "It became customary, then fashionable. And once Redout was set up, expedient."

"Huh," Markusz said. "So a whole bunch of Garians could disconnect from the augment network and hide down here." It wouldn't go unnoticed, but it could be done. Firmin was certainly confident it could.

Elly sat at the spare workstation and picked up a field analyser. Clearly she knew all about Firmin's plan.

"That doesn't bother you?" he asked.

"I know it bothers you," she said defiantly.

"It should bother everyone. Do you hate outsiders that much you'd be happy to see them die?"

"You don't know what happened here," she said. "All because of Redout. We had no choice in it."

"Do you think the people that fled here had a choice?"

"It's not up to us to save them."

"I know that. And I know those in charge of Redout have done the wrong thing by your people. But the refugees. The children –" He almost said "like you" but stopped himself. "They had no part in that. All they're trying to do is live."

They were the same arguments he'd used with Firmin. But Elly didn't have all of Garia resting on her shoulders.

"The maths don't work," she said.

That sounded like Firmin. "*I'll* decide if the maths work or not," he said.

"How?"

He sat on the free workstation chair and swivelled it to face her. "I don't know yet. But they will."

She tossed the analyser to him and he caught it one-handed.

"Why Garia?" she asked.

"I don't –"

"Why will Garia be last?"

"Ah, well. It's still a theory. But based on a lot of observations …" He trailed off. A lot of this was going to be difficult to explain, but she looked interested. And he had fuck all else to do.

"Do you know much about how the Effect works?" he asked.

She shook her head.

"Okay, well, I'm not known for my teaching skills, but I'll give it a shot. Tell me if I'm losing you. You know that when we're looking at distant parts of the universe we're actually looking back in time?"

She nodded. "Because the light takes so long to get to us from there."

"That's right. What we're observing could look totally different from what that region of space is like right now if we could travel there instantaneously and observe it in real time."

"What's that got to do with the Effect?"

"The first recorded Effect happened in a region of space a hundred and twenty thousand light years away. A nebula collapsed within the space of a day. But it happened a hundred and twenty thousand years ago. So this isn't something new. It may have been happening since the universe began and we've just been sitting in a remote corner of space, oblivious to it. There may be whole parts of space we observe that actually don't exist any more. The light from the Effect destroying them just hasn't gotten to us yet. As to how it happens …"

He threw his arms wide. Of course, nothing happened.

He looked at Elly and twirled a finger at the space between them. "Do you think you could … you know …"

Elly scowled at him.

"You did ask," he said.

She gave the barest gesture, but Markusz felt his augment engage with the local network. Not full access, but enough for this.

He threw his arms wide again and the galaxy filled their shared space, spinning slowly, but speeding up as he brought his arms together again, shrinking the image and revealing more of the space around it. Not just a single galaxy but another and another. The image shrank again, or their shared vantage point pulled further and further back to see more and more. Galaxies – thousands of them, each a hundred thousand light years across — became mere dots of light, stringing together and twisting through interstellar space. And between the bright points, smoky filaments of matter linking everything in a pattern that looked like tree roots or a frond of coral.

"The Laniakea Supercluster," Markusz said, "contains our galaxy and more than a hundred thousand others. You can't really see those shadowy limbs among the stars because they're made of dark matter. It was the gravitational effect of dark matter that condensed normal matter into galaxies and stars in the early universe, and it still forms the scaffolding of everything we *can* see. Teel, my old boss, theorised that dark matter may be involved in the Effect. That didn't mean much — we were knee-deep in theories when the Effect was first identified as a threat. But Teel was on the earliest CSTO team, so there was funding to test *his* theory. And the observations confirmed there is a definite change in the dark matter field during the Effect."

"Is there a point you feel like getting to?" Elly said.

"Soon. Just one more piece of cosmology." He wiped a hand across the supercluster and it disappeared, replaced by a very bright sphere. "The beginning-ish of the universe," he said and clicked his fingers. The sphere jumped in size in an instant before proceeding to grow at a more leisurely rate. "Again, not what it looked like — we think — but that rapid jump in size was the period of cosmic inflation when the whole universe grew faster than light."

Elly took a breath to interrupt, but Markusz beat her to it. "I know. Our ships have to go into the dimensional substrate for FTL travel. Inflation didn't break that rule. The universe itself expanded that fast, not anything travelling inside it."

He paused. "Yes, not explaining that very well. It would help if I could show you the maths." He thought about that. "Actually it wouldn't. You could flash a primer?"

"I'd sooner watch you totally fail to explain anything," Elly said.

"Doesn't matter. My point here is that early inflation was driven by a dark energy field."

"And that matters because …?"

Markusz smiled. "I'm glad you asked. All those solar systems smashing together – it's the opposite. It's deflation."

"You get paid for this stuff? It seems obvious."

"It is obvious. The hard part is working out the mechanism. The harder part is working out how to stop it. That's what I get paid for. *Got* paid for."

"And the mechanism?"

"Something is increasing the gravitational pull of the dark matter framework by several factors. Actually probably bringing it to the state it was at during the creation of the universe. And at the same time the dark energy field is creating a localised deflationary force that – to an observer outside the Effect – seems to break the light barrier but probably doesn't."

"So this something that increases gravity – you worked out what it is?"

"Not as such. But we don't need to. I mean, ideally, yes, it would be good to know that. But the next best thing is to understand the second-order effects, like what's happening with dark matter and dark energy *because of* that something, and then experiment until we work out how to negate those."

"And that's what the annulus does?"

"In a sense."

Elly gave him what he considered to be an above-par eye-roll.

"And there you have it," he said.

"Except you haven't explained why Garia is going to be last." She sounded more than mildly pissed off.

"Ah, yes. Sorry. That was Helena actually. A superb piece of work." He glanced round the room on the off-chance. Nothing. "The red glow left after a collapse –"

"The Teel-Attar radiation," Elly corrected him.

"Yes. Even early observations showed the radiation dispersal pattern was anisotropic along a single axis. That means the radiation field was always stronger in one direction. By the time Helena joined the task force, they'd observed well over a hundred and fifty thousand collapses, all of them with anisotropic glows. These events had happened all over the observable universe and at very different time intervals. But she was able to work out all those anisotropic axes were pointing at the same location, or rather the location where Garia was situated with respect to the spatial and temporal location of each Effect."

"Why?"

"We don't know. But a couple of years later, I came along with a mathematical proof for quantum entanglement over large areas of space persisting since before inflation. One of the outputs was a predictive model for where the Effect would strike next. With a little help from Helena and her experimental team we were able to predict the next three events and also retrospectively predict every event that had been witnessed thus far with ninety-eight point eight per cent accuracy. Projecting our modelling forward – while admittedly decreasing accuracy the farther out we pushed it – also indicated Garia would be one of the last systems hit."

"And that's why Redout came here," Elly said. "*You* fucked up my life."

"That's one way of looking at it," Markusz said. "But if it's any consolation, I've fucked up my own life a whole lot worse. And I had no idea what would happen to your planet."

Elly shook her head. "That's okay. If it hadn't been you, it would have been someone else."

Markusz doubted that. He was a singular genius after all. But he thought it best not to press the point.

"And I guess I can't blame your dead wife either," Elly said.

Markusz winced.

"And … Oh shit." Elly flicked an open hand towards him and he sat down hard as a shared augment window unfolded around them.

Deep space, but as he turned he saw the same region out by the heliopause: the borderspace with M-Def pickets and refugee ships facing off across a golden-hued barrier. Except the barrier was on the move. It roiled. Then shrank in quickly – almost like a reverse of the inflation image he'd shown Elly – so it was behind the picket ships and deepening to a dark amber.

A bright flash off to the left. One of the pickets lagging behind the others had exploded, sheared in half by the hardening barrier. It *must* be hardening for that to happen. People and broken walls and machinery poured into space from the ragged hull.

Then all hell broke loose. Spinning on their axes, a handful of pickets fired at the barrier but their beams glanced off in all directions. Caught by a stray shot, one picket exploded, cartwheeling back and ploughing into a long cargo hauler, crushing a nacelle which vented atmosphere in frozen clouds. A private liner, caught in the sudden storm of debris, had its front section caved in and fired thrusters to get away, only to smash into a mining tug. More ships tried to get away from the mayhem, causing more collisions and damage.

"What the hell," Elly said.

Markusz agreed. But he was staring at the annulus field and wishing he had real time data on this. Twice now, Teel and Rachik had produced an annulus effect he hadn't foreseen. Admittedly, both times with catastrophic results. From an experimental perspective, it was intriguing and possibly quite promising. From a real-world perspective it was fucking terrifying. After what happened to Paradis how could they keep tinkering like this?

"They weren't entirely unforeseen," Helena said.

She was back. Markusz felt ridiculously happy about that. It probably indicated he was succumbing to some deepening mental psychosis, but what the hell.

"Not unf–" he began. Then the augment window collapsed around him and he saw her standing at the workstation behind the still seated Elly.

Helena smiled. "Nice set-up," she said.

He smiled back. "Well, you know. But … not unforeseen?"

Elly stood. "Christ, is your dead wife back?"

"I told you before, you can call her Helena," Markusz said, more than a little pissed off. "Not unforeseen … yes."

He remembered now. There had been a side project. Early on, as he and Helena worked together on the equations that would eventually build the annulus. Teel and Rachik had gone through a door whose threshold Markusz and Helena had stood on before. They'd been distracted by the need to perfect the annulus, which had led them in an altogether different direction. Perhaps there was more to discover in the room beyond that door. Or perhaps there were more doors.

He needed that feed from the annulus. And he needed to talk to Rachik.

16

By the time she'd exited her apartment, Sylfe had known there was no point warning Rask. She'd seen what was happening out at the edge of the system and knew the commander must already be too well aware. All she could do was get to the council chamber. Fontaneau's plan would be in full swing now. She couldn't be the one to show any weakness.

Her private mover flew through the chasms of the inner city. There was barely any other traffic in the air. People were too afraid to venture out. The sky was too strange. The Teel-Attar blooms were tinged a dark amber due to the annulus field, with only the brightest stars shining through.

Her mover dipped towards the ring of lights around the council building's landing skirt. It had started to rain and Sylfe walked quickly towards the pavilion, pulling her coat tight against buffeting gusts of wind. The glass and metal building was in darkness. A light flared from a passing mover and she was confused for a moment by her reflection in the window.

As the glass slid aside to admit her, she almost walked into Asymptote Eleven coming out. The Haibeu's eyes were wide with wonder.

"It can only get more beautiful now," she said, then dipped her head and walked past Sylfe into the darkness.

There had been very little beauty in what Sylfe witnessed at the heliopause.

A lumen glided down to light her way and she could see another further off, hovering above a pacing figure. She could hear voices too. Or a voice.

"Stupid. Stupid. What are you? Why can't you –"

The words cut off as the figure stopped pacing and looked her way. Sylfe saw it was Leeuwin. He looked haggard.

Light was seeping round the council chamber door behind him. Someone was already in there and it wasn't hard to work out who. Leeuwin clearly knew and was trying to screw up the courage to confront him. He was also totally failing and berating himself for it. Sylfe thought he looked a little ashamed to be found this way.

"Ind Cachand," he said.

"Ind Leeuwin. I assume you're here for the same reason as me. To find out what the hell Ind Fontaneau has done."

Leeuwin paused for a moment, then straightened. "Indeed," he said, his voice a full octave deeper than a second ago. There was safety in numbers, after all.

We'll see how long that lasts once we get through the door, Sylfe thought.

"Shall we?" she said.

He paused again, then stepped aside – ever the gentleman even *in extremis*. She swept forward and the doors parted for her.

Fontaneau sat in his usual place at the centre of the curved council table. Teel had pulled up a chair to sit at his right side, and Rachik sat a little behind and between the pair, while Beltran sat to Fontaneau's left. Team Fontaneau was present. Denantes was there too, but seated at his favoured position on the extreme right end of the table, an edge dweller ready to swim either way depending on the current.

Sylfe knew by the slightly wheezy breath behind her that Leeuwin had followed her in. The door parted again and she half-turned to see Mayor Firmin enter, looking consistently stern. What did she think about events, Sylfe wondered.

Firmin stopped level with Leeuwin but said nothing. Fontaneau's group just stared at them, Fontaneau himself looking as stern as Firmin. They were in tableaux it seemed, and it was up to

Sylfe to move things forward.

"What have you done, Ernes?"

Fontaneau tilted his head back and looked down his perfectly gene-tailored aquiline nose at them. "I have made the hard decision," he said. "For *all* of you. And so I absolve you of all guilt. Even you, Leeuwin, though I know how much you revel in it."

"Fuck. You."

Sylfe turned to see Leeuwin's face red with anger.

"You've done whatever the fuck you want to do as usual and fuck everyone else. Don't dress this up as some kind of noble act to spare the rest of us."

Sylfe couldn't fault Leeuwin's character assessment, but confronting Fontaneau with the truth wasn't going to achieve anything. Fontaneau didn't care.

"I'm sorry you feel that way, Jan Pieter," he said. "I know you wanted to do otherwise, and I know your family is still out there. That pains me on a personal level. I don't desire to see anyone suffer."

Leeuwin let out a strangled gasp, whether from sheer incredulity at what he was hearing or simple disgust, Sylfe couldn't say.

"And you may not believe Beltran's report," Fontaneau continued, ignoring the interruption, "but thankfully your belief is not required. The facts are the facts and the action I took was both necessary and timely."

Facts *were* facts, Sylfe thought and one fact in particular was very telling. The fact that Fontaneau was even bothering to defend his actions. It told Sylfe that – at least for now – he needed the council, or those members of it he could sway, on his side. It told her he was not yet sure of his authority. He needed Beltran and the Haibeu if he wanted to keep Redout's administrative wheels turning; he needed Sylfe to keep the sun under control; he needed Firmin to keep the locals in check; and he clearly needed Denantes for *something*, though Sylfe couldn't imagine what. General deceit and backstabbery? But he didn't feel he could count on any or all of them to back him without at least some soothing narrative that spoke of a man thrust into an invidious position and forced to silence his softer side (*hah* – there was a joke) to do what "had to be done" for "the good of all".

The other fact that was indisputable was that, with the barrier impermeable, Fontaneau didn't need the Galactische Handelsonderneming or its sector governor-general any more because Redout would not be receiving any further deliveries.

Perhaps that thought was dawning on Leeuwin, because he looked a little shocked that he'd said what he'd said out loud. Or maybe he'd just realised how out of character he was acting right now.

"But I won't hold it against you," Fontaneau said. "Emotions are running high and I know you fear for your family."

Sylfe was pretty sure he *would* hold it against Leeuwin at the earliest opportunity.

As for the rest of the council, they had two choices: back Fontaneau or declare civil war. Whatever happened, the billions on Redout would bear the brunt of it. No-one here had the right to rule. Not even Firmin, because the influx of migrants meant native Garians were in the distinct minority.

Sylfe doubted airing her revelation that Fontaneau had destroyed Paradis would make the slightest difference. Only Denantes was a fellow Paradisan, and he didn't give a shit about anything as long as it didn't impact his libidinous pleasures. Besides, Fontaneau could always attribute the destruction to an unforeseen if tragic side effect of keeping them all safe.

"Thankfully there are others on the council who are a little more clear-headed," Fontaneau continued, nodding affably to Beltran and Denantes.

The door opened again and Rask entered with two armed officers.

Sylfe, Leeuwin and Firmin stepped aside as Rask swept past and halted in front of Fontaneau, flanked by his soldiers who unshouldered their rifles but didn't bring them to bear on anyone. Yet, Sylfe thought.

"Lower the barrier, Teel," Rask said. "Immediately."

Teel looked slightly taken aback, and glanced at Fontaneau before blustering, "I'll do no such thing. I am acting in accordance with the council's wishes."

Of course he thought he was, Sylfe knew. She'd seen the whole conversation. But Teel hadn't exactly done his due diligence to make sure Fontaneau *was* speaking on behalf of the council. And if push came to shove, would he really care? From what she'd seen of the private meetings, Teel seemed very enamoured of the idea of being under Fontaneau's protection.

"Are you really stupid enough to believe that?" Firmin said.

Teel reddened, and it was the only response anyone in the room really needed.

"Come, Mayor Firmin," Fontaneau said, "I expected you to be favourably disposed to the fact that the tide of migration has come to a halt."

Firmin snorted and walked past the soldiers to take a seat beside Denantes. Clearly she didn't care what Fontaneau did.

Rask, however, was looking fed up at being ignored. "Fontaneau, have your man do as I say."

Fontaneau looked pained. "Commander Rask —"

"Enough of this!" Rask shouted. He pulled his sidearm and levelled it at Fontaneau. "I'm invoking martial law and placing you under arrest for treason against The Thousand Worlds."

Sylfe flinched as a blast of heat sizzled past her and the tiny hairs in her right earhole curled up. When she looked again, Rask was no more. But there was a spreading puddle on the floor. The nearest soldier moved his boot to avoid stepping in it.

Sylfe turned. Tane was standing behind her and Leeuwin with the biggest handheld plasma cannon she'd ever seen hanging from one shoulder.

His tattooed face folded into a smile as he saw her looking at him. "Your pardon. I regret you had to witness that."

She nodded. Tane was traditional Opitauan through and

through. They revered the Great Families of Paradis.

"Leave the guns on the floor, boys," Tane said to the soldiers who had accompanied Rask. He tilted his weapon to left and right. "Return to barracks. You'll get new orders soon enough."

The soldiers did as they were bid and left.

"Another necessary action, I'm afraid," Fontaneau said, "but one I hope the council will ratify. The on-planet M-Def command structure has been replaced with Opitauans loyal to the council."

Loyal to Fontaneau, Sylfe thought, but Tane's deferral to her was a little heartening at least.

"Rask and the commanders under him would of course insist that we open our borders and do whatever Congress wishes," Fontaneau continued. "But that would be suicide, particularly now. The rank-and-file soldiers will fall in line. They're safe like us and we'll look after them."

And execute those that don't like the new management. What the hell, Sylfe thought as she took her place at the council table. She had to hand it to Fontaneau. When he decided to stage a coup he didn't hold back.

That left Leeuwin still standing and staring at the liquid remains of Commander Torhild Rask. He looked up finally, realised he was alone and took his place beside Beltran.

"Excellent," said Fontaneau. "We owe it to the people of Redout to show a united front after this latest unpleasantness. They must know that everything we do is directed at keeping them safe. I am both relieved and gratified that we've been able to see eye to eye on this important issue. And, I might add, not a moment too soon."

Sylfe's attention shifted as her sunbarques alerted her to a change in the substrate. Something big was arriving.

She opened a private augment window. Out at the heliopause the chaos had ended — at least for the moment. Those ships damaged beyond repair were being given a wide berth, but there were rescue efforts evident in small pockets as some refugee ships aided others. There was still room for common decency, it seemed.

The M-Def picket ships were spread out among the refugees, the better to maintain order while presenting a diffuse target. Whoever was in charge out there was doing a better job than the late Commander Rask ever could.

Her focus shifted to a point above the mass of ships, where space puckered and twisted. It started like a normal transit from the substrate, but the telemetry she had access to told a different story. The liminal region of spacetime was not thinning but … congealing was the only word she could think of to describe what she was seeing. Instead of opening briefly onto the delicately folded dimensions of the substrate, there was pushback. The influence of the annulus?

Then whatever it was reversed, spacetime behaved, and a ship emerged. A big one. Sylfe saw at once the M-World Congress seal on the vessel. This was the arrival of Deputy Speaker Rao that Rask had warned Fontaneau about when the annulus was first activated.

Not a moment too soon indeed. Fontaneau had orchestrated everything. He'd made sure the annulus effect stopped at the heliopause. Then he'd taken advantage of the ensuing carnage *and* Leeuwin's objections to undermine Rask. That had cleared the way for him to lock the bulk of M-Def outside and replace their command structure with Opitauans.

All of this had to be done before Rao arrived. And he'd succeeded. Just in time. What an industrious schemer he was.

17

Deputy Speaker Rao's ship had descended and was rendezvousing with one of the picket ships but spacetime still registered an event. Sylfe again witnessed that odd congealing between the substrate and normal space. She set her scopes to gather every shred of data on what was happening. Then spacetime corrected itself again and more ships were coming through. A lot more. All M-Def. Battleships, heavy cruisers, dreadnoughts, corsairs. Her augment registered them all, naming them and providing a tally of ships' complements, tonnage and firepower.

By the time space had snapped back to normal, the refugee ships were overshadowed by the biggest conglomeration of firepower Sylfe could imagine. More than half the current total military might of M-Worlds, based on the records she had access to. What. The. Fuck.

A shared augment window opened in the space before the council and Deputy Speaker Rao looked down upon them. He was old, his skin brown and deeply wrinkled. Bushy white eyebrows shot up from deep-set eyes and his mouth was pinched as if he'd just sucked on a lemon. Sylfe wasn't sure if this was his normal expression or because the current state of affairs wasn't to his taste.

"What is the meaning of this, Ernes?"

Okay, Sylfe thought, he seemed to have been properly briefed and wasn't in the mood for pleasantries.

Fontaneau looked completely unfazed by the firepower that had just arrived in local space. "I might ask you the same thing. I understood there was to be an inspection, not an invasion."

Rao's mouth puckered even more. "It is nothing of the sort. But it seems we are in need of the military. I ask again: what are you doing?"

Fontaneau took a moment to look around the table at his council, because that's what they surely were now. His.

"The council is doing what Congress requires it to do: build and maintain a viable repository for humanity against the encroachment of the Effect."

"You will drop your barrier. Now."

"That would not be wise," Fontaneau said. "Firstly it would cause a stampede amongst the refugee ships you see here, and they have already been subjected to far too much unpleasantness."

Sylfe heard Leeuwin utter a brief squeak of despair or frustration. Maybe a bit of both.

"And secondly, to drop the barrier would compromise our ability to deliver on Congress's requirements."

"What do you mean?"

"It is simple and I am appending the report prepared by our Fordana representative and fellow council member Ind Beltran. As you will see, to admit further persons will destroy the viability of everything we have built and consign those souls we have saved to a slow and agonising death. We cannot, in all good faith, allow that to happen. It pains all of us deeply. But humanity must survive. That need must transcend all other considerations, even the suffering and death of those like yourself who are unfortunate enough to be outside our barrier. If it is any comfort at all – and I sincerely hope it is – know that your sacrifice means the human race will survive."

Sylfe half-expected a choir of angels to accompany Fontaneau's last words. He was certainly waxing lyrical enough.

"This report is preposterous," Rao said.

"Tell me," Fontaneau asked, "why did you come with so many M-Def ships?"

Another level of puckering. At some point, Sylfe thought, Rao's lips would fuse together.

"The garrison here is due furlough," he said. "We simply took the opportunity to bring a replacement force."

Which was a complete lie. There was no way this was simply a replacement force.

"I'm curious, Deputy Speaker," Sylfe said. "You say Ind Beltran's report is preposterous. But M-Worlds must have done projections on the viability of Redout. If you refute his findings, what *is* the tipping point?"

Rao's eyes flicked to her. "That information is classified."

"But the modelling does exist." Sylfe hadn't really given the topic much thought when she'd arrived. She'd been more intent on doing her job and leaving planetary management to others. But she also knew that Beltran's report and the data it was derived from was factually correct.

"We understood you were coming with a small delegation to inspect Redout and report back," she continued. "But you come with an armada of ships, and your own vessel is far bigger than a simple delegation would need. I'd venture it's large enough to carry the entire M-World Congress. And their families. Are you evacuating?"

The image of Rao disappeared, replaced by the face of Congress President Miran Ferlow. Famed negotiator Miran Ferlow, the woman who held M-Worlds together with grace, common sense and good humour. Her short-cut blonde hair, clear eyes, high cheekbones and full lips telegraphed a puckish demeanour. Sylfe had long been an admirer of hers and to see her here and now was something of a shock.

"I think we can come to an accommodation," Ferlow said in her pleasantly honey-coated tones.

She really was quite beautiful, Sylfe thought. And she was sure the whole physical package that was President Ferlow contributed a great deal to her political success. But that was in no way to discount her intellect and skill at finding the middle way between opposing views and making it palatable to all. Except this situation was a little more unusual.

Congress had been planning this, Sylfe thought. If not all along, then at least for quite some time. They'd maintained order, kept the population calm with a systematic program of evacuation and resettlement to Redout, and – above all – given the people of M-Worlds hope that they would be kept safe. But they'd known all along about the projections for Redout's viability. Information so explosive, they'd no doubt justified keeping it secret to avoid a general panic.

Sylfe wondered at what point Ferlow and those in her inner circle had decided to save themselves ahead of anyone else. She could understand the logic behind such a decision, but she couldn't grasp the callous disregard for others required to put that decision into practice. They'd brought enough firepower with them to beat off anyone still waiting for Congress to save them. Including the last highliner from Paradis, which would have still been en route if the Effect hadn't claimed it.

"You've cut and run," Leeuwin said.

"Indeed," Fontaneau said. "The mighty Congress has decided discretion is the better part of valour."

Fontaneau had simply reached the same conclusion as President Ferlow, but he'd been a bit quicker off the mark and – because he had control of the annulus – he didn't need a fleet to keep others away. The fact that Congress had been caught out in such an outright betrayal of every living person in the M-Worlds had a kind of poetic justice to it, Sylfe thought.

Ferlow's calm expression clouded a little as she said, "We're not proud of what we've done. But it's true. Redout could never have provided refuge for everyone that needed it."

"There seem to be quite a few of you, Madame President. On that point alone, I'm afraid you would be denied entry," Fontaneau said.

"With all due respect to Ind Beltran, our calculations and projections are a little more rigorous than those he produced. We do have the resources of the M-World Institute to call upon after all."

Sylfe felt the deposit of a new report from the Institute land in her augment. She didn't bother reading it.

"We bring enough supplies and the newest generation of retaskers," Ferlow continued, "which will guarantee that – even with the addition of the people we brought and the existing garrison – there will be enough resources for us all to survive."

But not the poor refugees out in the heliopause, Sylfe thought. Would any on the Congress volunteer to remain behind and send a refugee in their place if the barrier were lowered? She suspected not.

Denantes cleared his throat and wiped a handkerchief across his lips. "We already have enough resources to survive," he said. "I don't know if it's worth the risk of letting you in. After all, there's only room for one set of leaders."

"We *are* the group best suited to run Redout. We were handpicked for the job," Beltran said.

He sounded a little testy. Perhaps smarting at Ferlow belittling his report.

"It's a good point," Fontaneau said. "What can a shipload of politicians and soldiers do for us other than introduce more mouths to feed, regardless of how many supplies they bring. Do you have any more useful skills, Madame President? Airflow technician perhaps? Nutrient synthesiser?"

Fontaneau could be an annoying dick. But in this case, Sylfe knew, he was right.

Ferlow knew it too and it seemed she didn't like it because good humour was suddenly off the table. "Drop the fucking barrier or we'll blow it away and you with it."

"That seems a tad aggressive," Fontaneau said. Again, he looked along the table to left and right and appeared to see no strong objections.

Much good it would do anyone if they did disagree, Sylfe thought, with Tane standing by the door with his still-warm plasma cannon. Either way the refugees at the barrier were fucked – at least for the moment. Sylfe might be able to do something to help them if she only had Fontaneau to contend with. But if Congress took over, she'd be completely powerless. So for the moment, she was content to keep quiet. After all, Fontaneau was acting entirely within character. Congress, on the other hand, were trashing everything they stood for simply to save their own skin. They deserved everything they got.

"I think we are unanimous in deciding that we won't be dropping the barrier any time soon," Fontaneau said. "Blast away if you like. But I feel that something designed to hold back the destruction of spacetime isn't going to be too fussed by missiles or plasma blasts. And once you're done with that, feel free to hang around. I'm sure the refugee ships out there with you, and the many more doubtless still on their way, would like to understand what their entire Congress is doing hanging out there in space while M-Worlds collapses around them."

The augment window closed and Fontaneau stood, regarding his fellow council members with an expression that Sylfe identified as the textbook definition of schadenfreude.

"A momentous day indeed," he said. "Now we are truly free to do what we have been chosen to do. And I have you, my fellow council members, to thank for that."

Sylfe was pretty sure that when Fontaneau said "we" he really meant "I".

She glanced around the table. Teel, Beltran and Denantes looked sanguine about this new world order. Were they all so lacking in humanity?

Leeuwin at least had the good grace to look utterly bereft, though some of that might have been due to his personal situation.

Sylfe kept her own feelings in check, unwilling to betray what she really thought. Firmin, it seemed, was taking a similar approach. Fontaneau had won this round and the calculus of human suffering was already inestimable. Sylfe was determined he would not win the next.

18

"I've lost track of how long we've been down here."

"How long *you've* been down here," Helena said. "Strictly speaking, I'm nowhere."

"There's no need to keep reminding me."

"More like you're reminding yourself."

"Just don't," he said and pointed at the shared window. "This transform. It's … quite elegant actually. For Rachik and Teel, I mean."

"But they stumbled on it. I mean, you've seen the data."

They'd seen a *lot* of data. Firmin had come through with the feed. Not just realtime, but complete logs since the annulus was installed. Including every little tweak and twitch Teel and Rachik had made.

The first deviation was to constrain the field to the heliopause. *That* was what had led them to the doorway Markusz and Helena had found and left unentered. But Teel had gone through it and — reading the logs — it was possible to follow the faltering steps he and Rachik took as they walked further into the room beyond.

The mathematical architecture the room contained was familiar at first, but the further Markusz went the stranger it got. And as he studied the way it reacted to Teel's transformations he felt both sick and excited. Sick because, while they'd succeeded in doing what Fontaneau wanted, he could see second- and third-order feedback in the changes they'd made that echoed through spacetime in unexpected ways Teel was ill-equipped to correctly intuit. Rachik certainly couldn't. He was a plodder. But with some study, and some very esoteric chats with Helena – she was always an excellent sounding board – Markusz saw the connection between constraining the annulus and precipitating the collapse of the Paradis system. And after he saw that, several other things had become clearer to him as well. That was where the excitement came in.

There were signs that further transformations were possible. Some could cause complete annihilation, and they must tread carefully. But others suggested novel outcomes.

The hardening of the barrier was one. That was a logical extension of the constraint transform, simply constraining the annulus in another way to become non-porous. And it had certainly proved effective. The massive M-World fleet pounded away at it for days and it remained resolutely opaque. The data they got from such a massive expenditure of energy and how that energy was suborned and twisted into other planar extensions was an education in itself. But proper study of *that* must wait for another day.

Helena was with him the whole time and they worked together as they always had, each pushing the other to be better. To think further than either could on their own. Together they discovered a way to generate pocket universes as an offensive weapon encircling an enemy; and a method to close down incursions from the substrate – another aspect of the constraint transform. They even found a way to reverse or stop the flow of time at a molecular level – cool, but not practical. Or not yet anyway.

For whole stretches of time Markusz forgot Helena was dead. What did that say about him, that he was so empty and needy he had to conjure her to be with him? And when he did remind himself she was a hallucination, there was a part of him that questioned if that really was the case. They were discovering so much together, it felt more than just a memory when they talked. Maybe she was something else. Maybe he was losing his mind. But did that really matter if it meant they could be together?

He dived back into their work, and things became clearer and clearer until …

"Come on," Helena said, "articulate what you're thinking."

He came to himself and realised he'd been standing hunched over his desk for an unknown span of time.

"You know, if you are my subconscious, you're a relentless taskmaster," he said.

"Isn't that the definition of a subconscious? Now stop deflecting. I know that look. You've found something."

"It's just …" He thought about the maths, the transforms, the architecture. All the data they'd sifted. "Once you 'go through the door' and do the things Teel and Rachik have done, it changes the relationship between the annulus and spacetime in a way that can't be reversed. Like something stretched beyond its ability to snap back."

"And what does that mean exactly?"

"I don't know yet, other than bad stuff is going to happen. Stuff we haven't envisaged."

"So let's work it out before it happens so we can stop it."

He looked at her. "Are you more than my memory and my subconscious ganging up on me?"

"Oh really, Markusz, how do you expect me to answer that?"

"Truthfully?" He really needed to know.

She smiled and his heart felt a little lighter. So pathetic.

"Maybe you're a dream that *I'm* having – have you thought of that?" she said.

"I don't feel like a dream."

"But would you, even if you were?"

"Are you sure you're alright?"

Markusz turned towards the door. It was Elly and he wasn't sure how long she'd been standing there. He glanced at Helena – still there – and shrugged. "Debatable, but we are getting somewhere, so does it really matter what my mental state is?"

"I suppose not."

"But we can't get much further on our own. We need to – I need to talk to Rachik."

"Who's that?" Elly asked.

"He works on the annulus. I need to warn him. He's started something that could be not good."

"Not good?"

"Catastrophically not good."

"Were you always this bad at communicating with children?" Helena asked. "You don't need to talk down to them, you know. In fact —"

"Alright!" he said, then instantly regretted raising his voice. He focused on Elly again. She had that look he was getting used to. That look that said *keep your distance or I will cut you*. And he was pretty sure she carried a knife somewhere about her person.

"I'm sorry," he said. "I've been down here working on this for quite a while and sometimes I forget how to talk to normal people."

"Normal?"

"He means people who aren't mathematical geniuses," Helena said unhelpfully. Though it *was* helpful that Elly couldn't hear her.

"I mean non-scientists. The annulus acts on spacetime to keep us all safe. But the team that control it are changing the settings to produce different effects."

"Like the hard barrier," Elly said.

"Yes."

"It's still ignoring everything they throw at it," she said and raised one palm.

The shared window showed a very familiar scene. The refugee ships had moved back – or been moved – to a safe distance and the M-World fleet was ranged along the edge of the barrier, pummelling it with every imaginable directed energy and projectile weapon in its seemingly limitless arsenal. Rainbow shards played across the face of the barrier. The attack was very pretty but, beyond that, ineffective.

Elly had let Markusz keep his limited augment connection to the local network. He raised his own palm, curving his index finger to modulate the view into the quantum. Here the barrier glowed uniformly bright. The ships beyond and the energies they expended were barely visible as a smoky blur, but something else was happening. Streaks of burning wire coalesced to twist around the barrier then shoot off into open space, where they disappeared. But not before they left a glowing blemish on the vacuum, like a bruise that slowly dissipated.

"What you see isn't because of what the fleet are doing," Markusz told Elly. "It's an unintended byproduct of hardening the barrier. Those changes to the settings I mentioned are doing something to local spacetime and I'm worried if we don't stop it, something bad will happen. I'm talking about Paradis-level bad. Or maybe worse. So I need to talk to the team to get them to stop. Or try anyway. It could already be too late."

"Firmin won't allow that," Elly said.

"Is there perhaps a way you could help me *without* telling her?"

He tried not to sound wheedling, but wasn't convinced he managed it. The look Elly gave him confirmed that.

"Why don't you just build another annulus and take over?" she said.

It was a reasonable question for a normal person to ask.

"I mean, every planet could have had an annulus if you'd mass produced them, couldn't they?"

"That was the original intent after we perfected the prototype," he said. "But as soon as we created a second, the first one collapsed. It seems the universe can only accommodate one annulus at a time. That's why I wanted to keep working on the one we have to see how far its influence can be extended. To see if we can reverse the Effect even."

"Could you make the planets come back?" Elly asked.

"See," Helena said. "She's really a sweet child, still full of hope. I don't know why you insist on thinking of her as a murderer."

"I don't know if that would be possible, though running time backwards might be an option. But risky." He shivered at the thought of an out-of-control temporal reversal. "But it definitely won't be if the annulus team kills us all. If I could just get a line to them, we may be able to stop all that."

"You really want to save everyone," Elly said, sounding surprised.

"Umm," Helena said as multiple alert windows opened above Markusz's workstation.

In Elly's shared window, the twisting wires were spinning faster, multiplying until the whole expanse of barrier was wrapped in an eldritch lightshow. Markusz focused on the readouts and saw a pattern he'd seen too many times before. The dark matter field was off the scale. Dark energy was rising too. But the annulus was holding steady.

Markusz became aware of a growing rumbling noise coming from overhead. Then the floor started to shake. They were in a supposedly stable magma chamber. Was that about to change?

"What the hell is that?" He had to shout above the rising thunder. He grabbed for his chair to sit before he fell.

"It's just alien stuff," Elly said, sitting on Helena's chair and holding tight to the armrests. "It's happened before. But not quite as loud as this."

The shaking grew worse. The sound was deafening, like some shrieking giant bird. It made it hard to think, let alone read the augment windows that were vibrating in front of Markusz's eyes. Or was he vibrating in sympathy with whatever was happening up above?

Suddenly the shriek cut off, replaced by a deep roar like a huge flywheel that had decided to reach equilibrium rather than tearing itself apart. The room stopped shaking. But he could still feel vibration through the floor.

Elly tuned her window back to the visible spectrum. At the heliopause, ships were scattering. They could tell something was happening, but Markusz was sure they had no idea what was about to hit them. His own windows were running through novel transforms the annulus was throwing out. It didn't look good.

"We'll be alright," he said, not sure if he was reassuring Elly or himself.

"It's not localised," Helena said. "It's all around us."

"I know."

"You know we'll be alright?" Elly asked.

"What? Yes. No. It's different. But the annulus is doing what it's meant to do."

"Except it's causing this too," Elly said.

"Yes," Markusz said. It was. In fact … He opened another window, modulated the scalar flow and overlaid it with a predictive transform he and Helena had been working on based on the new architecture. He swiped at slides and radiants, looking for something that matched what they were seeing.

Oh. That wasn't good. The overlay and the realtime flow were trending together.

Most of the fleet was on the move now. The M-World Congress ship was turning slowly to follow. The view juddered, the ship's movement appearing to stutter, then the whole scene shrank as if their viewpoint was accelerating back at dizzying speed. Markusz grasped his chair against a sudden feeling of vertigo. Then everything was gone and a thousand crimson flowers of Teel-Attar radiation bloomed. The sound from above suddenly silenced.

"What the fuck just happened?" Elly said.

Markusz swivelled in his chair. Helena leaned on his seat back as he reordered windows, ran readings back and forward. This was the Effect writ large. And he was sure it had been precipitated by what Teel and Rachik had done. But what exactly was the extent?

"There's at least two possibilities, but it'll take some time to verify," he told Elly. "Number one is that we've been surrounded by a simultaneous wave of Effects which have cut us off from the rest of the universe."

"And number two?" Elly asked.

"There is no rest of the universe. So I *really* need to talk to Rachik. *Now* would be best."

Elly was still for a moment, then she crossed to Markusz's workstation and began setting up a comm window.

"This had better not be a trick, because if it is I will personally gut you," she said.

"She doesn't mean that," Helena said. "Poor kid. It's hard for her to trust. But see what happens when you at least *try* to connect with another human being?"

19

Three days had passed since the council had assumed complete control of Redout and locked Congress and everyone else out. Fontaneau – and the rest of the council for that matter – had been quiet since. Sylfe had kept an eye on things, of course, but she'd also allowed herself some time to sit with the reality of never seeing Maman or Yvette again.

She was angry and grieving, but beneath all that she was terrified she'd start to forget them. She had recordings, full sensory holos, but it didn't feel like "being" with them. The way they were together; the gentle ease of loving and knowing you were, in turn, loved. Everything had been so right. If they couldn't be here with her, she wanted at least to hold on to that. So she'd interfaced with her augments perhaps more deeply than she ever had before, chasing down every memory she had, every scrap of thought, feeling, sensation she'd experienced through her entire life with her family from her first conscious thought in the crib to the very last day they spoke. She pulled all of it together and created a complete sensorium she could immerse herself in. She could be with her maman and sister at any moment they had shared at any point in their lives together.

Immersion in the sensorium was healing. There were so many things she had forgotten that came back to her as fresh as the day she'd first experienced them. And while that brought its own sadness, she also felt joy and gratitude that nothing had been lost, or would ever be lost as long as she lived.

But she was careful not to disconnect from the world as it was now. Her part of the Palisades was particularly well-heeled, and out on street level everything had the semblance of normality. The apron of her apartment complex looked out across a river plateau – though it was impossible to see the river any more. But the elevation still offered a view and the cafés ranged along the parapet were close to capacity.

Walking past the tables and along the promenade, Sylfe watched others enjoying the evening air – a couple holding hands, a family with one toddler and a babe in arms – and hoped they realised how lucky they were. Everything felt so tenuous now. But people were getting on with their lives, or trying to.

The sky too felt peaceful. Not eighteen light hours away, Congress's fleet still pummelled away at the annulus barrier. But nothing of that conflict was visible from her vantage point. The ever-present blooms of Teel-Attar radiation added a kind of beauty to the view, as long as one didn't consider what they meant. The stars themselves shone with a sepia tone, coloured by the annulus field, but that too was far from out of the ordinary. Different planets had different-coloured skies. It was an easy thing to ignore.

A scream behind her was joined by shouts. She turned and the family she'd seen was hunkered down on the ground, the adults pulling their children close and all staring at the heavens. The stars had disappeared. Instead, the sky was a dark scarlet textured like rumpled satin. Folds highlighted lighter and darker patches, and these folds were rippling slowly so that every segment of the sky was in motion. It was like being inside a giant stomach. Or a brain. Neither image was comforting.

Her sunbarques. She opened a window that fizzed before her then shut down. She tried again and this time it persisted, showing the SolEng logo. Then Roche – commander of her sunbarque group – appeared.

"Are you all safe?" she asked.

"Yes, Matri, we're –"

"Please, Roche," Sylfe interrupted, wincing. "I understand why, but please don't call me that. Not yet." There were some changes she wasn't ready to accept.

She saw Roche's eyes glisten with sudden tears and hoped he could keep it together, because if he broke down she wouldn't be far behind.

"Of course," he said. "The ships are all perfectly fine. The sun is behaving, but the visible universe … It's gone."

"Hold position," she said. "I'll try to find out what's happening."

She closed the window and opened another, this time to annulus control. There was no response even with her council priority. She swore. Fontaneau wasn't answering either.

This was down to more meddling with the annulus, she was sure of it. Things had been bad and now they'd gotten worse. It was time to get busy.

Elly finished setting up the comm window and gave access to Markusz. He saw the bottom left-hand corner displayed the icon that meant his location and identity was shielded. He input the ident string.

The window blurred and fuzzed. There was a lot of interference. Finally Rachik appeared. The space behind him was the grey moire of a privacy screen. Good.

Rachik's eyes widened as he saw who was calling. "Where the fuck have you been? They told me you were dead."

"It's a long story," Markusz said. "And we don't have time for it."

"Wait. Where are you calling from?"

Markusz gave an exasperated sigh. "Again. No time. You *do* see what just happened, don't you."

Rachik slumped in his chair and Markusz almost felt sorry for the poor idiot.

"Teel's had you tinkering, hasn't he?"

"He's intent on doing whatever Fontaneau wants. He ordered me to apply a new approach to the transforms to harden the barrier."

The architecture beyond the doorway, Markusz thought.

"It's radical *and* experimentally unsound given we're not in a test environment any more. I tried to tell him that —"

"But he didn't listen. You know Paradis was destroyed because of the last bit of tinkering."

Rachik's eyes narrowed. "I do. But how do you know that? Where *are* you?"

"That is *not* important right now. Focus, Rachik. We're trapped!"

Rachik looked in that instant like someone who'd been thoroughly beaten down by circumstance. "Is there a way out?" he said.

Markusz saw what it cost Rachik to ask him for help.

"I don't know. What we just witnessed was an outcome of the barrier hardening, but we didn't have enough data to pinpoint its probability and I'm still not sure what it really means. We have to work together, Rachik. I need your help too."

"That's really quite sensitive of you, darling," Helena said. "I think you're making excellent progress on the 'treating people better than slugs' front."

Well. Maybe. He was doubtful Rachik could add anything constructive by way of original thought. But there were other ways that even a slug could be useful.

"I need you to share everything Teel's given you on his new approach," he said. It could be there were variances to the path Helena and he had discovered. "And I need you to stop him ordering any more tweaks."

Rachik winced.

"Okay," Markusz acknowledged. "That may not be possible. But if he insists, I need to know beforehand what he wants you to do. That way we may be able to ameliorate any negative impacts."

"Alright," Rachik said.

"I'll send you some transforms soon. Something to keep things ticking over without any more nasty surprises. Nothing Teel will notice."

"Alright," Rachik said again, then, "Thank you." He closed the connection.

"He won't tell anyone about you?" Elly asked.

"It's not in his interests to do so."

"And can you do what you told him you would?"

Markusz swivelled in his chair to look at her. "Yes. I'm going to get us out of this. But I need you to keep helping me. I need you to trust me."

20

As Sylfe re-entered her apartment, her augments registered a message from Fontaneau. She opened it immediately and his larger-than-life head loomed out of the augment window, dominating the living room.

"Ah, my dear Sylfe. I apologise for interrupting you, but I wanted to keep you apprised of events."

This should be interesting. But as the message spooled on, she realised it must have been recorded before the sky disappeared.

"Firstly to the question of civil order. You will be glad to know Tane and his lieutenants have taken up the slack in the M-Def command structure."

Nice way of putting it, Sylfe thought.

"They have an increased visible presence where required. As for the augment-locked, they are none the wiser. So you can continue to go about your business safely. Ind Beltran and his team are functioning like the well-oiled machine we've come to expect from the Fordana. And we must do the same. This is the culmination of all our planning. It just came a little earlier than we anticipated. But I know I can count on you."

His accompanying smile was colder than space. But Sylfe supposed she should be glad she was part of the group he felt it important to "keep apprised". He still needed her.

"On that note," Fontaneau continued, "I'm suspending our regular round of meetings until things have settled into a routine. Don't hesitate to contact my office if you need anything at all."

The window closed, and Sylfe made sure there were no

lingering Fontaneauan fingers in her apartment systems.

None of what he'd said was entirely unexpected, but the question remained: why had the sky disappeared? Was it something Fontaneau had planned, or was it another fuck-up like Paradis? If the former, what did he gain from it? And did anything remain beyond the barrier?

Whatever the case, it seemed she could "continue to go about her business". Hopefully Fontaneau didn't suspect what that really was.

If Sylfe was going to stop him, she needed allies. And she couldn't be too fussy about where she got them. First stop was Leeuwin. Yes, he was weak and completely ineffectual and ordinarily she wouldn't give him the time of day. But he lived close by so what the hell. Also, Sylfe had to admit she was worried about him. He'd lost his family too. And after his outburst at the council meeting he was probably the least safe of them all.

Back outside, she'd expected the cafés to be deserted. But a few souls remained, though the atmosphere was distinctly muted and every so often someone cast a worried glance at the sky. Now she looked for them, Sylfe saw duos of M-Def personnel interspersed with an Opitauan here and there, keeping close to the buildings where they would be inconspicuous.

Up and down the apron, augment windows blossomed and closed, all issuing the same bland message: *Remain calm. All systems are functioning normally.* The people in this area were used to being well looked after and, disquieting sky notwithstanding, no doubt expected everything to continue as it should. There was nothing on the feeds, but Sylfe was sure there must be panic now – maybe even rioting – in those areas that were less well cared for. There was nothing she could do about that.

Leeuwin's apartment was only a couple of blocks in from the apron, though she had never visited him. Never even thought to. Building systems admitted her and she knew her every move in public spaces was being tracked and assessed. Fontaneau wouldn't let his puppet council go about without a little oversight, and there was nothing she could do to block this kind of passive surveillance without revealing too much about her own systems. But she hoped her reason for coming here was plain. One concerned council member looking in on the welfare of another.

Leeuwin's door knew her and must have relayed her presence inside without comment. And Leeuwin must still be alive because a moment later the door opened, but stuck halfway. Sylfe pushed on it and heard the tinkle of broken glass. The entry hall carpet was littered with shards of broken mirror. She trod carefully, little pieces of glass crunching underfoot.

In the main living room, chairs and side tables were overturned, curtains torn from windows, empty liquor bottles lying like abandoned soldiers. Stretched across a padded easy chair was Leeuwin, one hand plastered across his forehead and eyes, the other hand clutching an all but empty bottle of absinthe. He groaned.

"Big night?" Sylfe said.

Leeuwin groaned again.

"I uh … thought I'd check in on you. See how you're going."

Leeuwin looked at her between splayed fingers. "Splendidly. I can't even drink myself to death properly."

Which was entirely in character, she thought. Poor Leeuwin. And also pathetic Leeuwin.

She brushed detritus off the other easy chair in the room and moved it to sit opposite him, making sure her augments bolstered the apartment's systems to prevent unwanted snooping. Again, nothing to cause surveillance concern. Private domiciles were supposed to be sacrosanct, particularly for the upper classes.

"You don't need to kill yourself," she said. "Fontaneau is managing that admirably for all of us."

Leeuwin gave a short bitter laugh, then clutched his head again. "I just don't understand how it all went so wrong so quickly," he said, drawing himself up in his chair. His GH uniform was rumpled, unbuttoned and stained with a variety of liquors. Maybe even a little vomit. "I loved my job. I mean, I was grown for it but I loved it anyway. I loved my wife and daughter. I felt myself to be a very fortunate man and I tried to do good to others less fortunate. It was my way of giving thanks. I don't understand why I'm being punished so."

Poor me, Sylfe thought. Still, in less extreme situations, he had been quite decent. Professional, kind and – yes – dull.

He gestured to an open door opposite the hallway. Through it she could see a cot. "That was to be our new baby's nurs–"

His voice broke into sobs and Sylfe looked away. Jesus.

She waited until he'd collected himself again. "I didn't know your wife was pregnant," she said. "I'm sorry."

"She stayed with her parents. They'd decided they were too old to come to Redout and she wanted to spend what little time she had left with them. And now it's too late."

"I thought they were waiting their turn on the GH highliners."

"That was just publicity. GH liked to show everyone was equal in the eyes of the company, even the wife of a sector governor-general."

And now it was too late. Just another tragedy in a constellation of tragedies.

"I'm sorry for disturbing you, Jan Pieter. I just wanted to see you were alright. And I know you're worried about Fontaneau. I'll do what I can to protect you."

So long as it doesn't compromise my own position, she thought.

Leeuwin barked a bitter laugh. "Oh, I'm not worried about *him*. He needs me."

"I don't understand."

Leeuwin looked at her through the alcoholic blear and she saw calculation in his eyes. No-one trusts anyone, she thought. Not even Leeuwin. But he came to a decision all the same.

"It's to do with the ship. The last highliner."

"The last one to arrive? I understood it was slated for dismantling."

"Yes. It had reached the end of its serviceable life and GH donated it to the construction effort here. But Fontaneau had it repurposed."

That was something that had escaped her scopes. Now, her augments showed her the dock records and footage of the highliner taking to the air again, set on a deep orbit.

"As Sector GG, my augments were grown with the continually updating algorithm to access and control any GH ship," Leeuwin said. "It's a quaint security feature from the old days to dissuade mutiny. Not much use rebelling against the commander if it renders your ship dead in space."

"So the ship's captain would have the same augment?"

"He does. Or he did. He walked out an airlock with no suit after Paradis disappeared."

Oh. "And the first officer or whatever you call the second-in-command? Surely they–"

"Shipped out-system after debarkation," Leeuwin said. "Non-essential personnel for a skeleton crew. He's somewhere out there, if 'out there' exists any more."

"So Fontaneau diverted a massive highliner into deep system orbit and you are the only person with executive control?"

"That's it." He took a swig from the absinthe bottle and grimaced. "Fuck knows what he's going to make me do with it."

"Well," she said, "that is quite something." Perhaps Leeuwin could be of use after all. She knew he despised Fontaneau. "I wonder if you might let me know if you receive any orders about that highliner? Just between you and me, that is."

He gave her that look again. "I suppose I could."

She stood and patted him awkwardly on one rumpled epaulette. "Look after yourself, Jan Pieter."

"And you, Ind Cachand."

She looked back at him as she gained the hallway, but he was leaning precariously out of the chair and rummaging underneath it. He pulled out a full bottle of something.

She left him to it.

Firmin was a long shot. Sylfe knew that. But then she hadn't counted Leeuwin as a possibility and that little tidbit about the highliner might come in useful. Beltran was unlikely to bend her way. The man was as soulless as his spreadsheets. Denantes would denounce her if there was advantage in it. Asymptote Eleven might be useful, but she wasn't sure how – or what approach might be best with the Haibeu.

The mayoral offices of Garia were typically understated. A brutalist low-rise block surrounded by a narrow moat studded with stepping stones to the building's many entrances. Inside was a broad and empty public space, with no stage or raised dais. Sylfe knew about Garian government. It seemed designed to be a complete repudiation of the Byzantine hierarchies of Paradis. Here the mayor was only first among equals, and anyone could raise and debate issues, hurl criticism and demand accountability in this common space. All activities that would get you shuffled off to a quiet room for a beating on Paradis.

Except there were no Paradisan quiet rooms any more. Nor any secret police operating at the behest of the Great Families. But then there wasn't an operating Garian commons any more either. Only the council was left now – since M-Gov had self-immolated – and that temporary structure wouldn't last long. Sylfe wouldn't put it past Fontaneau to recreate the Paradisan system of patronage and serfdom, with his house at the top of course.

The administrative offices were below street level and accessed by a brick staircase. There was no secretary in the mayoral antechamber and the door to Firmin's office was invitingly ajar.

"Come!" Firmin's voice rang out in the empty interior.

Sylfe entered the office. Firmin was sitting head down at a large wooden desk. A beautiful piece of craftsmanship, constructed in highly polished and finely grained dark wood. It made Fontaneau's desk look like a cheap fairground reject.

Between Firmin and Sylfe were several light sculptures.

Holographic scenes, which … Well, the violence portrayed seemed jarring in such a sober bureaucratic environment. The closest showed two figures, both arched back, hands extended above their heads in the act of throwing flaming cylinders as an Opitauan in heavy riot gear rushed them with a shield thrust forward to take the brunt of the blast. Beyond that was a scene of complete chaos. Bodies blown apart; others caught in a suspended moment rushing from the scene as a fiery explosion tore through a building, windows and doors blowing outwards in deadly shards. Sylfe's augment tagged the first as *Garian settlers protest the destruction of the Monument des Fondateurs*, and the second as *Redout security building bombing*. There were three other scenes, all of which echoed the theme of a violent invasion of Garia for the sake of the creation of Redout. It wasn't a pretty story.

"These scenes are … provocative to say the least," Sylfe said.

Firmin put down her stylus and regarded her coldly. "You obviously haven't visited our National Museum. The Paradisan exodus was far more violent. Even though your kind wanted us gone, it wasn't enough just to let us leave."

"I know you see me as 'of that kind'. The kind you despise."

"Despise." Firmin considered the word. "That would require more energy of me than I can spare. Are you here to convince me you're not like the others?"

"No. Any such words would be meaningless. Only actions can prove that."

"Actions can be deceiving as well, young Ind."

"And yet it was a member of the Great Families that enabled your ancestors to leave Paradis and colonise Garia."

"You're no Herku Depharian," Firmin said.

Sylfe nodded thoughtfully. "Perhaps not. And yet there's no harm in talking. Our situation—"

"Don't presume to know what my situation is," Firmin snapped.

Sylfe nodded again. No point being oppositional. Firmin had enough of that for both of them. "*The* situation with Fontaneau would seem to threaten anyone on the council not willing to toe his line without question. I assume – and I'm sure you'll correct me if I'm wrong–"

That elicited a pale smile from Firmin.

"– that you would rather not have Fontaneau or any Paradisan as your lord and master."

"I'll concede that. For the sake of conversation."

"And so at some point, someone will have to push back. Convincingly and in a manner that leaves no space for retaliation. I hope you appreciate I am being entirely candid with you."

"Either that or you've come from Fontaneau to flush me out," Firmin said.

"That's more Denantes's function. But I expect I have no way of convincing you otherwise."

"None that I can see."

"But on the slim chance that I am being truthful, I can say this. Whoever goes against Fontaneau must be sure of landing the killing blow. Not just on him but the instrumentality he commands. I am not without my own resources but I am no match for him alone. If you feel similarly, please know I am open to cooperating."

There was a quiet cough behind Sylfe and she turned to see a white-haired Garian woman standing in the doorway.

"I'm sorry my assistant wasn't here to welcome you, Ind Cachand," Firmin said. "But she will be happy to escort you out." She picked up her stylus and bent once more to her work.

The woman walked Sylfe back over the stepping-stone moat and nodded pleasantly enough before returning to her duties.

Sylfe summoned her private mover and looked back into the common space, thinking while she waited. She had the feeling Firmin was serious in rejecting her overtures. That puzzled her. Was the mayor so blinded by hatred of Paradisans that she refused what Sylfe had to admit with all modesty was a resourceful ally? That seemed like a luxury Firmin could ill afford if she wanted to save her people from Fontaneau's rule. So there were two ways this could play out. Either she'd come around and make an alliance with Sylfe for the common good; or she already had a plan in place that she believed would get her what she wanted without the need for an alliance. Now that was an intriguing prospect.

The mover landed and its doors swung wide for Sylfe to step inside. Idly she wondered how secure Firmin's systems were and set a number of passive scopes running to test them out. By the time she pulled into her apartment's below-ground garage she was sure system infiltration was a dead end. Interesting that the Paradisan mayor had better system security than Ernes Fontaneau. Perhaps she had more to hide.

Still, there were more old-fashioned ways of gathering information. Sylfe linked with Redout records and accessed information on Firmin's staff. The woman was no fool. She'd make sure those who worked for her were beyond bribery. But one couldn't pick and choose family members.

A few minutes later Sylfe had a full dossier on Abel Durand, brother of Firmin's secretary, Elise Gagnon. He was unemployed but that wasn't unusual. Even so, residents of Redout had no need for money unless their tastes ran to hard-to-get luxury goods. Or gambling. Abel had an unfortunate interest and lack of luck in the ancient card game of Trente et Quarante, which meant he was in debt to certain notables of Redout's demi-monde who were notoriously short on patience. It may be worth talking to Ind Durand.

21

"Nothing's left," Markusz said, sagging against his desk. "Everyone else is dead. Every star system. All the galaxies beyond our own. Gone. The entire universe has been reduced to a sphere thirty-six billion kilometres wide with Redout in the middle."

"It still sounds like a lot when you put it that way," Helena said.

"It's less than nothing."

How had things gone so wrong? Well, he knew how. Teel and his fucking meddling. The universe brought low by a mediocre scientist-cum-petty-bureaucrat. It would be laughable if it wasn't so damned depressing.

"Markusz. You can't give up now. I died and you kept going. This can't be worse than that, can it?"

He looked at her. Stood a little straighter. "No."

"Well then, let's do what we do best. Look at the numbers and work out how to fix things."

Markusz pushed his chair over to Helena's workstation so they could sit together. He opened up analysis windows of every possible view of what had transpired and together they pored over the raw data.

"It's like you said: the Effect and the annulus are in lockstep," Helena said.

"Action and reaction on both ends," Markusz agreed.

"Speaking of reaction," she said, "I thought the base was going to shake apart."

"Yes. That's worrying me too. It suggests a connection between this place and the Effect."

"Or this place and the annulus somehow."

"But why? I mean, if the base was built as more than some alien refuge, what's it for?"

"We need to find out. And that's not going to happen sitting in this lab. But first things first," she said, pointing at an analysis window. "These numbers are at least promising. It could suggest —"

"Another stabilising transform, yes. I'll send it to Rachik."

The fact that Elly had allowed him to keep a line open to Rachik showed just how far their relationship had come. Markusz was touched that she was willing to trust him. Or she was terrified enough to go against her better judgement. Maybe both.

"But it may not be enough," he went on. "I'm just worried the annulus is moving down a path that we can't predict, let alone control."

"We need more help," Helena agreed. "The solar harmonics are interesting. Look at this point here. There's an intersection in the substrate. What about that good-looking woman, the solar engineer?"

Markusz swivelled in his chair, drawing back from Helena. "I never said she was good-looking."

"Well, clearly you thought it because I'm from in there." She pointed at her temple but clearly meant his.

Markusz felt distinctly uncomfortable. "She's pleasant to look at, but I certainly haven't considered her in any romantic context."

Helena barked out a laugh. "Romantic context? You sound like such a stuffed shirt."

"But I see what you mean about the solar angle," Markusz said, ignoring her. "SolEng could provide us with another set of levers to directly affect the substrate."

Helena coughed and continued in a gruff approximation of Markusz's voice. "Yes. Of course. Sans any 'romantic context' naturally. But come on, Markusz. We both know it's been a while."

"I'm not having this conversation," he said. "Anyway, it's unlikely Elly will help us contact Ind Cachand. I get the feeling we've pushed her to her limit."

"Have you got a better idea?"

Markusz opened a window and entered Firmin's string. She appeared immediately.

"You have a solution for this latest clusterfuck?" she said.

"We're working on it. But I have a couple of requests for you."

"That doesn't sound like something I'm going to like. But you're in luck. I'm on the base so I'll be there in a few minutes."

Markusz sat back, wondering how best to approach this with Firmin. She wasn't going to do anything that might jeopardise her secret bolthole. And he didn't want her to know Elly had been helping him – albeit grudgingly so far.

"The direct approach," Helena said. "She's not the kind of woman to fuck around."

Markusz nodded just as the door opened to admit Firmin. Elly was with her, looking around the lab as she entered and not making eye contact. Interesting.

"So what's this about?" Firmin asked brusquely.

Don't fuck around. Okay. "It's about the fact there's no universe left. They keep fiddling with the annulus –"

Elly flashed a look at him, but he had no intention of revealing the contact she'd allowed.

"The datafeed shows the transforms they're using and I need to be able to influence that." More than I can with just Rachik, he didn't add.

Firmin folded her arms and stood straighter. All the better to say no, Markusz thought, but instead she said, "How?"

"It has to do with solar harmonics. Something as big as the sun impacts spacetime in a number of ways. If we can act on the sun, we can cause changes in the substrate which will in turn impact the annulus. I'm sure I can make this work, but we need Ind Cachand's SolEng sunbarques."

"Out of the question. I've already had her snooping round offering an alliance against Fontaneau."

"And what's wrong with that?" Markusz said. "You know he's going to end up killing us all if someone doesn't stop him?"

"Only if he can find us," Firmin shot back. "Besides, he's done us a favour keeping the rest of Congress and all their military out."

Markusz couldn't believe his ears. "At the expense of every other planet in the universe! This man is responsible for the deaths of more people than the sum total of despots and dictators in the whole of human history. We don't need those kinds of favours."

"You're shouting, Markusz," Helena said. "Maybe dial it back a little."

But Firmin had already closed down. Her next words were as cold as steel. "We don't need Cachand, Fontaneau or any other oligarchs to help us. When the time c—"

The floor shook beneath their feet and Firmin and Elly took a step back, Firmin grasping the edge of Markusz's workstation. But Markusz barely noticed. He was staring at the analysis windows.

Then the sound from above came again. Not as bad as last time, he thought. It sounded more like heavy machinery spinning up, then jumping in intensity as if a massive turbine was close to leaping clean out of its housing. Okay, admittedly it was still quite bad. The shaking got worse too, like a smaller earthquake than last time but an earthquake all the same. Markusz grasped Helena's desk, unable to do anything more than hold on.

Out in the region where the heliopause had been, the Teel-Attar blooms twisted and shredded and reformed. Then they leaped forward all at once.

The shaking stopped.

The machinery shriek descended through the octaves and sank into silence once more.

"That's not good," Helena said.

"What's happened?" Firmin asked, releasing her grip on the workstation and standing tentatively, as if worried the shaking would begin again.

"Well, a minute ago, the space enclosed by the annulus was a sphere of diameter thirty-six billion kilometres," Markusz said. "Now it's down to thirty-three billion. We just lost ten per cent of the remaining universe." He took a deep breath. "Mayor Firmin, I understand it's distasteful, but we need to do everything we can to save what we have left. We need help."

He glanced at Elly, willing her to intercede. The girl looked scared, but she was scared of Firmin too.

"You will not contact Sylfe Cachand," Firmin said. Each word could have occupied its own stone tablet.

"Okay, well … what about the shrieking from above and all the shaking? This place reacted when the universe disappeared, and again now when it shrank. Have you experienced that before?"

Firmin looked thoughtful, then nodded. "There's a lot of alien tech above this level and most of it is beyond us. We've studied it for centuries but we're not scientists."

Markusz resisted the temptation to bury his head in his hands; he didn't want to antagonise this woman. The Garians had found this place — one of the most mind-blowing engineering feats in history — so long ago, but they'd kept it to themselves. It should have been studied to the nth degree by the finest minds in M-Worlds. Instead it had been tinkered with by cleaners.

"That's not fair," Helena said. "They weren't all cleaners. And you can't really blame them. They'd been beaten into submission by the Paradisan oligarchs, finally escaped against all the odds, founded their own planet and then found this. If they'd invited anyone from outside to see what they'd discovered, they'd have been without a world again in a flash. Try again, Markusz."

He took a breath. "Mayor, would it be possible for us – me – to look at this machinery? It's alien technology that seems, somehow, to be reacting to what's happening with the Effect and the annulus. If we can study it, it might suggest a solution. It's a long shot, but right now I'm desperate enough for long shots."

"I think it's worth letting him look at it," Elly said quietly.

Firmin held up a hand. "Wait," she said. Her gaze shifted to the middle distance, no doubt reacting to a private augment window.

"Alright, that's not happening," she said finally to whoever was briefing her. "Get kitted out. Elly will go with you."

Then she turned to look at Markusz again and sighed heavily. "You can see the machinery, but it's going to have to wait. Elly, with me."

The two Garians left.

"I don't like the sound of that," Helena said.

Markusz was forced to agree.

22

Out in the corridor, Firmin said to Elly, "I told you I'd give you a mission. There's a situation developing. Brak's waiting topside."

Elly didn't have to be told twice. She flashed her grandmother a grin and stopped off at her quarters to grab her gun.

The elevator took an age, but when the door opened on the supply tent, Brak threw a Fabrika SA onepiece at her.

"Transport's outside," he said and pushed through the tent flap.

Typical Brak. Action first, talk later.

She followed him into the oppressive heat and through the warren of tents to an automated maintenance mover, which took to the sky as soon as they were aboard.

It was only when they were safely in the air that Brak spoke again. "You actually got permission for this one." He grinned.

"Fuck you," Elly said. "You'd have done the same."

He chewed that over for a moment, then nodded. "In any case, this is a milk run. Got to pick up an Abel Durand."

"I know Abel. He's Elise's brother."

Brak grunted. "Got a tip he's agreed to meet council member Cachand. Firmin wants that not to happen."

Elly considered that as the Fabrika SA mover made for Redout Central. Mamie had said Cachand was already snooping. Abel didn't know much; Elly was sure of it. But she knew they didn't want their people taking unnecessary meetings with incomers. Which made her feel guilty she'd let Markusz talk to the annulus engineer, Rachik. But he'd made it sound so important.

Fuck, it *was* important. She only had to look out the window to see that. The sky had *gone*, and what was left of space had just shrunk again. She didn't understand all the science, but she was certain now that their lives depended on Markusz. He was crazy. But he was also trying to save them.

Across from her, Brak grunted again. "Durand's on the move. On a submover headed for the Palisades."

Their mover altered course and accelerated.

Elly knew Mamie only trusted Markusz so far, which was why she wasn't doing much to help him. He'd said he needed to talk to Cachand; Mamie had closed him down. He wanted to see the alien tech; Elly was sure Mamie would have refused that too if she hadn't sided with him. The thing was, she didn't want to be stuck on this planet for the rest of her life, and there was only one person who'd said he could fix that.

The mover descended into a maintenance depot close to the submover station for the Palisades. Fabrika SA had these locations all over Redout and the organisation was riddled with Separatists. Fabrika specialised in menial tasks. What better workforce for it than the rejects of Paradisan society?

Elly placed her gun in Brak's work tote and they exited the depot into a broad lane between residential towers. Brak shared a window tracking Abel's ident code. The fool hadn't turned his augments off. The window tagged him among a knot of people coming out of the mover station at street level, just ahead.

Brak increased his pace and Elly lengthened her stride to keep up. Abel was oblivious they were following him, and Elly drifted apart from Brak so they could catch up to him on both sides.

"Hey, Abel," Brak said in a not unfriendly tone as he cinched Abel's upper arm so they walked in step. "What you doing all the way out here?"

Abel stared up into Brak's face looking startled, then turned to register Elly. As he recognised her, his features fell into their natural melancholic state.

"Ah," he said. "I wasn't going to say anything."

"Then why take the meeting?" Brak asked, more curious than accusatory as he steered Abel out of the flow of pedestrians and into a narrow alley between a power substation and an apartment block. He pressed Abel against the wall, one hand resting on his chest.

"What are we going to do with you?" Elly said.

Elise was always complaining about her no-good brother. Personally, Elly had liked him the couple of times they'd met, but she also knew that he couldn't be trusted.

"I'll go home," Abel said. "I won't talk to her."

"But you've opened the door, haven't you?" Brak said. "She's going to keep calling you. And she's a powerful woman."

Then he looked past Elly and swore softly. "Tat-têtes," he said.

Elly turned to see two Opitauan security personnel entering the mouth of the laneway. Masked by Elly's body, Brak flipped open his work tote and reached in for his pistol.

"What's going on here?" the closer Opitauan asked.

"Friendly chat. No law against it," Elly said.

The other Opitauan had the blank look of someone consulting an augment window. It would be seconds before he realised Brak and Elly weren't broadcasting ident codes. They were running out of options.

Then Abel removed all their choices but one. "Help me," he said. "I don't know these guys."

"Free Garia," Brak said, levelling his gun and shooting both Opitauans in the head before doing the same to Abel.

"Fuck," Elly said, wiping Abel's blood and brains from her face. "What's our exit?"

Things had fucked up very quickly. M-Def and Opitauans would be converging on this location and the only edge they had wouldn't stand up to line of sight. They had to get off the street.

Brak grabbed a rag from his tote, mopped his own face and handed it to her. "This way," he said and ran deeper into the alleyway.

Elly followed him, through a service door into the substation.

The walkway inside was tight. This was original Garian infrastructure for the Palisades, but a lot more conduits and piping had been shoehorned in by the Corps d'Ingénieurs to support the Redout expansion. Brak raced along, turning corners seemingly at random.

A final turn and they were staring at a blank wall.

"We have to get out of here," Elly said, forcing her voice to sound calm.

"Don't worry," Brak said. "We built this, remember?"

He hit the wall panel with the heel of his hand and it popped open. A ladder inside led down. He turned and smiled at her. "Always know your exits *before* you start any trouble."

"And when were you going to tell me about this? What if they'd killed you?"

"Pfft. Wouldn't happen."

Elly loved Brak, but fuck – she also hated him sometimes.

She pulled the panel shut behind her and descended the ladder.

At the bottom, Brak activated a lumen. A narrow tunnel ran off into the darkness.

"It's quite a walk," he said.

Staring at the back of Brak's head for the next however long held zero appeal for Elly. She was still pissed with him. "I'll go first this time," she said.

As they walked, she thought about what they'd done. Abel had sealed his own fate, and he was already living on borrowed time as he wasn't on Firmin's list to evacuate to the base.

But if Markusz could fix things, maybe that wasn't the case any more. She remembered him saying, *I'm going to need you to keep on helping me.*

If Elly listened to Mamie and did what she ordered, everything would go on exactly as it had been. They'd be safe in the base, could close the doors when they had to. But then what? They'd all die eventually.

Elly didn't want that. She wanted a life with places to go. That's what Markusz was offering. She knew he wasn't lying to her when he said he could do it. He might be lying to himself, of course, in which case they were all dead anyway. But she wanted that chance.

23

"We located the highliner lingering in the outer asteroid belt," Roche told Sylfe. "Regardless of its size, it wasn't easy to find. It's on a course back to Redout orbit."

"Thanks," Sylfe said. "Have the sunbarques on the far side break off and join you this side. I want you all together and safe."

He nodded. "Of course, Ind. Let's hope there's no more shrinkages. We'll alert you if we see anything. Roche out."

Sylfe smiled at the commander and cut the connection. She worried about her crews. At least they had their families onboard, but now things were more uncertain than ever.

This latest failure of the annulus had surpassed "concerning" and was in the region of "terrifying". She had to do something, but she wasn't clear yet what that was. Fontaneau had effectively sidelined them all.

Her mover informed her the traffic through Redout Central was heavier than usual and it was taking a roundabout route back to the Palisades for her meeting with Abel Durand, so there was time for a little check-in on Teel. After recent events, she'd included him on her list of people to watch.

Her scopes opened a window onto the annulus control room. The insipid Rachik was checking off items on a pad while watching the annulus. The ethereal ribbon glowed in all its multi-hued beauty as if everything were perfectly fine.

Teel entered, pulling at the front of his severe justacorps, smoothing imaginary wrinkles. He still had that maddeningly superior expression on his face, as if none of the annulus's now growing list of failures were his fault. Sylfe wondered how long that defence would continue to work with Fontaneau.

"What in heaven's name are you doing, Rachik?" Teel snapped.

Rachik turned, looking blank and possibly a little disoriented by the anger directed his way. The poor sap was only doing his job from what Sylfe could tell. But perhaps this was Teel's "out": any annulus stuff-ups could be laid squarely at his subordinate's door.

"I'm running the diagnostics to understand the shrinkage," Rachik said.

It seemed eminently reasonable to Sylfe.

"Give me that." Teel snatched the pad and swiped away the program Rachik had been running. "What about these transforms you've been applying?"

"They didn't cause the shrinkage if that's what's worrying you."

"I'm not worried," Teel sneered.

"They're stabilising transforms. They were thoroughly checked in simulation."

"But the maths isn't familiar. This transform here," Teel pointed at the pad, "how did you come up with it?"

Rachik blinked rapidly. "It's derived from the shield equations. The new maths–"

"I know it's the new maths," Teel snapped. "What I want to know is how you came up with it. And this one too. It's not a direct application. I want to see your workings."

Rachik blinked rapidly again. "My workings?"

"Yes!" Teel shouted. "I'm still in charge. Any changes need to be passed through me. So, your workings."

Rachik was looking pastier by the minute. Then he straightened and bowed. "I'll have them to you by shift end, sir."

Teel sniffed. "See that you do."

That was curious. Just what problem did Rachik have with explaining his work, Sylfe wondered. She'd keep tabs on developments, but right now her mover was landing.

She debarked and took the elevator to her floor.

Hugo Denantes was loitering in the corridor outside her apartment.

"If this is another sympathy visit, I'd rather you didn't," she said, sweeping past him.

"It's not."

For a fat, old man he could move surprisingly quickly, Sylfe thought, as he dipped and half-twisted to navigate his gut round her rapidly closing door.

The hallway flooded with red light as her apartment systems armed.

"I only have to think it, and you're dead," she said.

He held his pudgy, short-fingered hands up in front of him. "I don't doubt it and I assure you I am not here for violence."

She watched him for a second longer as her apartment reported he was unarmed and his augments were dormant, then turned and walked into her living space. He followed and sat. His hands were still held palms towards her.

"Put those down," she said shortly. "What are you here for?"

"Fontaneau has achieved what he set out to achieve. As you said, his rising tide has lifted all boats." He grinned at her toothily. "But it will not always be so."

"If you're offering an alliance, you can fuck right off, Hugo. I'm not an idiot and I can't imagine a person least worthy of my trust."

"I know you have been spying most effectively on Fontaneau for some time now," he said. "And I know he is completely unaware of that fact."

"And?" She hoped her demeanour showed Denantes she had run out of fucks to give. Because it was the absolute truth.

"You misunderstand me. I'm not threatening you or blackmailing you. I'm not going to tell him. I also know you haven't infiltrated my systems."

"And you haven't infiltrated mine," Sylfe said. "Though not for want of trying."

"I admit ..." He licked his lips. "I have long wondered what it might be like to penetrate your defences."

She favoured him with her best eye-roll.

"But I know that must remain a simple fantasy for me. Or perhaps a sim—"

"You've told me what you won't do and can't do," she said. "What *can* you do for me? What good are you?"

Denantes sat back, stretching expansively, and unbuttoned his waistcoat before the fabric ripped under the strain. "You're building a coalition, or an insurrection. You haven't succeeded yet, but I have the feeling you will. So I'm backing you."

"You're backing both sides. That's how you ensure your own survival. The only thing you're not doing is playing one side against the other because you at least have the intellect to know you don't present as a viable third alternative. No-one's going to back you, Hugo. You've never been a natural leader."

She saw him flinch ever so slightly. That, she knew, was his weak spot: the feeling of inadequacy that was the undeniable birthright of coming from a minor family. The fact his family had banished him here only compounded it.

"That may be true. But I am not without teeth," he said, any false bonhomie or air of innuendo suddenly missing from his demeanour. "My company may not be sexy like your SolEng or Fontaneau's Destruction sur Commande, but Fabrika SA plays an important role. There isn't a machine or system on Redout that doesn't rely on our devices. And our weapons division has been a major supplier to both M-Def and the Opitauans for years now. Everything we make is designed with a back door that no-one except a Denantes can access."

Now Sylfe could see the cold calculation that lay below his florid manners and affectations, and she had to admit she was a little scared of what someone like Denantes was capable of.

She sat on the lounge opposite. "Even if you render their weapons useless, we can't exactly hand-to-hand the Opitauans into submission."

"Devices can be made inert, and devices can be made to explode," he said.

"And you would do that for me if I asked you to."

He held her gaze for a moment and it was like looking into the eyes of a gutted fish. Then he transformed into the mannered caricature of an aristocrat again. "I would do that if it looked like serving me well, my dear Ind."

"Well." Sylfe stood again and extended a hand. "It's nice to know what options are on the table."

He rose and took her hand, bestowing a cringeworthy kiss on her knuckle. "Indeed. And now I shall take my leave of you. Good luck!"

She waited until the entrance door closed behind him, then sank into the lounge again. A scope nudged at her consciousness and she read the message. Abel Durand was dead. Fuck. As one door closed …

What was it Leeuwin had been drowning his sorrows in? Absinthe. She wondered if she had any in the drinks cabinet.

Three drinks in, she picked up a line of thought she'd been too distracted to follow since M-Def had shot up a bunch of refugee ships. Just where *was* Markusz Zielinski?

She pulled up the latest from her scope. *Markusz Zielinski: recorded killed during the recent terrorist attack on the highway.*

The deadest of dead ends. Still, that was only one datapoint and her scopes would have found it quicker than this if it was a simple matter of scouring the news feeds. This smelled like information inserted after the fact. Someone covering up their tracks.

She'd already accessed the death records from the date Zielinski disappeared onwards. The mortuary listed three corpses from that highway attack: Opitauans, not M-Def as had been reported. Fontaneau had told Teel he'd "deal" with Zielinski but his body still hadn't turned up, despite this latest report.

She flash-scanned the breaking news report from the scene again. *Garian Separatists.* Did Firmin have him, or at least know the whereabouts of the separatists who did? The mayor wasn't going to help Sylfe no matter how nicely she asked. And she obviously kept a close watch on her people given Abel Durand's sudden expiration.

It was time, Sylfe thought, to talk to Asymptote Eleven.

24

Elly had returned fairly quickly from whatever Firmin had her doing – though she was typically close-mouthed about it – and taken them directly to the "machine level". It was above the living space Markusz had seen when he'd first arrived here. Above the massive rotor in the ceiling that – he assumed – kept the air circulating.

He'd imagined it would be quite a large room, packed with whatever was needed to survive and maintain position in the asthenosphere. But large wasn't the word. Huge, gigantic, stupendous didn't fit either. This place was wider than the living area below by an order of magnitude. But the height … He couldn't begin to calculate. This wasn't a machine level. It was a machine city.

"No wonder the whole place shook," he said, glancing at Helena.

They'd come up through an entrance in the floor somewhere near the middle of the space. Above them, maybe a couple of kilometres away, was a vast sculpture of blades, interwoven and bent into an egg-shape. It spun slowly and inside, masked by the base thankfully, was a harsh actinic light that brightened and dimmed as the blades revolved. Reaching up from floor level on six sides, but not touching the egg, were long, curvingly articulated appendages that ended in bulbous thorns a little like a scorpion tail. They clicked and flicked in and out between the blades then left and right in a hypnotic dance.

"What the hell is that?" Markusz whispered.

Elly, standing beside him, sighed. "Yeah, we don't know. Come on. This way."

Past the scorpion tails was a curved wall easily a kilometre high. It looked organic, riddled with holes and tubes like coral or a microscopic image of bone marrow. It was humming lowly – a ghostly sound like wind blowing through a discarded flute.

"We think that's the atmosphere reprocessor," Elly said.

"Good job you don't need to repair it," Markusz said. "This stuff has been here for how long?"

"The base was discovered a decade or so after Garia was settled. So almost five hundred years."

"And who knows how long it's been running since before then," Helena said.

"Come on," Elly said. "This is an access way."

A quarter-turn around the scorpion tails there was a straight corridor leading right through the reprocessor. Markusz calculated it was fifty metres deep.

On the other side, the vaulted space above was filled with glowing globes turning slowly, bouncing and brushing against each other in a random dance. Some were a few metres above his head and looked to be ten metres across. They were all the colours he could think of and each time one touched another, they swapped hues. There were thousands of them, disappearing up into the dim.

"We have no idea what those are either," Elly said.

Markusz felt small and vulnerable, pressed down by the weight of all that strangeness hovering just above his head.

"Now we go through these," Elly said.

Because his attention had been drawn upward as they cleared the atmosphere plant, he'd missed what was spinning a few metres in front of them. He was reminded of a child's gyro toy: a whirling disk pierced by a spindle. There were rows of them – twice as tall as a human – extending left and right as far as he could see, possibly round the whole space. As well as spinning, all of them were moving: left, right, forward, back. A dance complicated by the need to keep from running into each other, because every gyro was moving to a different sequence.

"That doesn't look safe," Markusz said. "Why do we need to go through them?"

"You wanted to see the machine room. I'm taking you to a vantage point," Elly said. "And it is safe. I used to play here when I was a kid. Keep behind me. Move when I move."

She stepped in front of him, close to the first line of spinning gyros. "Ready?" she said, glancing back.

She stepped forward and Markusz, who was by no means ready, jumped to catch up, almost running into her back – which would have been disastrous. Child's game or not, being hit by one of these things would hurt.

But he was ready for her next move. Left. Left. Back. Left. Right. Forward. Right. Back. He kept his gaze focused on her shoulders because if he looked at what the hell was spinning past him, he'd stumble and that would be it.

Another left, then back, right and forward, and suddenly he was in the clear and Helena was standing in front of him.

"Well done, you," she said. "I haven't seen you move so fast in ages."

"I notice you took the short cut," he said testily. He was panting and struggling to conceal it.

"If you two are finished," Elly said, obviously inured by now to Markusz talking to thin air, "we're here."

A broad staircase led to the top of a high wall. Markusz and Elly climbed to a circular platform. The reprocessor wall was still behind them, but from here they could see the curvature of the distant outer wall of the base. Beneath the platform and running almost to the edge of the space were concentric circles of what to Markusz looked like database banks, though looks could be deceiving. Still, the hum of machinery and flashing lights seemed familiar in all this weirdness.

"That's what I call some serious propulsion," Helena said.

Running from as far as he could see above and down against the outer wall to disappear beneath the edge of the floor were massive cylinders. Their surface was studded with cabling, and thick housings bulged at regular intervals along their length. Markusz reckoned he could see maybe a fifth of the curvature of the outer wall from his vantage point. He counted twenty in that space.

"You think that's what they are?" he asked.

"What?" Elly said.

"Helena thinks those tubes are engines," he explained.

"That's what we think too."

Helena smiled and winked at Markusz. "Definitely propulsion systems. I am an engineer, you know."

"But you're also a dead memory in my head. I'm *not* an engineer."

"Well, it's nice to know that some of my knowledge rubbed off on you," she said. "But look. You can't tell me all that engine power is needed just to hold this base in position. If it was we'd be deafened by now."

"Well, I doubt they built the base here. They're advanced but they're not gods. They built it above ground and used the engines to move it here," Markusz said.

"Or maybe they came from somewhere else," Elly said. "Another planet even."

"Those engines look powerful enough to haul this whole structure into space," Helena said.

"It's a bit of a leap from tunnelling from the surface to flying here from another world," Markusz said. "But I suppose it's possible."

He looked at the steps behind them. The risers were of a size that were easy for humans to climb. The builders must have been humanoid at least.

"Is there a control room for this base?" he asked Elly.

"There is, back down below. But I don't think I'm meant to take you there."

"I won't touch anything, but I need to see it. Most of this machinery is a mystery, but we know there's a connection with this place and what's happening outside. A control room could help us figure out what these machines are for."

Elly's lips pressed in a thin line, so Markusz pushed a little more. "I can't even begin to work out how to get the universe back if we don't know what this base does. I'm sure it's something vital. It could even be the key. You want that, don't you?"

"Be very careful," Helena said. "You shouldn't toy with her hopes and fears."

But Markusz wasn't lying. He couldn't give up on this. "Please, Elly. It's that important."

"Okay," she said finally. "I'll take you."

Retracing their steps was far from easy, but Markusz navigated the gyro maze without incident and soon they were back under the scorpion limbs.

"Can we get a video feed of this whole space, now we know it's here?" he said.

"I suppose," Elly said shortly. "I'll add it to the list."

"Thank you. I really appreciate it, Elly."

"Since when did you find the time to take a people-skills course?" Helena said.

They climbed down into the vestibule beneath and entered the lift that had brought them here. It went down. Further than before.

The doors opened on another vestibule with two doors. Markusz made for the one immediately across from the elevator.

"Not that one," Elly said.

He turned. "No? What is it?"

"It's a way out."

He looked at the door again. The actuator was at shoulder level. He could just –

"I *am* armed," Elly said. "Not that I'd need to be."

"Of course." He smiled weakly. "I'm sorry." He nodded at the other door. "Lead the way."

"You first," Elly said in her best guerilla separatist warrior voice.

The door opened on another circular space, but this one was reassuringly room-sized and contained things that seemed to at least make sense. Tilted surfaces projected from the walls around hip height, and in the centre of the room was a circular table at the same height. The surfaces each had two chairs, though the bases cantilevered out from the wall on a gimbal.

"We call this place the control hub," Elly said. "And they've spent centuries figuring out a little of what it does."

She showed them the surface just left of the entrance, which was decorated with coloured finger-width patches, some grouped together and all bearing a notation in an unfamiliar script. Not unexpected, Markusz thought, but it did suggest something.

"This is environmental control for the base," Elly said, pressing a couple of coloured patches. A holo-window opened above, displaying a matrix of three graphs, each in motion and labelled with the same script. "We worked that out through trial and error. And this next workstation is the computer database interface. We use it for all our operations because it's off the Redout network. It's got a whole heap of directories we can't access though."

"And what about this? It's not original," Markusz said, pointing at a standard comm unit patched into the station by a myriad of cables.

"We needed to run comms for intraship and outside. If this place has its own comms station, we couldn't find it. As for the rest of the room …" She shrugged.

Markusz took a turn round the control hub, looking at the surfaces, the coloured controls, the gimballed chairs, and then joined Helena at the central table.

"This is a very human or humanoid-centred design," he said. "Did the Garians find any bodies when they discovered this place?"

"No," Elly said. "It was functioning but empty."

"And what about in the tunnels that led here?"

Elly shook her head. "Whatever lived there died so long ago there was no trace of them. Just tunnels, caves and hints of structures."

"What are you thinking?" Helena said.

"As if you didn't know." He sat on the nearest chair. It was quite comfy. "These coloured controls and the displays – they make sense to someone who can see in a human spectrum. I don't know, but if a species evolved here under high UV, wouldn't their eyes function differently?"

"I suppose," Elly said.

"What was the air mix like here when it was discovered? Did it match the high hydrogen concentration of the planet before the Garians settled it?"

"I don't know. It was hundreds of years ago. They made changes – that's why they had to work out how to use the environmental station. But whether the air was the same as topside …" She shrugged.

"And everything else the native Garians built is barely discernible dust," Markusz said. "But this place looks brand new, even though it's been here for more than half a millennium at least."

"So?" Helena said. "If they grew their habitats out of plant material like the rooms here, maybe they just rotted away outside."

"Maybe," Markusz conceded. "But I don't believe so."

"Are you going to tell me what you're thinking?" Elly asked.

"I think you're right. This place wasn't built by the aliens that built the tunnels. I think it came from another planet. Piloted here by humanoid aliens who were able to fly through M-World space undetected."

"Couldn't it have been built by humans?" Elly asked.

"No." Markusz jumped up again and joined Elly at environmental control. "No humans we know could build the machines we saw. There's nothing in the Thousand Worlds to equal them. And we know at least some of them react to the Effect. We don't know *why* though. It's fucking weird, but," he pointed at the alien script, "this is very good news."

"We haven't been able to work out the language," Elly said.

"You haven't had a genius mathematician to help you before," Markusz said. "Translation is just code breaking and code is just maths. Besides, these words describe functional things not esoteric concepts. This is environmental control, so whatever those signs say is about that. We'll just scan all the labels and I'll set up a translation protocol.

"This helps, Elly. Bringing me here. It definitely helps."

25

The Haibeu were playing to type when they'd insisted on a purpose-built facility to house their contingent of the Redout Confederation. Somewhere they could live together shielded from non-Haibeu neighbours. Conversely, Sylfe thought, the non-Haibeu were equally happy not to have to rub up against Hivers when they ventured out of their apartments.

The high windswept mesa was an industrial area set aside for this hemisphere's atmosphere-scrubbing infrastructure: rows and rows of ugly and literally skyscraping blocks of tightly packed glassy vanes arranged around massive turbine towers. Set amongst the scrubbers, the Haibeu Commons took advantage of the same strong winds but it was something altogether more spectacular: a sinuous, undulating tower that rotated in the breeze, its curves lengthening as it turned, then breaking apart in a jumble of shapes before reforming into another beautiful arc.

Sylfe's mover deposited her at the base of the building and she stepped out into the buffeting breeze. Up here the air smelled fresh and bracing, and she paused for a moment, feeling some of the tension she'd been holding in her shoulders fall away. She looked up as the building transitioned from a tightly wound corkscrew to a flowing integral curve and felt a little dizzy.

Normally her council ident gave her automatic access to any public area, but the doors to the ground-floor atrium waited until she spoke.

"Asymptote Eleven."

There was a moment, then the doors opened onto a glowing

path directing her to one of a bank of glass elevators. Once she was safely inside, the car moved off, entered an enclosed tube and accelerated slowly. So slowly, in fact, she wasn't sure it was still moving. But three seconds later it opened onto a hallway with organically curving walls festooned with plants.

Sunlight shifted across the open space as the building rotated. Again Sylfe felt a little dizzy and hoped she'd get used to it. Then she realised her augments were completely dead. She'd lost all connection with her instrumentality.

She heard soft footsteps and Asymptote Eleven appeared, wearing a beautifully patterned yukata in red, navy and gold.

"Please forgive me for the privacy shielding, Councillor Cachand," she said. "It is a requirement of the building."

"Sylfe, please. And don't apologise. I understand how important privacy is for the Fukei."

Asymptote Eleven smiled. "It is kind of you to call us that. Please, come in."

Sylfe followed her along the curving hallway and into a broad living space that was devoid of flat planes and angles. The walls, the furniture, even the picture window looking out on the slowly passing atmosphere vanes curved and undulated in pleasing ways, and everywhere there were plants – succulents and glossy-leafed ficus mostly – so she felt she was in the most peaceful indoor space.

Asymptote Eleven sat on a polished wooden lounge that curved around a table sprouting like a leaf from the floor. A spouted earthenware pot and two cups sat on the table.

"Sit, please. And you must call me Eleven. Tea?"

Sylfe nodded and sat. The wall opposite the window displayed three holo images of the most marvellous architectural buildings Sylfe had ever seen. Their shape and form seemed to echo and accentuate the landscape around them. She pulled her gaze away when Eleven handed her a cup.

"Pictures of our home on Fukei IV," she said. "Gone now sadly, like so much. Your world too."

Sylfe felt a rawness in her throat and sipped at her tea, watching Eleven. The woman really was quite beautiful. Her bald head was flawless, and her eyes were piercing blue above strong cheekbones and a thin, straight nose. Her lips parted as she drank her own tea. She met Sylfe's gaze for a moment, then looked away.

"If you don't mind me saying, you seem very different from how you act in the council chamber," Sylfe said.

"In public we are expected to be a certain way so we are not threatening."

"You're not threatening here and now."

"But others are less … discerning than you. They hear the stories about the Haibeu and they're afraid. They prefer those stories to the truth revealed by their own eyes."

Sylfe sipped her tea again. She'd heard those stories too: that the Haibeu were barely human hive-mind drones ruled by some secret cybernetic overlord. It was meat for the holodramas, but nothing so devoid of humanity could create the buildings she saw on the wall or create a room like this that made her feel so completely relaxed.

She paused. Yes, she did feel relaxed in this space. Even cut off from her augments, potentially at the mercy of whatever the monstrous Haibeu may have planned for her, she was at peace here. It was a blessing after the last few days.

"I love your apartment," she said.

"So do I," Eleven said. "Everything here, this building, the buildings you see in the holos, follow a mathematical principle. It's a truth the Fukei discovered when we finally arrived at our colony world. We lived in our ships for three years after planetfall, not building, taking time to debate how we could truly live in sympathy with our new world. How what we eventually built could sit in the landscape and be 'as beautiful' and 'as perfect'."

She paused, lifted the pot and refilled both their cups.

"It was one of our leaders, the architect Obe Tanka, who finally showed us the way. The forms he designed were physical expressions of the same mathematical equations present in the life of the planet. Their simplicity and beauty was stunning, and we Fukei embraced the mathematics that drove those forms and began to apply them to the design and construction of everything we could see and use." She smiled. "In a way, what we made re-made us. We began to prioritise mathematical function, appreciation and calculation in our implants. The deeper we went, the more beauty we saw. And beauty was efficient. When it came time to link to the Consource, we brought the talents we had built in ourselves to market in the best way – the only way – we knew how."

"Your ability to create the most functional systems imaginable," Sylfe said.

"Yes, all in the service of beauty. The beauty of the universe."

Sylfe frowned. "There's not much of that left. But you reminded me of what you said when we saw the annulus."

"I said it was beautiful. The mathematics that drive it are different from any we've experienced."

"Beautiful but not perfect," Sylfe said.

Eleven paused and some emotion flickered across her eyes. Embarrassment perhaps? "It's … not something I can explain. More an intuition, but one born of close association for many years with mathematical forms. The equations. Even the changes we've noticed with the barrier and the shrinkage–"

"You studied the annulus during those events?"

"We – all of us – did. We have access to the systems and records and we – not just myself – are fascinated by the annulus."

Sylfe paused. Knowing now what she did about the Fukei, she supposed it made sense.

"But I interrupted you," she said. "Please, continue."

"Even the changes in the equations feel 'right', regardless of the damage they've wrought," Eleven said. "The annulus is on the path to becoming."

"Becoming what?"

The woman smiled. "I don't know. It's only a feeling I have."

"And the others. The other Fukei?"

Eleven nodded. "And the others too. I should tell you that some of what the rest of M-Worlds think about us is true. We do share a deep link with each other through our augments, particularly during system design and other problem-solving activities. Beltran and other higher-level Fordana know this, of course, but it's not really spoken about."

"Are your … the others. Are they listening now?" Sylfe asked.

"Yes."

Sylfe hesitated, not quite sure how to proceed.

Eleven said, "They're listening because you have come to me with a problem. And if we are to solve it, I need their help. But we will not betray your trust if you choose to place it in us."

Truth be told, Sylfe's list of trustworthy people on Redout was vanishingly small and things were getting desperate. But she did trust this woman. She didn't know why. Call it a feeling.

"I'm trying to find Markusz Zielinski," she said.

"The creator? Yes, we'll help you."

"He disappeared but I found a few leads. If you could …" Sylfe pointed skyward and raised her eyebrows.

Eleven nodded and Sylfe sensed her augments re-engage. She parcelled up what she'd discovered about Zielinski, the Separatist attack, the dead Opitauans, and felt Eleven's systems open to her.

"I see," Eleven said. "The death report is obvious fabrication. Messy. Inconsistency in the mortuary records. Not the work of Haibeu."

"I'm glad it's not," Sylfe said. "I'd probably have no leads at all if that were the case. I think Mayor Firmin knows where he is. But I haven't had any luck getting into her systems."

"Let us see," Eleven said. She became quiet, her gaze somewhere else.

Sylfe felt ashamed of the impression she'd formed of the woman from the times they'd met before. She'd seen her often enough in the council rooms but hadn't really bothered to introduce herself. She'd just discounted Eleven as one of Beltran's minions.

And perhaps – even unconsciously – she'd bought into some of the disaffection many shared about Haibeu, that at some deep level they weren't quite human any more.

She realised Eleven was looking at her again.

"That is very strange," she said. "The standard Garian systems are analogous to those of Paradis, which makes sense given they originated from that planet. But the architecture of Mayor Firmin's systems is very different. I've seen nothing like it before. And it is impervious. At least so far. We're looking at it some more but I don't hold out much hope."

She paused, thinking. "It might help if we review the raw surveillance footage. We have priority access to those records. There are multiple sources but I'll thread together the best we can get. There."

A window opened between them showing the frozen image of a roadway. An armoured half-track hung tilted in the air, the blossom of an explosion behind it.

Time unfroze and the vehicle smashed into the road surface, shedding armour plating and breaking apart. Part of it burst into flames, sending thick black smoke whipping across the roadway. Two figures ran towards the wreckage in full body armour and helmets. One of them shot an Opitauan still strapped into his chair. Then ran to shoot the other two.

Another figure fell from its chair onto the roadway and the window zoomed in on Zielinski. He shouted, waving at the armoured terrorist, and when the figure approached him, he pulled at their gun and placed it on his forehead.

"What the hell?" Sylfe said.

The figure pulled back, leaned down. Smoke drifted across them and when it cleared there was no-one there.

The image froze again. Snapped to a different perspective, running back slightly and forward again. Then another. And another.

"Nothing," Eleven said. "The road surveillance is visible spectrum only. No real security need for more."

Sylfe slumped back on the lounge. "So it's another dead end."

But Eleven had that faraway look again. "Hmm," she said. "Reciprocal Six suggests a different approach."

Eleven swiped the window away and opened a new one. A time-based graph of a transmission. "This is the carrier wave for Zielinski's augments. It's at a low energy level because he wasn't actively engaged with them at the time."

"Too busy crashing and tussling with terrorists," Sylfe said.

"It ends here." Eleven pointed to where the line stopped scrolling and dropped to zero. "Normally we'd only see something like that if the body was completely destroyed. In an explosion, for instance. If he'd been shot in the head like the others, there would still be a carrier signal as the augments would continue to connect to the network. But this is a complete absence."

"Weird," Sylfe said. "How does that help?"

"On its own, it doesn't. Now look at this."

Another window opened, this time showing a row of different-coloured columns. Each column was topped with a "total" figure and this number, along with each column, was rising and falling as Sylfe watched.

"This is a representation of all the augmented citizens in the node where Zielinski disappeared and all the nodes surrounding that one," Eleven said. "In effect, it tracks the movement of citizens as they pass through the city using their augment carrier wave. Their augment connects with the nearest node as they travel. Now," Eleven said and the columns froze, "this is the moment just before Zielinski disappeared."

The node column read 36,423.

"And this is the moment immediately after he disappeared."

The node column read 38,929.

"Now if we remove all the people flagged as entering from another node in that split second, and add back in all the people flagged as leaving for a neighbouring node, we get this figure."

The node column read 36,423.

"I don't understand," Sylfe said. "If Zielinski's signal disappeared and you discounted all movement into and out of the node, shouldn't it read 36,422?"

"It should but it doesn't. There's an augment carrier signal being recorded by the node that isn't actually within the node's catchment area."

"They're spoofing his signal," Sylfe said. "How did you …"

Eleven smiled. "There are three hundred Haibeu on Redout."

"Many hands," Sylfe said, and then realised there were countless Haibeu not on Redout. "Did you feel …?"

Eleven shook her head. "It happened very quickly. I doubt anyone outside the heliopause had any idea at all when their universe ended. It could have been much worse. But we who survive still have much to do." She indicated the node column. "We've identified the hijacked signal. Or signals rather. Whatever was used on Zielinski cycles through other users' augments to avoid detection. It might produce a transient error for the user whose signal is hijacked, but probably nothing worth reporting. However, there is a moment as it jumps from one user to the next when it refers back to Zielinski's actual location. It's next to impossible to find but …"

"Three hundred minds are better than one," Sylfe said.

"We've tracked what we think is Zielinski to an end point, and it is an end point. After this he completely disappears and we have no idea how."

"Where is it?" Sylfe asked.

"Outside the city in a refugee area."

Sylfe sighed. "It would be nice to go there, maybe pick up his trail if we could. But if I left the city, Fontaneau would know at once."

"That is assuming the surveillance systems logged your departure. You've already seen the level of access we have."

Sylfe nodded, then smiled. "And I am very glad you're on my side. My mover is just downstairs."

Eleven said, "Let me change. We Haibeu prefer to blend in."

26

"You know I'm right," Markusz said after he returned to his lab from the control hub.

"I know you think you're right," Helena replied. "You have a theory about this place. It'll do until different proof comes along. But it's not exactly a priority."

Markusz sighed and leaned back in his chair. "You're no fun. Just my prefrontal cortex focusing on problem-solving. There was a time you were more willing to let your hair down and laugh a little."

"Well, I'm not me any more. If I'm no fun it probably says more about your current situation. You want my help more than anything, don't you?"

Was that all he wanted? No, but it was all he could get from an imaginary wife. That and the comfort her presence provided.

He sat straight again and opened a window on his translation program. "You're right, of course."

She sat beside him and a smile played across her lips. "But you were fun. And we had fun together."

"That we did," he said. "So let's see what we've got."

The window showed a representation of the control hub. He zoomed in on the environmental station and the translation program wiped the alien notation from the control surfaces and replaced it with Common.

It was pretty clear the control surface did what Elly said it did: the rows of coloured control patches were labelled *ventilation, heating, cooling, filtration, germicidal irradiation* and so on. Other controls isolated environmental options for different sections and levels in the facility, while readouts monitored gas mixture, airflow and temperature, recycling and recapture, and dozens of other functions needed to keep everyone in here alive. Each translated notation had a figure beside it – an indication of how sure the program was that the translation was valid. Pretty much all of them were high eighties or above.

"Okay, let's look at the next station over. Computer interface, Elly thought."

Again the program replaced the visible notation.

Markusz studied the image. "It's very …"

"Antiquated," Helena finished.

"Various input/output options. That section there, it's clearly a physical keyboard for direct command input. I've never seen one outside of a museum." He shook his head. "How do we reconcile this with the instrumentality we saw above the living area?"

"Unless it's a simple redundancy for just in case," Helena said. "Let's suppose this is an extremely advanced vessel from another planet."

"Yes, let's suppose I'm right," Markusz agreed.

Helena ignored him. "If it's that advanced, the computer system would be completely integrated and automated, maybe artificial intelligence level. But it's a ship. And things can go wrong, so they build in a redundancy. A next-to-mechanical way to interface with the computer system in case there's some kind of higher-level breakdown."

"Okay," Markusz said. "It's a theory that'll do until different proof comes along."

"Ha-ha," Helena said.

"Anyway, what about the rest of this stuff?"

They reviewed all of the stations. Some of it made sense. There was a guidance, navigation and control section, and the program was fairly confident about the translation there. As well as inertial measurement systems necessary to maintain position in the asthenosphere, there were global and astro guidance systems, sensors and propulsion controls well beyond anything needed for a static underground structure. There was also a monitoring and control station for power generation and routing. The vessel – as it now officially was – had a ring of fission reactors with a lot of redundancy built in.

"No in-built communications systems," Markusz noted.

"Maybe run through the computer?"

"But where's the redundant system if something happens? The Garians had to wire in their own."

"Hmm," Helena said. "Yes, that's strange. Nobody to communicate with? Or maybe your translation program missed it. That's the simplest answer."

"I'm not a fan of simple answers," Markusz said. "I find things are often a lot more complex than we expect."

"Like getting along with other people?" Helena said. "Sorry. Low blow."

"So," Markusz continued, ignoring her, "we've identified a fairly standard set of power, propulsion and environment control systems, and then there's four stations where the translation is a bit more hit and miss."

"*Energy transfer*," Helena said, reading the high-level functional translation the program had tagged for the group of stations. "I mean, we already have the fission reactor station over there with a pretty comprehensive set of controls for power routing. So what's *this* transferring?"

The control tags the translator had attempted to decipher all held a low confidence score below twenty. *Flux stabilisation*, *matrix coordinator*, *n-dimension buffer* and so on. It all added up to a word salad.

"Fuck!" Markusz said. "This is what controls upstairs and it's …" He sighed. "It's pointless. We're wasting time on this crap when what we should be doing is making sure the annulus is stable. Despite all the help we've given Rachik, there's another shrinkage scheduled in an hour. We need the solar engineers."

"We can't get them," Helena said. "Firmin was pretty clear on that."

Markusz stared at her.

"I know that look," she said. "No, Markusz. You'll get yourself killed."

"So what? We can't waste any more time." He opened a comm window. "Elly? I need to get back to the control hub. The translations have come through and I need to check the results."

"Can't you do that in your lab?"

Elly's voice sounded sleepy and Markusz realised he and Helena had been talking long into the night. In fact it was morning. Just like old times.

"No," he said. "Some of this stuff is analogue so I need to be onsite just to make sure."

Elly yawned. "Okay, I'll be right down."

"I told you not to toy with her," Helena said. "You don't disappoint an armed teenager."

"Maybe I know Elly better than you give me credit for."

"That'd be a first."

Elly made her way to the sink and splashed water on her face. It was stupidly early. There had to be an easier way to babysit a crazy mathematician. But it was simpler to just do what he asked otherwise he'd keep talking.

She'd slept in her clothes. Again. So she headed straight to the lab. Markusz was talking when the door opened – no doubt to Helena – and he didn't stop talking when he saw her.

"Ah, Elly. Thanks for coming down, I really app–"

"Shut up and let's just get this done so I can go back to bed."

For once, he did shut up and they rode the elevator down in silence, although he kept glancing at her like he was nervous about something.

When the doors opened, Markusz walked to the exit she'd warned him off last time they were down here and looked back at her.

"Stop fucking around," Elly said.

"I'm not. Elly, I'm going through that door. If I'm going to save everyone I need to speak to Ind Cachand and Firmin won't let me. I'm not going to let her stop me. And I can't let you stop me either. So shoot me if you have to. But I'm opening the exit."

He raised a hand tentatively to the contact.

Shoot him in the leg or help him, she thought. That's what it came down to. Fuck. She'd already made her mind up. *Sorry, Mamie.*

The door slid open and Markusz cringed a little, no doubt expecting to feel a blow or a stab or a shot.

"As soon as you go topside they'll find your augment," Elly said. "You won't have a chance."

He turned back to her. "Then give me a scrambler. I can handle it."

That would work, she supposed.

"Okay, I'll get one. Wait here. I'll only be a couple of minutes."

As she stepped back into the elevator she said, "Markusz."

He turned fully to look at her.

"I fucking mean it. Do not move."

"Okay."

She took the elevator back to her room level, ran to her locker and grabbed her gun and the scrambler. The lift was still waiting for her when she got back and she punched the button angrily. He'd better be there when she got back or she'd track him down and –

The doors opened to reveal Markusz still standing in the vestibule. Elly handed him the scrambler.

"I really appreciate this," he said.

"You'd better. If Firmin finds out, she'll skin you."

Which was probably preferable to what she'd do to Elly. Still, Brak had taught her: once you commit to the plan, you commit. No second thoughts. Not that there was much of a plan.

Markusz opened the exit door again. The space beyond wasn't much bigger than a closet with a ladder set into the wall.

"I don't have to climb right through the asthenosphere, do I?"

he said. "That's three hundred kilometres!"

"No, you idiot. This is a service way to the main exit. There's an easier access a few floors below your lab, but you didn't exactly tell me what you were up to."

"Oh. Sorry. Well, wish me luck." He placed a hand on the ladder.

"Wait," she said. "I'm coming with you."

"Really?"

Elly sighed mightily. "Yes, really. You're just going to get yourself killed otherwise."

"Funny, Helena said something similar."

She pushed past him and grabbed the ladder.

"I'll go first. Try to keep up."

They started climbing. Five minutes later, she stepped onto a narrow platform and tentatively opened a hatch set into the wall. It wouldn't do to get caught skulking around with their number-one hostage.

The chamber beyond was empty, and Elly led Markusz past two elevators big enough for heavy machinery to a more person-sized elevator at the far end.

"This place just keeps getting weirder," he said. "Airlocks I can understand, but what sort of ship has elevators that go outside?" He paused. "I suppose they were built later by whoever flew the ship here. Maybe that's why you didn't find any bodies. They all left."

They entered the elevator and Markusz slapped the cufflet around his wrist as the lift started rising.

"You're sure you want to do this?" Elly said.

"I have to."

"And you're sure you need Cachand?"

"I'm sure. I can't do it alone."

When they finally arrived at the surface and the doors opened, Markusz lifted a hand to his brow and groaned as the scrambler kicked in.

"Uh," he said. "I'm okay, but – Jesus – the things some people are interested in. The early Roman plays of Titus Maccius Plautus, a detailed 3D rendering of the black hole in the centre of the M87 galaxy – which doesn't exist any more – and a study of how E. coli can survive and thrive in a one hundred per cent hydrogen atmosphere. I mean, don't these people know the universe is ending? Shouldn't they be – I don't know – making their peace with whatever maker they believe in?"

"People are stupid," Elly said.

"Now that's something we can *both* agree on," Markusz said.

"Here, put this on," she said, handing him a bulky jacket. "And–"

"Keep the hood up and my head down. Yes, I know the drill."

They pushed through the tent flap to the outside. Markusz stopped dead, gazing at the rippling sky.

"Shit, just look at it," he said. "I mean, I've seen it in the lab obviously but …"

The refugees around them, standing in their perennial lines or sitting around on tatty camp chairs, seemed none the wiser and certainly not concerned. They were still experiencing their custom-built facility. She wondered if they even knew what the hell had happened over the past few days.

"We need to get to Redout Central," Markusz said. "That's where Ind Cachand will be."

"So, back the way we came," Elly said.

She took his elbow, guiding him through the nearest line and then along the dusty road between the tents. He stumbled and she grabbed at him to keep him upright.

"Fuck. Sorry. Hard to see through all these neo-quantum light sculptures from the Halsblad School of Art," he said.

"Ind! Ind!" a voice called out behind them.

Elly glanced back and managed to make out a figure with arm raised. She yanked Markusz between a couple of badly patched tents and veered him round a cooling fan to continue along a makeshift alley running parallel to the road.

"Ind!" the voice called again, closer.

"Pick up the pace," Elly said and started to run, her hand clamped around Markusz's wrist.

Markusz stumbled, falling headlong, and this time Elly was dragged down with him. They hit the ground hard, leaving Markusz winded and gasping for breath.

"Ind Zielinski!"

Elly let go of his arm and crouched to look back the way they'd come, raising her pistol.

Two women – one a Haibeu – stood together between the tents, arms non-threateningly wide.

Markusz grabbed at Elly's firearm, pushing it away.

"What the fuck?" Elly said.

"You have to come with me," the non-Haibeu woman and Markusz said at the same time.

Elly's gun was suddenly torn from her grip. She fell back and saw a man levelling his own weapon at her and Markusz. His face was covered in tattoos.

"Actually, you have to come with me," the Opitauan said. "Or I can kill you here."

27

Sylfe landed her mover in an open area of the refugee camp that was peppered with automated supply vehicles in various stages of unloading.

She and Eleven quickly entered the maze of tents that seemed to go on forever. There were so many people just wandering around, all with the blank look of the augment-locked. The sky didn't bother them. Nothing did, Sylfe supposed, as long as their illusionary lives persisted. What a depressing thought.

"We're never going to find Zielinski in all this," she said.

"I have the exact spot his signal disappeared," Eleven said. "When we get there, it might suggest what happened to him. It's a start at least."

"Alright," Sylfe said and smiled. Eleven was always so positive. Sylfe wouldn't have gotten this far without her help, and it made a nice change to have a friend. Her mind bumped up against that word, but as soon as she queried it, she knew it was true. Eleven was a friend. And she could rely on her. Absolutely.

"It's that large tent up ahead on the left," Eleven said.

As Sylfe looked, two figures emerged. A young girl – a native Garian by the look – and what she was sure was a man wearing a bulky coat with the hood pulled over his head. They pushed through a line of refugees, then hurried along the road away from them.

"The augment signal error is back," Eleven said.

"Then that's them." Sylfe raised an arm. "Ind! Ind!"

The girl looked back at them, and then the two figures dodged behind a line of tents.

"Come on," Sylfe said.

She and Eleven ran between the tents in pursuit of the fleeing figures. They weren't fleeing particularly quickly as the man kept stumbling, like he was drunk or something. Sylfe called again, but they clearly weren't going to stop. Then the man stumbled once too often and the two figures went flying, landing in the dirt.

"Ind Zielinski!" Sylfe called, but the girl rolled to kneeling and levelled a gun at her.

Sylfe grabbed Eleven's hand and came to an abrupt halt, pulling the woman behind her.

The hood had fallen from the man's head – it was clearly Zielinski. He pushed the girl's gun aside.

"You have to come with me," Sylfe said, at the same time as Markusz said the same thing to her.

Then Tane appeared from nowhere and disarmed the girl. He pointed his weapon at Zielinski. "Actually, you have to come with me," he said. "Or I can kill you here."

"Stay here," Sylfe said to Eleven and took a step forward.

Tane glanced at her but his pistol never wavered from Zielinski.

The Garian girl was crouched by Markusz's side, one hand on the ground for support, the other reaching slowly behind her back.

"Uh-uh," Tane said and the girl froze as he turned his pistol on her, resting a boot on Zielinski's chest to keep him exactly where he lay. "I don't know who you are and I don't care. I only want him. So you can stand up slowly and turn around."

The girl stood, hands apart and palms open, but didn't turn to leave.

Sylfe felt things were going to go bad very quickly. She took another step and Tane regarded her.

"Tane," she said, "put the gun down. And you ..." She raised her hand to the girl. "Don't do anything hasty."

"Do you think you could take your boot off me?" Zielinski said. "It's far from comfortable down here."

"Just stay where you are," Sylfe said.

"Of course I'm okay with being saved by a woman," Zielinski said. "Don't be ridiculous."

"What?" Sylfe said.

"Don't worry," the girl said. "He's arguing with his dead wife. It happens a lot."

"Her name is *Helena*," Zielinski said.

"Just shut up!" Tane said. "Ind Cachand, what do you think you're doing?"

What *was* she doing. Well, the only thing she could think of, and it wasn't necessarily going to work, but here goes nothing.

"It's *Matri* now, as you should realise, Kaito Tane," she said, using the Opitauan honorific. It all helped. "And I'm telling you to stand down. The Great Families of Cachand and Fontaneau are now *en concours*."

Seconds stretched and they all seemed frozen in place as the Opitauan warrior considered her words. Tane was a traditionalist, Sylfe knew. That was all she could count on.

Finally he pulled back, lifted his boot off Zielinski, and holstered his weapon. "Patri Fontaneau is looking for this man," he said to Sylfe.

"Well, he can't have him. I need him. I suspect we all do if we're to live beyond the next few days."

"What will—"

"What you tell Fontaneau is up to you," Sylfe snapped, more sure of herself now and bringing the full weight of the venerable Cachand Family behind her words. "I know you're loyal to all Paradisan Families, but that man is not worthy of your loyalty. I hope you realise that some day. Now leave us."

"Yes, Matri." Tane delivered a short bow and disappeared between the tents.

Sylfe let out a huge sigh.

"What the hell just happened?" Zielinski said, standing and brushing dust off his trousers and a wide bootprint off his jacket.

"The Opitauans have been in service to the Great Families

of Paradis for centuries," Sylfe said. "Titular heads of each Family – which I unexpectedly became when Paradis was destroyed – have certain authorities and obligations that Tane still believes in, regardless of everything else going to shit around us. I've given him notice that my Family and Fontaneau's are now formally in competition with one another."

"We were coming to find you, Ind Cachand. Uh … Matri," Zielinski said.

"You can call me Sylfe, and this is Asymptote Eleven."

"Eleven will do," Eleven said behind her.

"And this is Elly. And please, call me Markusz."

"A pleasure," Sylfe said, nodding to the girl. "And your dead wife is Helena. My condolences."

"She says thank you," Markusz said. "But don't worry – I'm not insane."

"I'm glad," Sylfe said. "We were coming to find you too."

"This is all *really* nice," Elly said. "But we need to get the fuck out of here."

"They can come with us, back to the facility," Markusz said.

"What? No!" Elly said.

"Yes," Markusz insisted. "It's shielded against sensors, it's the best place to talk in secret, and Firmin would rather have me back there than wandering around up here."

"Mayor Firmin," Sylfe said. She'd suspected as much. The mayor was somehow way ahead of all of them.

"Firmin will skin you," Elly said to Markusz.

"She won't. It's time she faced up to reality."

Going on her past encounters with the mayor, Sylfe wasn't sure that was the optimal approach for dealing with her.

"Come on," Markusz pressed. "There's nowhere else for us to go."

"*Fuck.* This way then," the girl said, and pushed between two tents to the main thoroughfare.

Markusz smiled sheepishly at Sylfe and she and Eleven followed on behind.

Now she had more time to look around, Sylfe felt utterly responsible for the shabby habitats and general ramshackle nature of the camp. It was even worse when she considered the lush apartments she'd arranged for Maman, Yvette and Suzanne. She'd been far too focused on her own work with the sunbarques instead of paying attention to what was happening on the ground. Though how much she could have influenced her council colleagues to arrange a more equitable division of resources was anyone's guess; and with Fontaneau in charge now it would be pointless. Best to concentrate on how to prevent everyone from dying and build from there.

Elly ushered them all into a large tent. "I just hope we haven't been tracked," she said.

"I've blanked us from any passive surveillance," Eleven said. "There won't be any trouble."

"So how did the tattooed goon turn up then?" Elly asked.

It was a fair question and one that had occurred to Sylfe.

"Yes, we've reviewed that," Eleven said. "He followed Sylfe and me by line of sight. It was the only way he could with the surveillance net under our control. He's probably been following you for a while, Sylfe."

"Damn," Sylfe said. "If Fontaneau doesn't already suspect me of treachery, he soon will."

"It's probably better if we continue this conversation downstairs," Markusz said, pulling aside the door of a large cargo pod to reveal an elevator.

"That doesn't look like Refugee Management infrastructure," Sylfe said.

"Believe me, it's not," Markusz said.

The elevator doors opened and they all got inside. Elly selected a level and the car started down.

"I know it's going to be hard to believe, but we're actually travelling through the planet's rocky mantle and down into the molten asthenosphere," Markusz continued. "There's a base down there that we suspect is an alien spacecraft, fully functional and buried for at least half a millennium. Firmin has it earmarked as a bolthole for her people if the shit really hits the fan."

"Hard to believe" was an understatement, Sylfe thought. Markusz was already talking to his deceased partner; was this another delusion? Still, this elevator obviously led somewhere and the bit about Firmin rang true. She knew the mayor had some plan up her sleeve that meant she could reject Sylfe's offer of an alliance out of hand. As to the unbelievable alien ship, it was probably best to humour him.

"So, this ship," she said. "What's it doing down there?"

"We've got some partial theories," Markusz said. "But we'd appreciate some fresh perspectives."

"We'll certainly try," Sylfe said.

She glanced at Eleven to see what she made of all this. She was gracing them all with her most beatific smile.

"You seem to be enjoying this," Sylfe said.

"Why not?" Eleven said. "More wonders to discover."

It was a good mindset to have, Sylfe supposed. But she didn't feel so sanguine about the situation. There was too much at stake to just kick back and enjoy the ride.

That thought carried her through to the end of the elevator ride, when the doors opened on a pissed-off Mayor Firmin flanked by two armed guards with rifles levelled at them. Sylfe grabbed for Eleven's hand again, but there was no way either of them would live if those guards opened fire. She was sorry she'd gotten the Fukei into this.

"Elly!" Firmin snapped. "Get out."

The young girl stepped – somewhat sullenly, Sylfe thought – out of the elevator car.

Firmin's focus was squarely on Zielinski now. "I should open fire on the lot of you."

"Go ahead," Markusz said.

Great, Sylfe thought. Delusional *and* with a death wish. He clearly didn't care who else might get killed along with him.

"And then turn the guns on yourselves," Markusz continued. "Killing me is tantamount to suicide."

"Oh, you are so fucking full of yourself," Firmin said.

The direct approach really wasn't working out, just as Sylfe had suspected.

"I am," Markusz said. "But not without reason, and you know it or you wouldn't have kidnapped me in the first place. You want me to save you, but you won't do what I ask to achieve that. Elly at least listened."

"I'll deal with her later."

"No, you won't," Markusz said. "I take full responsibility. This place isn't the safe haven you think it is. There's another shrinkage coming in nine minutes. It's too late to do anything about it now because you wouldn't let me contact Ind Cachand. Elly did what you should have done. She helped. And with the Ind's help, we can perhaps ameliorate the shrinkage after this one."

Okay, now he was starting to make sense, Sylfe thought. And she'd had a chance to look at their surroundings. The chamber they were in was a very odd design. Not even remotely Garian, and she was sure the Redout Project hadn't built whatever this was.

Firmin looked at Elly again, then down at the floor. Finally, she sighed and waved one hand. Her guards shouldered their weapons.

Then she focused on Sylfe and Asymptote Eleven. "If you or your friend tell anyone what you've seen here, I will personally kill you both."

"As I said before, I'm an ally. And if my silence doesn't prove that, I'll prove it by stopping Fontaneau," Sylfe said. She was quite sure she sounded far more confident of the latter than she felt.

Firmin snorted. "Another one that's full of themselves. Elly will help you leave quietly when you're ready." And then she was gone, her guards following along behind.

"Was that true what you said about the shrinkage?" Sylfe asked Markusz.

"Yes. Come to my lab. We can watch it there."

28

Whatever this place was, it certainly didn't feel like a spaceship from the limited parts Sylfe saw on the way to Markusz's lab. The walls were soft, with a felt-like covering and a fine organic patterning to them; and the doors were oval, with a trip-worthy raised threshold like an ocean-going craft. She had to admit she had zero experience of alien ships though, so her judgement was probably entirely useless.

Markusz's lab was at least familiar. There were two workstations, but it looked like he worked here alone.

"You might want to sit down," he said as they entered, then he turned to Elly. "I'm sorry about that. I didn't mean to–"

"Don't worry about it," Elly said and sighed. "I was going to have to deal with it sooner or later."

She grabbed a couple of fold-out chairs from the wall and handed them to Sylfe and Eleven, then sat at the spare workstation.

Meanwhile, Markusz busied himself opening a number of shared augment windows: a view of the current border with the Effect; a view of the annulus; and a number of windows that carried live data of the annulus function straight from Teel's own laboratory.

"The gravitic readout is the one I think might be of most interest," Markusz said. "It's something your SolEng sunbarques could influence if we get a chance. Oh, and since we're here, we may as well watch what happens up above."

He opened another window that looked down on a collection of weird shapes in motion: a metal egg floating above giant talons, a great circular sponge, dark spindles beyond, and in between them all, coloured balls of light floating around and kissing gently against each other.

"This is the machine level at the top of the ship," Markusz said.

"That's machinery? It looks like a child's amusement park," Sylfe said, all doubts about Markusz's assertions about this place falling away to be replaced by a stunned sense of wonder.

"Best to sit now," Markusz said, and quickly sat at his workstation.

Sylfe was aware of a throbbing beneath her feet and a growing sound of heavy machinery.

"There seems to be some kind of feedback," Markusz said, shouting above the rising hum, "between the annulus, the Effect and this ship. We've heard and felt it, but we haven't observed it up to now."

The alien egg glowed brighter and the talon things moved faster and faster, whipping in and out until they became a blur. The machine noise rose to a deafening level and the coloured balls suddenly all turned scarlet and froze in place.

Sylfe's gaze darted to the other windows, tracking the changing numbers and looking for a first visible sign of a change. Any change.

She felt a touch on her hand and looked to see Eleven's fingers enfolding her own. The woman sat beside her, staring just as intently at the windows.

"It's happening now," Eleven said, just as the engine sound around them reached a crescendo then cut off. The Effect leaped forward in its window. The annulus looked just the same, but the readouts were off the scale.

"We're down to a sphere of diameter a little under twenty-six and a half billion kilometres," Markusz said. "We've lost twenty per cent of the remaining universe."

With the ship quiescent again, Eleven let go of Sylfe's hand and stood to observe the windows more closely. Sylfe followed suit. As she stood beside Eleven she recalled the woman she'd been used to seeing – and ignoring – in the council chambers. This Eleven was so much more open; warmer, engaging and engaged. Freer to be herself here at the end of the universe?

Sylfe shook her head, then glanced at Markusz who was looking round the room distractedly. "Something wrong?" she asked.

"Nothing," he said. "But look at this." He pulled one of the windows closer and tilted it so she could better see. "This is what suggested to us that you might be able to help."

It was a map of the gravitic scalar flow across the whole system. As Markusz moved his fingers the inclines and declines of the flow bunched and stretched, running from a timepoint two minutes before the shrinkage occurred to two minutes after.

"So look here," he said, and the representation froze as he pointed at a false colour image showing a particularly energetic section of spacetime. "This is the annulus pushing back against the Effect, using a gravitic transform. You see the slippage there? That's why we lost more space. But if we could harness the sun's–"

"–magnetosphere to increase this transform through the substrate," Sylfe finished. "Yes, I see. We might be able to hold back the tide." She sighed. "When do you anticipate another shrinkage?"

"Tomorrow," Markusz said. "Give or take."

Sylfe nodded. "Time enough. You say we're on an alien ship – but what *is* this place? Maybe if we understood more we could help more."

"Well …" Markusz paused and looked at Elly, who was still seated.

The girl rolled her eyes. "It's a little late to get coy."

Markusz grimaced. "Yes, sorry about that. I kind of got carried away facing imminent death from an Opitauan. It gave me flashbacks of a certain exploding vehic–"

"It's like he said in the elevator," Elly interrupted. "This base has been down here since before Garia was settled. Early Garians found it when they were exploring tunnels left by a dead alien civilisation."

"None of which was reported to M-Worlds," Markusz said. "If

it had been, there would have been experts crawling all over it for decades and we'd have a better idea of why it's here, who brought it and what it actually does."

"And Garia would have no longer belonged to the Garians," Sylfe said.

"Yes," he said. "So I can understand why they didn't. Ironic that they lost control of the planet anyway when Redout was established. But the thing is, there's a connection between the machinery on this ship and the Effect. You saw and felt that yourself. Why the aliens came here, I don't know. Maybe they knew Garia was going to be the last planet."

"Where are they now?" Eleven asked.

"No trace. Maybe they died. Maybe they left."

"Why would you leave if this was a safe haven?" Sylfe said.

Markusz shrugged. "In any case, there's a control room that we've tried to decipher with varying degrees of success. And a ship computer system, but we can't access any of the files from the original owners."

"I might be able to help with that," Eleven said. "But really, I don't believe we have anything to worry about."

Markusz gaped at her for a moment before recovering himself. Then he said, "Sorry?"

Sylfe suspected she knew what was coming.

"You'll forgive me," Eleven said, eyes cast down in something approaching embarrassment, "you are a brilliant mathematician. Creator of the annulus. But I think perhaps your creation is outgrowing you in ways that you do not understand."

Markusz was blinking rapidly and Sylfe suspected he was struggling not to say something rude. She didn't share Eleven's conviction that the annulus was changing for the best, but she couldn't deny the woman's belief was genuine.

"The changes Teel made has forced the annulus in a direction we didn't originally envisage," Markusz conceded. "And it's changed it irrevocably, I'm afraid."

Teel might have made the changes, Sylfe thought, but really it was Fontaneau who was to blame. His ego had destroyed not just Paradis but the universe.

"The change is not yet complete," Eleven said. "The mathematics of the shrinkage only make me more certain. It is close to perfection now."

Markusz looked to Sylfe, no doubt for some indication her companion was completely insane. Sylfe, however, remained composed.

"I don't understand this as Eleven does," she said. "But I can't disprove her assertion either."

"Mathematical perfection is all well and good," Markusz said. "But it's a moot point if no-one is left alive to appreciate it."

"In any case," Sylfe said, "you won't find anyone better than Eleven to help with your alien computer system. And I'll be in touch as soon as I contact my sunbarques."

Markusz nodded.

Sylfe turned to Eleven. "You're sure you'll be alright?"

The woman smiled. "I will. And my colleagues will make sure your mover isn't tracked until you're safely back in Redout Central."

Now it was time to go, Sylfe felt sad that Eleven wouldn't be coming with her.

It seemed that Eleven felt the same way. She touched Sylfe's arm and said, "We'll see each other again soon."

On the way back to the elevator with Elly, a thousand questions sprang into Sylfe's mind about the alien technology around and above them, but she couldn't bring herself to ask any of them. She knew she'd been admitted here under sufferance and should be grateful for that much.

Still, the silence between them in the elevator ride up eventually became unbearable and she said, "You don't need to worry about me. I'll keep your secrets safe."

Elly just laughed. She'd clearly been brought up in the school of Firmin.

But overall, today had been a win. And it was only when Sylfe acknowledged it that she realised how desperately she'd needed one.

Elly rode back down in the elevator, recalling the look on her grandmother's face when she'd ordered her out of it earlier. *I'll deal with her later.* It was all calculated to put her in her place. And Markusz "taking the blame" for her was just another way to treat her like a child. It made her angry.

But she'd learned when she saw her parents killed in front of her not to let anger overwhelm her. Anger without control was pointless. Harnessed, it was a tool. She'd used her anger to become the best fighter she could be. To kill when necessary. It had made her strong. Not just her body, but her mind. She wasn't going to slink to her quarters and wait for her grandmother to summon her. She had nothing to be sorry for.

Elly's augment indicated her grandmother was in her chambers, so she went right there and rapped on the door.

Her grandmother looked up from her desk as Elly entered and said, "I thought we'd reached an understanding." She was clearly still pissed off.

"We did," Elly said. "You agreed to treat me like an adult."

Pissed off transitioned to full-blown rage as her grandmother stood, throwing the flimsies she'd been holding aside. "And this is how you demonstrate that? By bringing Sylfe Cachand here and exposing everything?"

"That … wasn't meant to happen," Elly admitted. Her grandmother had a point. But it wasn't *the* point. "If you'd just let Markusz contact her via augment like he asked, it definitely wouldn't have happened."

"So … what? You disobey me? You go behind my back?"

"Yes! When you're wrong and there's no way you'll be convinced otherwise."

Her grandmother pulled back at that, her eyes narrowing as she considered Elly. "You've been spending too much time with

Zielinksi," she said eventually. "He's poisoned you against me."

Elly felt her own anger surge, but she wasn't going to lose control. "You keep treating me like I'm a child who doesn't know their own mind."

"You keep *acting* like one!"

"You're wrong, Mamie. We should be doing everything we can to bring the universe back. Or at least *try* while there's still a chance. Instead, you want to give up, lock the doors and ignore whatever happens up there. That's not the life I want. And it's not one I'd choose without trying everything possible for something better. If that means working with the enemy, then let's do it. I've listened to Markusz, yes. And Cachand. They make sense. And there's still some things they can try to save us all."

Her grandmother sighed. "I forgot how young you are."

"I–"

"No, I don't mean you're still a child. I mean you still have hope for something better. I've lived through too many disappointments for that." She sat again. "That doesn't mean I condone what you've done."

Elly breathed out quietly. "I'm not asking you to. I just want you to understand why. And to see me for who I really am."

Her grandmother grunted. "You're just like your mother, you know."

"Yes. And she was just like you."

That was part of the problem, Elly supposed. Neither one of them gave way easily. She hesitated. She should probably admit to everything.

"I also helped Markusz connect with one of his old team so he could influence what they do with the annulus. It's all part of the same thing."

Her grandmother nodded, which Elly took as a good sign. "I don't suppose there's any point telling you not to do something like this again."

"You're right," Elly said. "I just need you to trust me."

29

In her mover en route to Redout Central, Sylfe received an urgent summons to attend an emergency council meeting. She knew there was every chance Tane would reveal her treachery to Fontaneau before that meeting began. And whether the Patri moved against her then or not, he may at the very least try to circumvent control of her sunbarques. Well, good luck with that.

She opened a window to Roche.

"I was just about to call you," he said. "All ships are together and we're making our way as close to Redout as possible while still maintaining operations. And the highliner is approaching the western hemisphere beanstalk."

"Interesting. Taking on supplies?" Sylfe wondered.

Roche shrugged.

"In any case, I need you to do two things for me," she said. "Firstly, please ignore any communications you receive from Ind Fontaneau or the council. And second, you'll be receiving new data for some special operations. Nothing too taxing, but please be ready when you get it."

Roche looked immediately concerned. "Of course, Ind."

"The data will come from Ind Markusz Zielinski. He's a friend. And you are to follow his instructions as you would my own. This is vital, Roche. Do you understand? And no discussions on this. Keep it to the seniors only."

"Ind Cachand," he said, then paused.

"Speak, Roche. You know you always can with me."

The older man smiled. "It's just that many onboard are worried for your safety. We could send a shuttle to bring you back to the ship. There's no need for you to be on the planet."

Sylfe would have joined them in a flash if she could.

"Please thank the crew for their thoughts. I have some unfinished business." She paused. "But it might be worthwhile bringing one of the sunbarques into Redout orbit. Just in case."

They weren't warships by any stretch, but what they did carry could be used offensively if she needed. Having the option might be useful.

"I'll bring my own ship in," Roche said and signed off.

Sylfe's mover descended to the landing apron around the pinnacle of the council building and she disembarked. The sky was all rippling scarlet. It would have been pretty if she didn't understand the cause. The annulus had slipped again and it wasn't something Fontaneau could brush under the carpet.

If the council knew the slippage was due to meddling at his behest, it might give even his most ardent supporters pause. But Sylfe wasn't ready to confront him on that openly. Not as long as he controlled the Opitauans and, through them, M-Def. But it may give her some leverage to sway Denantes a little further towards her side of the equation – not that it would make her trust him any more – and perhaps convince Beltran that he'd backed the wrong horse. Fontaneau could find himself isolated, and then, with the weight of the council on her side, Sylfe could work on Teel to let her take control of the annulus. It should make a nice change for him after dealing with a megalomaniac. It was a working plan anyway.

Looking across the city she could see isolated columns of smoke and hear the wail of emergency klaxons. People were panicking. She couldn't blame them.

Things were equally tense in the council chamber. As she entered, Leeuwin was in quiet discussion with Beltran. The GH sector governor-general was giving Beltran a run for his money in the gaunt-to-the-point-of-looking-cadaverous stakes. Sylfe wondered if he'd had any solids since she last saw him or if he'd switched his diet to pure eighty-proof.

She smelled Denantes before she turned to see him hovering by her right shoulder. She shied away to avoid breathing his odorous exhalations.

"Enjoy your trip, Ind?" he said with a toothy grin, and sauntered to his usual seat at the right-hand end of the council table.

He was fucking with her. He had to be. But the sight of Tane standing just inside the door, his attention focused on a private window, gave her some pause. If Tane could follow her … Well, even if Denantes knew what she'd been up to with Markusz, he could do her no more harm than Tane could and she'd already resolved to let those cards fall where they might.

Firmin entered the chamber behind her and Sylfe wondered how the mayor travelled around without being tracked. Did she have a more efficient subterranean route back to the city? In any case, she was studiously ignoring Sylfe. So far so normal.

There was another Fukei where Eleven usually sat. Sylfe's augments informed her this was Coefficient Eight. She would be surprised if Beltran had noticed the difference.

"I believe we have not only a quorum but a full house," Fontaneau said, beaming from his seat at the head of the table. "I thank the councillors for their indulgence and ask that we all be seated in order to commence this extraordinary meeting."

If Fontaneau was worried about recent events, he certainly didn't show it. The man was positively ebullient.

Sylfe sat in her usual chair beside Leeuwin, and Beltran sat to Fontaneau's left. She looked for Teel, who had taken to sitting at Fontaneau's right … Oh. So that's how it was. Teel was sitting at a small table to the right of the entranceway with Rachik by his side. To say the chief scientist of the CSTO Task Force looked sick with worry would be putting it mildly.

"There is, as you will have seen from the meeting papers," Fontaneau said, "only one item of business. The unfortunate state of affairs of the annulus and the devastating impact its repeated failings have had on the citizens of Redout."

He looked around the table, gathering the gaze of every individual like the first-class actor he was, Sylfe thought. They all had ringside seats to what she was sure was going to be a command performance. That said, it was possible Fontaneau didn't need to convince anyone of anything. If he couldn't bring "those he needed" along with him, he could simply compel them with force of arms at this stage in the game. But then there'd be no audience, just subjects. And he would have to give up the mask he wore. Sylfe realised that he relished the mannered performance he gave for its own sake. It was a private psychodrama he indulged in and played out in the real, to his own amusement and the terror of others. They were already screwed. This was just icing on the cake.

"The citizens of Redout, our most precious, indeed sacred children — for are we not, as council members, guardians to all who would seek refuge here? — are in very real fear for their lives. A fear which has only been made more acute by the latest news about the annulus. Twice now, its sphere of influence has contracted. And this on top of the mass destruction of the rest of the universe, which it was unable to stave off."

That wasn't exactly fair, Sylfe thought. No-one had said the annulus would stop the Effect dead. But neither she nor anyone else was inclined to object.

"We have reports of fires and looting as civil order breaks down under this burden of fear," Fontaneau continued. He raised his gaze towards the back of the room. "Kaito Tane is busy coordinating the emergency service, rescue and security efforts. But the panic we are seeing on the streets is a long way from abating."

Beltran cleared his throat. "If I might, Ernes?"

Fontaneau glanced at the Fordana before pursing his lips and nodding slowly.

"From a system level," Beltran said, "the flow of information is the problem." He looked around the table and was greeted with blank stares. "It's quite simple. The knowledge of the shrinkages has fuelled the current panic. But in the refugee-holding facilities, life continues as normal. You see?"

Sylfe considered how poor a communicator Beltran was when he didn't have his flowcharts to rely on. It stemmed from a basic lack of humanity, which in turn meant he could conceive of inhuman solutions like this one.

"You're suggesting we augment-lock the entire population and feed them a false reality where everything is okay?" she asked him.

Beltran's smile looked like something generated by a facsimile of a human. "Why, yes. Excluding the council, of course, and the security forces. We could make the sky the right colour for them again. We could even give them the stars back."

"Right. Well." Sylfe paused as her brain struggled to understand how and why Beltran might even consider this was a good idea, then gave up. "Apart from being fucking insane and inhuman, it also does nothing to solve the actual problem we have."

Beltran's eyes went wide and he looked to Fontaneau or anyone to jump in and defend him from what Sylfe imagined he saw as an unwarranted attack. But Fontaneau was nodding at Sylfe, a twinkle in his eyes that made her want to shudder.

"I understand you're only trying to help," he told Beltran, "but Sylfe is correct. We can't simply wave our hands and make the problem disappear, much as we might like to. We need to act. We need to show the people we are doing everything we can to protect them."

His eyes swept the table and rested on Sylfe before he intoned, "Ind Teel."

"Yes?" Teel's voice was barely a whisper.

When Fontaneau finally turned his head to look at Teel, his features were carved in granite. "You will stand when you address this council, Ind."

Already flustered, Teel almost jumped out of his chair, causing the table to lurch forward. Rachik looked up at him, his expression mirroring the fear plastered across his boss's face.

"Come forward." Fontaneau's tone was that of a disappointed

parent.

Teel walked to the centre of the room, stiff-legged and visibly sweating. Sylfe couldn't see how this would end any other way than badly for him, but she also couldn't look away.

"Ind Teel, this council took you at face value when you joined us," Fontaneau said. "We believed your assurances and gave you every support and resource at our disposal. When the first problems appeared with your performance, we gave you the benefit of the doubt. We did not expect miracles, simply that you execute your duties as promised."

"As I did," Teel said, forcing his way into the monologue. "But if the Ind might recall, it was you—"

"But problems recurred. They exacerbated." Fontaneau bit off each word, glaring now at Teel, who withered on the spot. "And as a result, we see pandemonium spreading across this last cradle of humanity."

"I only—"

"I am correct in stating that as lead scientist you are the chief decision-maker on every action relating to the annulus?" Fontaneau said.

"Yes, but—"

"There is no room for prevarication, Ind."

"You requested—"

"The consequences of those decisions are yours and yours alone. You were warned on your very first day. And the council has now run out of patience. Tane."

Tane broke off from his private conversation and strode to the centre of the room to stand alongside Teel, who regarded him wide-eyed and visibly quaking.

Tane unholstered his pistol and levelled it at the scientist.

Sylfe stood. "Ernes, you can't do this."

Leeuwin stood along with her, but his "no" was barely audible.

On the other side of the table Denantes was grinning, clearly entertained by the turn of events.

"You and Jan Pieter are too soft-hearted," Fontaneau told Sylfe. "It does you credit, but it does us and the people of Redout no good at all."

He nodded at Tane.

The pistol fired and Teel crumpled to the floor.

"Ind Rachik," Fontaneau said.

Rachik shot out of his chair and stumbled back against the wall.

"You are now chief scientist. I pray that your performance is better than your predecessor's. The people shall be told the annulus has now been stabilised and no further problems are expected. With the help of Tane's troops, I am sure order can now be re-established." Fontaneau turned to the council members and allowed a tepid smile to replace his stern expression. "Can the meeting be adjourned?"

If anyone had intended to interject or raise new business, the rapidly expanding pool of Teel's blood on the floor had clearly given them second thoughts. The room cleared quickly.

As Sylfe was on the way back to her mover, Leeuwin fell in step with her.

"Just to let you know," he said quietly, his face a mask, "I've been ordered to bring the highliner into close orbit and dock with the beanstalk."

Sylfe already knew that, but didn't want to disappoint Leeuwin. They'd all had a rough day.

"Thank you," she said. "Did he tell you why?"

Leeuwin only granted her a pale smile and drifted away.

30

Markusz woke. As he rolled over, he saw Helena sitting on the end of his cot.

"Were you watching me while I slept?" he said.

She smiled. "That would be weird."

He took a deep breath. Let it out and rubbed sleep from his eyes. "I dreamed I was falling down a well. And you were at the bottom waiting to catch me."

"That's nice," Helena said, arching one eyebrow. "If a little Freudian."

"You know, I can't help feeling there's more to you than just my memory. You died in a collapsing annulus field. I'm here inside another collapsing annulus field. Couldn't there be some … connection? Across time? Across fields?"

"Now that is wishful thinking. I'm not some princess in an enchanted sleep, waiting for your kiss to waken me. That's just romantic twaddle."

"So says the rational side of my brain." Markusz pulled himself up and leaned back against the soft wall.

Helena regarded him levelly. "The sane side. And the side that says we need to focus on the task at hand."

She was right of course, but Markusz couldn't deny the feeling he had. Okay, so maybe it was wishful thinking. But maybe it was intuition. That sense had served him well all through his career. The feeling that he was reaching towards an answer. That he'd get there if he just kept going.

"Maybe, maybe not," Helena said. "If there is an answer, it'll come. That's the way it works, isn't it? Forcing it won't help."

"Where did you go anyway? Last I saw you we were running through tent city. I turned round and you were gone."

Helena pursed her lips. "I didn't want to cramp your style when you met the lovely Ind Cachand."

"Oh, please," Markusz said angrily.

"Or you sent me away for the same reason. Which story do you prefer? And before you say anything, I'm not jealous."

He pushed off the cot and strode to his workstation. The annoying thing was, if Helena was part of him then he *was* attracted to Sylfe. Which meant he was annoyed at himself for feeling that way. But he didn't. He wasn't.

"I don't have time for this." He opened a window and checked the feed from Sylfe's sunbarques.

Firmin was pissed off with him, but she was also a pragmatist: she'd allowed Markusz more augment access and set up the line to Sylfe. There was no chance of being detected. Everything here ran through the ship's computer, which had proven impenetrable.

He opened another window showing a datastream from the annulus.

Helena leaned on the workstation beside him, watching the lines of data.

"If Asymptote Eleven is right, we shouldn't meddle with this," she said. "It's changing, we can see that. But maybe it's changing for the better."

"Is that your intuition?" Markusz said.

"The Haibeu have an extraordinary facility with mathematics. Everyone knows that. We've learned so much working through the new maths that Rachik and Teel applied to the annulus."

"The maths that got us into this mess."

"Yes. But it's possible there's more to it. It's all so new."

Markusz nodded. "There are rooms beyond that room. But if we allow it to go further, there's no going back. We've already seen that with the shrinkages. There's no do-over here."

He shook his head. "I can't believe I'm debating with myself whether Eleven's idea has merit."

"I think it's a good thing," Helena said. "The old Markusz would have rejected her out of hand."

"You're saying you've changed me for the better?"

"Or you've changed yourself. If Eleven is right, the trick is for us to do nothing."

Markusz shook his head. "No. I can't do that."

"And that's what I love and hate about you."

He checked the data from the sunbarques again and the annulus. It looked good but he couldn't be sure until the next shrinkage either happened or didn't.

A private window opened displaying Rachik's ident.

Markusz accepted the call and was shocked at the man's demeanour. He was wild-eyed, his usually carefully arranged hair standing up like a cockscomb.

"Zielinksi," Rachik rasped, "he's *dead*. Teel. Fontaneau had him gunned down in front of us."

Markusz sat heavily in his chair. "Poor bastard."

Beside him, Helena said, "He didn't deserve to die."

He kind of did though, Markusz thought, and savoured the fact he maybe wasn't as reconstructed as Helena liked to think he was. Well, well, well, Teel had finally met a situation he couldn't use to his own advantage.

Rachik was still peering out of the window like a frightened rabbit.

"But that means you're the boss now? That's a good thing," Markusz said.

"But for how long? Another shrinkage and I'll go the way of Teel."

"No, you'll be *fine*," Markusz said. "Besides, replacements are a bit thin on the ground. Look, we're doing some more work from this end. We'll know soon if it's successful."

"No."

"No?" Markusz wondered if Rachik hadn't heard him right. "Look–"

"You need to come in, Zielinski. I need you here."

"So you can put me between you and Fontaneau?" Markusz looked at Helena, who shook her head slowly.

"You come in here or I'll tell Fontaneau about you anyway," Rachik said.

The nerve of him after everything Markusz was trying to do. Really, some people … Mind you, even if Fontaneau did know about Markusz, it was unlikely he could find him.

"Go ahead and tell him," he said, "because there's no way I'm coming within spitting distance of that madman. Or here's an alternative. Why don't you grow a backbone, get some common sense and keep doing what I tell you to do? Do you think you can manage that?"

Rachik glared from the window, which suddenly closed.

"That went south rather quickly, darling," Helena said.

"Fuck him," Markusz said, still angry.

"No, forget him. There's no reasoning with him in that state. He'll come around. Look, why don't we go and check in on our resident Haibeu?"

Markusz sighed. "I suppose."

He could have handled Rachik better, he knew that. But there was also something deeply satisfying about cutting loose in the face of such deep ingratitude.

Eleven sat at the main table in the centre of the control hub. She smiled as Markusz entered and asked, "Did you manage to get some sleep?"

He felt the last of his anger fall away under the brilliance of that smile. Eleven really was a remarkably calming influence even if she did come across as a bit weird.

"I did. Thank you." He looked around the room. "So what do you make of all this?"

"I could spend a lifetime here. The computer architecture alone is … It doesn't seem like it should work but it does. Such complexity. More than the human brain. But at the same time more robust. More connected." She brought her focus back to Markusz. "The Garians are using it, you know. A parallel network to our own that extends as far round the planet as the Redout council's own systems. It's remarkable they were able to use it without really understanding it."

"A testament to their native cunning, no doubt." He sat at the table and Helena stood by his side. "Like the environmental system. It's lucky they didn't blow up the planet."

Eleven smiled. "I suspect this place would have fail-safes for that." She hesitated. "I haven't been able to get into the original databases yet."

"So, no user manual?"

"No, but we're not completely in the dark and your translation program's helped. The computer contains a set of routine diagnostics to track, test and verify ship systems. I used these on the environmental station to trace and match the translated controls to the functional machinery they're connected to. Confirming the 'heating' controls connect to actual heaters and so on."

"That's reassuring," Markusz said and exchanged a look with Helena. He was thinking of many similar conversations they'd had, with her explaining how the devices she designed would test the equations he'd developed.

"Next I applied the diagnostics to the stations you've flagged as 'energy transfer'. It was rather more difficult, but the key device that has the most linkages to these stations is the floating egg structure on the machine level."

"So it 'does' the energy transfer, whatever it is." He leaned back in his seat and the gimbals rearranged to support his shifting weight. "If this was planetary infrastructure, I'd say this place is designed to tap geothermal energy in the asthenosphere and transfer it to the surface. But it's not. It's reacting to the Effect, and the Effect translates matter to energy."

"But we don't know where that energy goes," Helena said beside him.

"Huh," Markusz said, then focused on Eleven again. "Sorry, my wife has just reminded me that the energy the Effect produces seems to disappear. Apart from the Teel-Attar radiation, we don't know where it goes."

"And Garia is at the anisotropic centre of every Effect we've observed," Helena said.

He looked at her and felt pieces fitting together in his head.

"And again," he said almost apologetically to Eleven, "she reminds me that Garia is at the focal point of every Effect we've ever tracked."

"She's quite brilliant, your wife," Eleven said.

Markusz wondered if she was just humouring him. But she looked pleasantly free from judgemental thoughts in true Haibeu fashion.

"She is," he said. "Although she'd say I'm quite brilliant because she's simply a helpful figment of my imagination. But I don't feel like she is."

"You were obviously deeply connected when you were both alive," Eleven said. "That energy doesn't just disappear – like the Effect energy. There's a connection that persists."

"I don't believe in life after death," Markusz said.

"Nor do I, in the conventional sense. But there's a deeper truth beneath the reality we experience. I've seen enough to know that much. We may not understand it. But accepting it, I think, is healthier than rejecting what doesn't fit our 'rational' world view. And if we are lucky and remain open, we may be rewarded with an answer."

"She's nice, if a little loopy," Helena said.

But Markusz found comfort in Eleven's words. Though he would never admit it.

He took a breath and mentally shook himself. "So, purely theorising here, but a lot of this ship is given over to energy transfer.

It's located in the dead centre of the Effect. When the Effect devours space, it reacts."

"And that's putting it mildly," Helena said.

"Or specifically the machinery linked to the 'energy transfer' stations react. Is the missing energy channelled somehow to Garia and then transferred somewhere by this ship? And if that's the case, is the ship causing the Effect or simply utilising it? Diverting the energy from wherever it's meant to go to somewhere else?"

"Whew," said Helena. "Big theory. Lots of holes."

"It fits the observations as far as they go," Eleven said.

"But we still don't really understand the Effect," Markusz continued. "We understand some of the impacts it produces, which helped in creating the annulus, but we haven't been able to crack the underlying cause. Without that, there's no way to prove this or any other theory."

"Except things have changed," Eleven said. "The mathematics of the annulus was altered by Teel and that brought it into a closer relationship with the Effect. They're in lockstep now: annulus and Effect. So the mathematics of the Effect could at least be partially intuited as the mirror of the annulus mathematics."

Markusz didn't remember standing, let alone rounding the table to grab Asymptote Eleven by the shoulders and lift her to her feet. His mind was too busy spinning off into infinities.

"That's very simple. And very brilliant," he said.

Eleven smiled. "And I think I may be able to open the alien databases if I could contact the other Haibeu," she said.

"I won't tell Firmin if you don't," he said, returning her smile. Then he sat again and turned his mind to Effect mathematics.

31

Sylfe had returned to her apartment after the meeting and tried and failed to sleep. She kept seeing Teel's murder over and over. Hearing Leeuwin's faint objection, as powerless as her own against the schemes of Ernes Fontaneau. They were all but trapped and the exits were closing. Soon they'd be at the mercy of a madman. And much sooner perhaps, she'd be dead.

That was another reason she couldn't sleep. She knew from her scopes that Tane hadn't yet reported the protection she'd afforded Markusz Zielinski. But as soon as he did, Fontaneau would likely sign her death warrant.

She imagined her mother saying *that's the spirit*, and felt a smile tug at the corner of her mouth. Matri Adele Cachand was an extraordinary woman and she hadn't raised slouches. Sylfe wasn't going to give in to despair. If worse came to worst, Roche would carry on without her and help Markusz save everyone left alive. Assuming he could. And if Fontaneau did move against her, he'd discover she had teeth.

A scope pulled at her awareness and her heart suddenly beat hard in her chest. Her link to Fontaneau's rooms was active and as the augment window opened, she saw Tane enter.

Then she blinked and looked again. The room had been a standard bureau, albeit gaudily decorated to the point of nausea. But now ... it was a throne room. Fontaneau sat opposite the entrance on a heavily padded and gilt chair, his feet resting on a brocaded foot pillow. The "throne" stood on a raised platform, three steps up from floor level. Rich drapes hung above and behind it, suspended from a circular abomination of gilded metal and stylised ostrich feathers, and on either side stood two thin gilt columns supporting a capital F surrounded by a laurel wreath on which perched a stylised eagle. In short, Fontaneau had gone "full monarch", at least in his own mind.

Tane slowly and deliberately unholstered his pistol, then drew his curved khukuri – which always struck Sylfe as a particularly vicious-looking blade – and lay both on a small table just inside the doorway. He then stepped forward, head bowed, and kneeled on the bottom step before Fontaneau's throne. Fontaneau stood, extending one hand, which Tane took and pressed to his forehead. Tane, still kneeling, shuffled back off the step and sat back on his haunches on the floor, finally looking at Fontaneau who had resumed his seat.

Good gods, Sylfe thought. It had been obvious for a long time that Fontaneau wanted ultimately to rule, but she didn't think he'd take it this far. These were deep dynastic forms from early Paradisan history she was witnessing.

Although, as with most things Fontaneau did, there was reason behind it. Centuries ago the Paradisan Families had exercised a kind of ultimate power, which had become ameliorated over the generations by reintegration with the rest of humanity in the form of M-Worlds. But if M-Worlds was gone, why not reintroduce that power dynamic, particularly if it reinforced one's position in uncertain times. It was also something that the Opitauans, and perhaps Tane in particular, understood very well.

The necessary formalities observed, Fontaneau finally spoke. "I thank you for your action at the council meeting, ridding me of that annoyance."

Tane bowed again. "It was my honour to serve, Patri."

Fontaneau nodded once, gravely. "Has order once again been restored across my provinces?"

Provinces! Sylfe thought. Oh, he was loving this.

"What unrest there was has been swiftly dealt with, Patri."

"And what of the mathematician, Zielinski?"

"The search continues, Patri. To find one among so many is a difficult task. The Fordana have been unable to help."

Sylfe let out a breath she didn't realise she'd been holding. Well, well, well.

Watching closely, she saw colour flush Fontaneau's cheeks. But to unleash such anger would be unseemly. A king knew his rule would prevail no matter what temporary obstacles may stand in their way. Or such was the fable of power the Paradisan Families had woven into the fabric of their society back in the day.

Instead Fontaneau said, "This situation will be corrected."

"It shall," Tane agreed.

Sylfe sat back. What had just happened?

Traditionally, Opitauan warriors acted in accordance with a simple code with three principles – duty, honour, service – and a single rule: that an Opitauan would never act directly or indirectly against a Family head. That was necessary to ensure Families could trust their Opitauan guards. But beyond that, things got a little murky. Opitauan cadres – and even individual Opitauans – were free to interpret the spirit of the code as they saw fit, depending on the specifics of a situation and what action they believed would be the "moral" choice.

The destruction of Paradis meant Sylfe was now head of the Cachand Family and equal in stature to Fontaneau as far as the code went. Fontaneau, deeper than Sylfe had imagined in his fantasy of sovereignty, believed that what was good for him was good for everyone. He'd lost sight of the fact there could be genuine alternatives. Yet, Tane had witnessed Sylfe and Fontaneau clash a number of times about how to use the annulus and, by extension, Markusz. And Sylfe had doubled down on that mutual antipathy by telling Tane the Families were *en concours*, which meant the two Family heads were now in complete opposition.

Tane was required by the code to keep out of it. He'd agreed with Fontaneau's summation that the "situation would be corrected" but it seemed he personally wasn't going to do anything to assist that either way. It was up to Sylfe and Fontaneau to nut it out. One or the other would prevail, and Tane would then recommence serving whoever was in the ascendant.

This was good, Sylfe thought. It was a chink in Fontaneau's armour. The first she'd been able to find.

But Fontaneau was still talking. "… Leeuwin and have him placed in protective custody and ready to move at a moment's notice. And beef up security around the annulus and double the guard on Rachik. No-one is to access the facility without my express permission."

Tane stood and bowed, then reversed to the doorway, eyes still on the ground – no doubt to ensure Fontaneau's divine gaze didn't smite him, Sylfe thought – pausing only to retrieve his weapons.

For his part, Fontaneau rested an elbow on his throne and cupped his noble chin in his hand, gazing into infinity. No doubt pondering weighty thoughts that only he could possibly understand.

Sylfe cut the feed and pondered her own thoughts. The highliner was docking with the beanstalk and Fontaneau was making sure Leeuwin, the only person who could control the vessel, was exactly where he needed him.

She opened a secure window to Firmin. And was surprised when the mayor accepted her call immediately rather than routing it through some functionary to give the vile Paradisan the runaround.

"What?" Firmin said.

Okay, not exactly smiles and welcomes but it was a start. "I've just been observing Fontaneau."

Firmin stared at her for a few seconds before finally saying, "And?"

"If you have an evacuation plan, you might want to set it in motion. There's a good chance things are going to get worse very quickly."

Firmin glanced down, possibly at something on her mayoral desk, then looked at Sylfe again. "Thank you," she said. "You didn't have to do that."

"No," Sylfe agreed.

"And what are you going to do?"

"I'm going to visit Hugo Denantes to see if he can be any help."

"Well, good luck." The window closed.

Baby steps, Sylfe thought.

The afternoon sun shone brightly, in complete disregard to the billions of Redout inhabitants contemplating their incipient deaths. Nature didn't care about humanity and that was as it should be.

Sylfe left her mover on the council tower's landing apron, entered the building and took a broad circular staircase down to the domicile levels. The M-Def guards at the bottom nodded acknowledgement as she passed them. The one on the left looked like he needed a shave and his uniform was spotted with food stains on the collar. Standards were slipping and she wondered what other details might be escaping their newly minted monarch's attention. Taking control was all very well but it often wasn't as easy as one thought. Or maybe Fontaneau was concentrating on what mattered most and devil take the rest.

As she approached Denantes's door it was opened by a muscular man wearing a pointy-nosed Scaramouche mask and not much else. Sylfe wasn't a prude by any stretch of the imagination but she was annoyed because Denantes was obviously trying to shock her. It was childish. Well, with any luck she'd be able to sour his afternoon for him.

She swept past the man and through the hideously decorated entry hall – red velvet drapes and priapic satyrs pursuing nymphs across trompe l'oeil walls – and walked into the reception room. This at least provided some relief from the libidinous decor of the entry. It was light and classically furnished, with only a modest amount of gilt on the cornices and ceiling roses. The pastoral scenes on the painted wall panels spoke less of the demi-monde and more of an age of innocence.

The juxtaposition was odd, Sylfe thought as she sat on an overstuffed lounge. Perhaps Denantes conducted augment meetings of a more formal nature here. Or perhaps this reflected the real Denantes and what she'd witnessed outside was protective colouring only.

That line of reasoning collapsed when the far wall split along an invisible seam to admit the sole surviving member of the Denantes Family in déshabillé. His face was flushed, his hair – what there was of it – in disarray and sweat beaded his brow. He pulled at the front of his brocaded dressing gown and Sylfe caught an unwelcome flash of hairy, sweat-slicked belly. Beyond she saw a luridly lit room festooned with ropes and pulleys, with two naked women suspended upside down above a water-filled glass tank. An octopus clung to the tank wall, its tentacles reaching up to entwine them.

Her view was thankfully cut off as the wall resealed.

Denantes towelled at his brow, then threw the flannel to the ground. He arranged himself on the lounge opposite Sylfe, propelling a waft of sweat her way. She tried hard not to wrinkle her nose.

"This is a delightful surprise," he said. "If I'd known you were coming I would have made ready."

Sylfe was glad he hadn't. She had no desire to be offered the opportunity to wrestle octopi.

"I'm sorry to interrupt your … downtime," she began.

He raised a hand and graced her with a toothy grin. "Please. You never need to apologise for gracing me with your lovely presence."

She didn't have time for this. "Let's cut the shit, Hugo. I'm here about Fontaneau."

"Ah!" Denantes let his hand drop to his lap and assembled his face into a more serious expression. "By all means, Sylfe. Let us talk plainly if that is your wont."

Sylfe knew she had to step carefully. Denantes was a loose cannon, more prone to indulging his vagaries than erring towards rationality if he had a choice. She had to push him but not too far.

"You said some time ago you would be willing to back me against Fontaneau. I've gathered some allies and we have an opportunity now to move against him. Before it is too late for all of us."

Denantes regarded her for a moment, then his whole body shook with a single grunt that turned into a chuckle. "Oh my dear Sylfe, I like your spirit. But time moves on and after Ernes's … shall we say decisive action against Teel, I feel the pendulum has rather swung back in his direction. I think I'd need a little more convincing."

"So you can betray my compatriots to Fontaneau?"

"Nothing so gauche. But perhaps I can offer *you* my protection against him. You could stay with me. I'm sure we could find many … diversions together." His flaccid lips twisted into a smile.

If Sylfe had a weapon handy, she would have burned him to the ground right then and there and to hell with the consequences. His "offer" was disgusting, boringly predictable and enraging all at the same time.

But she buried her rage before he could read it on her face. "Then you know what Fontaneau has planned?"

Denantes's smile grew wider. "Of course."

"And you have a berth on the highliner?"

The smile faltered. "Highliner?"

"Ah. Perhaps the pendulum has swung further than you realise, Hugo. Fontaneau sequestered the last highliner for his own purposes out in deep orbit and it's now taking on supplies at the beanstalk. He also has Leeuwin under house arrest because, as GH governor-general for the sector, he's the only one with the genetic authorities to command the ship. The annulus is under heavy guard and I think very soon Fontaneau, Leeuwin, the annulus and the highliner will be departing Redout for good. Without you it seems. I take it there's nothing on the highliner you can backdoor?"

Denantes's carefully constructed artifice dissolved into something much more feral. He glared at her. "GH have always been very careful about their ships. So, no. That motherless bastard! I'll bring the fucking sky down on him."

"*We* will bring the sky down on him, Hugo. We need a plan if we are to out-scheme Fontaneau. My group has one, and we're almost ready to put it into action." Which wasn't true, but she was sure they'd think of something. "You can play a vital part in that. But you must wait for my signal."

Hugo's eyes had gone glassy and distant. No doubt he was spinning what uniquely horrendous revenge fantasies he would visit on Fontaneau given half a chance.

"Hugo!" she said sharply and he focused on her again. "You wait for my signal."

He nodded, then reached fumblingly to an onyx box on a side table and grabbed an ampoule of something which he pressed to his neck. There was a hiss and his whole body shuddered. He slumped back on the lounge, fingers loosening so the empty drug tube fell to the floor.

"Good," Sylfe said rising.

And when we're done with Fontaneau, she thought, I'll personally finish you.

32

Markusz worked in a frenzy. Pushing, always pushing. Helena beside him, never leaving. Talking to him in his dreams when he finally grabbed a few minutes' rest. Then into it again. Calculations, leading to more calculations. Checked and rechecked and on to the next. Eleven helped too. Her insights were useful. As useful as Helena's, and he felt – even as the universe contracted around him – his own internal world expanding in ways he'd never thought possible.

There was so much that was new. Rooms beyond those he'd ventured into following Teel's and Rachik's stumbling steps. More and then more, going beyond what those two idiots had wrought, and finding arcades, galleries, vast promenades of calculation. He tracked the changes to the annulus through these spaces, seeing its ghostly dance with the Effect, step for counter-step, understanding more of the underlying equations that drove each of them.

Each time they changed, new ways of thinking were required, new numbers, new operators, whole new branches of maths. He felt the answer proceeding in front of him, just beyond his outstretched grasp. But unlike Eleven, he wasn't at peace with that. He was desperate to know, but there was no simple way to leapfrog beyond his latest piece of understanding because each change made predictive modelling useless.

Eleven was still sure the end point would be perfect. Perfect in what way she couldn't say. Perfect oblivion? Perfect preservation? Whatever happened, Markusz didn't see a way they could survive unless they did *something*. But what?

Keep going was all he could come up with, but then he looked at his current calculation and thought, finally, he saw a kind of sense to it all.

"I think," he said to Helena, "that—"

"Coffee?" Elly stood in the open doorway with a steaming mug on a tray.

There was some sort of hubbub behind her. Markusz could see people passing along the corridor. Lots of people dressed mainly in work clothes.

Elly stepped forward and the door closed.

"What's happening outside?" Markusz asked.

"Things are turning to shit," she said, placing the mug on his workstation. "Firmin's ordered the evacuation. This is the first of them arriving."

"Really?" Markusz wondered what that meant. Would they lock the ship down once everyone was onboard? And what about his work?

"Yes, really. So if you're going to save us you'd better hurry the fuck up."

"Right. Well, I will," he said, taking a sip. "You not having one?"

"Too busy." Her eyes narrowed. "And so are you."

"Absolutely. Talk later." He gulped at his drink and it burned all the way down.

Elly left, and Markusz turned back to Helena. "It's just another deadline, I suppose. It's not like we aren't already on the clock."

"Speaking of. You were about to say something?"

"Well, yes, umm …" He grimaced. "You know how you can say things inside your head and they seem perfectly sensible, but when you say them out loud they sound really insane?"

"Out with it," she said.

"I don't know." Markusz eyed her warily. "You can be really critical at times."

Helena tutted. "Aww, are you feeling a little precious?"

"It's just … I feel I understand, but it all seems …"

"Look, you need a sounding board," Helena said. "The good

thing about talking to me is it's all still happening inside your head. The only judgement you need to fear is your own."

"Okay." He took a deep breath. "So the latest calculations point to a reason for the Effect. And that reason supports the many worlds hypothesis."

"Which states that every time there's a subatomic interaction, the universe splits to enable all the possible outcomes to occur in their own universes," Helena said. "The cat is dead *and* alive. Just in different realities."

"Right. But one of the key criticisms of that theory was, where does all the energy come from to continually create new universes? And it looks like the Effect is the answer. It winds spacetime back and collapses it. We were never able to track what happened after that apart from the minimal amount of energy that bled out as Teel-Attar radiation. But that was before the new maths. The Effect doesn't transfer matter into energy; it combines it into a different kind of … *thing* that can't be detected. I call it a 'Zielinski coherence'."

"Of course you do," Helena said.

"So anyway, this coherence can't exist in-universe. As soon as it's created, it appears at the 'siphon point' for that universe. The anisotropic centre of the Effect occurrences, which in our universe is right here inside Redout. The coherence then leaves our universe through the siphon point and is used to power the creation of new universes."

Helena looked at him for an uncomfortably long moment. Then she said, "Yes, that sounds totally fucking insane. Why is *our* universe experiencing the Effect?"

"Ah. Well, after they're created, certain universes have a lower probability than others. The ones with the lowest probability are candidates for pruning, and they start getting eaten up when the creative pressure for more universes rises to a particular level."

"And you've proved this with the maths?"

"Yes. I'm pretty sure this is what the numbers are telling me. Eleven can check but —"

"You want a sympathetic ear first."

"I want your ear. You always told me when I was going too far, and I've fucked up enough to know you were always right. But if you are just my memory of you, there's a chance I might not be as hard on myself as you would be."

"Oh, I don't know. You can be pretty hard on yourself."

He smiled. "But if there *is* something of the energy we shared that still exists, it would be nice to know what that thought too."

"I can't help you with that, but let's test things. Say the Effect is as you say it is. What is this ship doing here?"

"This is going to sound even more insane. The Effect is a natural mechanism of what I'm calling the 'oververse', the collection of all universes. The ship isn't creating the Effect and it isn't stopping it either. It was built by humanoids like us, but it's way beyond any technology CSTO has. You and I both know that. I think it comes from another universe."

Markusz waited, watching the scenario play out behind Helena's eyes.

"It still could have been built and put here by aliens we don't know about from this universe," she said.

"To what end? It's not stopping the Effect. But it is reacting to it. And the mechanism reacting to it is for 'energy transfer'."

"So you think …"

"It's located at the siphon point to somehow divert the Effect energy for some other purpose."

"We're getting quite 'creative' here," Helena said.

"I know. There are things I'm sure of. The Effect is a natural process supporting universe creation. Redout is at the epicentre of the energy transfer process for our universe. This ship is here. Beyond that I agree it's conjecture, but educated conjecture. It's not beyond the bounds of possibility to imagine another universe like ours that has fallen prey to the Effect. Let's say science has evolved differently there. Maybe they had fewer wars or more wars – whatever was necessary to speed scientific progress beyond our own. They understand what drives the Effect. They can't stop it in their own universe. If they could, there wouldn't be any reason to come here."

"So why do they come here?"

"You really want me to say it out loud?"

"I really do," Helena said. But she didn't look cross. If anything she was encouraging him to take that next step.

"They come here because their universe is doomed. Our universe is doomed too. But with this ship, they can divert the Effect energy drained from our universe and feed it into theirs. It's hard luck for us, but they're saving their universe. I can't think of a loftier goal."

"And what happened to the crew?"

"Maybe they went home. But the existence of exits to the surface says otherwise. Some of those elevators could move a shuttle to ground level. I think it was a one-way trip. They set up the base and then left Garia to blend into our society, live out their lives and die knowing they saved everyone and everything they loved."

"I always loved your romantic side," Helena said.

Markusz smiled. "So, what do you think?"

"I think you should keep most of this stuff to yourself. Share the maths with Eleven for sure. But as for the rest … You still have to work with these people, you know."

Markusz considered. "Okay, maybe I got a little carried away. It's not like I can prove any of the ship stuff. I just like to know why things are."

"I get it. You're a completist."

"I'm not interrupting, am I?" Asymptote Eleven stood in the door. The corridor behind still showed significant traffic. "I thought you should know we finally managed to open the computer databases."

"And?" Markusz asked.

"There are mission log files, but they're all blank."

"But that tells us something," Markusz said, looking at Helena.

"There was a mission."

Helena simply put a finger to her lips.

"And … if we live long enough, we might find out what it was," he finished. "But at least you're into the computer proper."

"Yes," Eleven said. "And I've been able to access the ship's motive controls. The vessel is spaceworthy and capable of flight."

"Nice," Markusz said. "Pity there's nowhere left to go."

33

Sylfe fumed as her mover made best time to the refugee camp and Markusz. She couldn't believe the remains of the human race were at the mercy of Fontaneau and Denantes: two men with huge egos and zero empathy. Or rather she could. Hadn't it always been that way? It was just so disappointing humanity hadn't been able to evolve past it.

Congress President Ferlow would have made a much better fist of things if she'd had the chance. True, she'd rather tarnished her reputation by deciding to abandon the rest of M-Worlds to their fate, but that was one mistake after a faultless record of actually doing good, using the power of the Congress to rein in the more wayward members of M-Worlds and guarantee a baseline of decent living standards for everyone. Besides, Maman had always liked Ferlow and that was a good indicator of character. She'd just been in a shit position at the end.

Warnings blossomed across Sylfe's augments and suddenly the mover descended. Not a power loss; an automated grounding due to an alert. The turbine towers of the atmosphere scrubbers were below her and she glimpsed the rotating tower of the Haibeu Commons as the mover banked quickly, selecting a safe landing site close to the edge of the mesa.

As soon as the mover was at rest Sylfe tried to make sense of the multiple feeds crowding for her attention. Something was happening at the western-hemisphere beanstalk. She selected an aerial view: a drone swooping in with the setting sun behind and the tether in front. Usually there was a slight bowing due to the Coriolis effect of cars moving up and down the space elevator. But this section of tether was drifting too far. And it was rising. Suddenly the end whipped past. Sylfe froze the vision, focusing on the image. Either it had broken – which was unheard of – or it had been cut.

She selected another feed from a few minutes ago. Vision of tether mechanicals – maintenance robots that ran the length of the tether – but they were swarming, concentrating on a single section of the cable, and then it split. Mechanicals fell away, the upper tether whipped out of view, the bottom section fell. The newscaster was trying to work out what had happened. The mechanicals had stopped responding shortly before they swarmed.

Sylfe's mover shook and off in the distance she saw a plume of smoke. It wasn't the cable coming down, she knew that. The tether was immensely strong but also incredibly light. Too light to cause that sort of damage. But the cars … They were falling.

Another shock. Another column of smoke. These cars had been close to the break; others would be falling for quite some time yet. The split had occurred twenty-five thousand kilometres from the surface. The remaining eighty-seven thousand kilometres of the tether was heading up, dragged higher by the counterweight. And the terminus station too. Which meant the orbital rings were in danger.

Sylfe opened another window to look at the twin rings of the orbitals, which were spaced either side of the tether and above the terminus station. The majority of the rings housed solar collectors and wave transmission, but a significant portion was overflow refugee habitats.

Another window opened. The same thing had just happened to the eastern-hemisphere beanstalk. She watched as the western terminus station leaped up towards the twin rings, veering as it tracked along gariostationary orbit, and – miraculously – passed right between them.

Her relief was short-lived. The eastern terminus wasn't so nimble. It impacted one of the rings, which immediately crumpled, the circumference bending as it spun. It clipped its sister ring and both structures disintegrated, whirling wildly, destruction rippling round the rim, the mayhem punctuated by exploding clouds of vented atmosphere carrying debris and bodies.

Sylfe cut the feed, unable to watch. Then opened a window again, scanning the debris for the highliner. It was there, below where the rings had been. Presumably it had been docked to the terminus station when the tether broke. But it was a big ship and it looked like it had survived intact.

Had the highliner been the target? She checked the specifications of the tether mechanicals. Manufactured and serviced by Fabrika SA. Denantes had decided not to wait for Sylfe after all and was doing whatever he could to stop Fontaneau leaving on his ship. And she doubted Denantes would leave it at that.

She heard and then saw a large transport heading directly for the mesa. It had a fluidly organic design and looked spaceworthy. The ship manoeuvred quickly through the atmosphere stacks and landed beside the Haibeu Commons. Between the stack bases she saw people – Haibeu – streaming out of their building and moving in orderly lines towards the vehicle.

She opened a window to Markusz.

"You're safe," he said. "Good."

"I was coming to see you, but it's too late now. Denantes has backdoored everything built by Fabrika SA. He's out to stop Fontaneau, and we're likely to be the unfortunate casualties of their little war if we don't do something."

"Denantes broke the tethers?" Markusz said, eyebrows rising.

"He did. And it looks like the Haibeu are on the move."

Another window opened. Eleven. "They're evacuating to Redout orbit," she said. "It seemed prudent."

"I don't blame them," Sylfe said.

"We're tracking multiple infrastructure system failures," Eleven said. "A lot of M-Def seem to be locked in barracks. Doors aren't working. Others are being attacked by augment-locked refugees. Power relays are melting down. Structural fires are out of control.

Emergency services are already overwhelmed."

"Denantes is acting out," Sylfe said. "I thought I could control him. Fontaneau won't be hanging around for long. I'm going to try to stop him, but I'll need some help."

"I know just who to ask," Markusz said and the windows closed.

To Sylfe's left, the Haibeu transport took off. She wished them bon voyage.

Satisfied it was safe to fly again, her mover lifted and the city spread out before her. The fires Eleven had mentioned were obvious now. A patchwork of destruction. Everything they'd built to keep humanity alive and Denantes was willing to burn it all down in a fit of pique.

As she climbed higher, more explosions bloomed. A building – her augment tagged it as a fission relay – erupted in flames, pieces of wreckage flung wide in fiery arcs, gouts of black smoke spreading over the surrounding buildings. Above her, a debris storm was ramping up, chunks of the orbitals painting the sky with flaming fingers. This was what Armageddon looked like.

She had to get to the annulus. The sooner she could stop this madness, the sooner they could start saving people again. That was what they were meant to be doing here after all. But the longer this went on and the more infrastructure got damaged, the worse things would get. That tipping point Fontaneau had been so worried about would be something looked back on fondly as a marker of quieter and more hopeful times.

Her scopes enhanced her view as she came into line of sight of the control centre where the annulus rested.

The building, looked unscathed, thank Christ. The tower tapered elegantly to a split point with a flat landing pad between the tips for movers and smallish craft, and a platform suspended off one side of the left spire for larger craft. The immediate airspace around it was crowded with M-Def Spitters – small offensive fighters. It was possible they'd warn her off or even just shoot her down. But turning back now wasn't an option.

It seemed her bona fides with Fontaneau were still good, because the Spitters closest to her approach turned to track her, but that was all, and then she was down on the pad. Still, she couldn't expect a warm reception inside.

As she stepped out of her mover, four anti-personnel wasps hatched from the hull and buzzed to follow her, one of them venturing towards another mover as it landed.

Evan Beltran stepped out, looking glummer than ever.

"Ind Beltran," Sylfe called, waving the wasp back. "I assume like me you're here to find out what the fuck is going on."

Beltran's lips pursed, no doubt shocked by her "unseemly" language. But if you couldn't swear at a time like this, when could you swear, Sylfe thought.

Beltran recovered enough to say, "Indeed. I'm at something of a loss to explain it. Systems are down, controls are locked out. I'd say we were under attack if there was such a thing as an enemy here."

"Oh, but there is," Sylfe said. "Shall we go and see if he's up for a chat?"

She swept on towards the heavily guarded entry, with Beltran running to catch up. Again, her luck held. The M-Def and Opitauan guards waved her through. She was a council member after all. They didn't even question her about her wasps. Maybe they thought she was being prudent under the circumstances. Or maybe Fontaneau was that sure of himself.

The doors parted and Sylfe entered the control centre proper, which was a scene of quiet industry. Technicians trotted about, crating and stacking instruments. She saw Rachik on the raised central platform, lit by the annulus as he manoeuvred a housing around it. And on the far side, framed by the exit to the extended landing platform for larger vessels, was Ernes Fontaneau.

He raised an arm in greeting and shouted across the space. "Ah, my fellow council members. So good of you to come see me off."

Sylfe's wasps alerted her to something she'd missed. Dotted around the room were several armed Opitauans; and as she passed the platform where the annulus was being crated up, she saw Tane next to the exit, holding Leeuwin by the arm. Poor Jan Pieter looked halfway between bereft and petrified. She couldn't really blame him. He was Fontaneau's puppet now. Just as they all were in one way or another.

Fontaneau flourished a pocket kerchief and a flight of his own wasps appeared around him as if he were a stage conjuror.

"What are you doing, Ernes?" Beltran asked, sounding bewildered.

Sylfe thought it rather obvious, but Beltran was into more straightforward equations: *if A then B.* Perhaps the mathematics of betrayal were beyond him.

"Simply being prudent, old friend."

Old friend? Fontaneau was positively ebullient with good humour. Perhaps because he was enjoying the last laugh on all of them.

"You may have noticed, the planet is no longer safe," he continued. "We must protect the annulus above everything else. And if we are unable to stall the shrinkages, the sun will eventually fall victim to the Effect. That won't be a good time to be on a planet's surface. I have faith it won't come to that." Here his gaze fell on Rachik, who, Sylfe noticed, visibly blanched. "But it's not something we can take risks with."

"But ... but ... we can't *all* leave the planet," Beltran said. He was really struggling with reality today it seemed.

Fontaneau thrust his lips out and nodded sadly. "Very true. I'd like you to know I appreciate the service you've given me and the project, Evan. Onboard ship we have no need for a Fordana systems administrator, of course."

Fontaneau's eyes moved to Sylfe. His smile returned as he took in her wasps. Perhaps he recognised a fellow predator when he saw one. "And if the sun does disappear, sadly we have no further need of SolEng, my dear Sylfe. But it has been a genuine pleasure to work alongside you."

For once, Sylfe was at a loss for words. She could protest that he couldn't leave everyone else to die, but clearly he could. Or that he wouldn't get away with it, because he was.

"Despite the ungrateful Denantes's efforts," Fontaneau continued, his expression souring, "my highliner is now fully stocked with supplies, retaskers and personnel. It's smaller than a planet, I admit, but it will be quite comfortable enough. We'll be back if the situation improves, but if not …" He shrugged. "Rest assured, those of us who survive onboard will remember your valuable contributions to humanity."

A gust of wind ruffled his hair as a large cargo transport settled on the landing apron behind him. He smiled. "That's our ride to the highliner. I hate long goodbyes, so … adieu."

The door burst open behind Sylfe. She turned to see M-Def and Opitauan guards firing back into the entrance hall at an oncoming horde – that was the word that came to mind. A wild, frenzied, screaming mob, eyes rolled back in their sockets, clawing stiff-fingered at the guards even as they fell under concentrated blaster fire. Most of the screaming was incoherent. Animalistic.

Eleven had mentioned augment-locked rioting, but this was something else. None of those running to their death seemed at all worried by the prospect.

Tane and the other Opitauans in the room moved to support their comrades.

Sylfe grabbed Beltran and dragged him to cover. She'd just ducked behind the platform holding the annulus when the room lit up with sharp explosions, followed by screams of pain and more screams from the attackers. The guards were on the ground, bloodied and writhing, limbs blown apart – and fighting for survival as the augment-locked fell on them, biting and gouging like wild animals.

Sylfe saw twisted and blackened weapons lying among the bodies, and remembered Denantes's words: *Our weapons division has been a major supplier to both M-Def and the Opitauans for years now.*

Beside her, Beltran whimpered and skittered away from the

fighting on hands and knees, making for Fontaneau.

The remaining guards were overwhelmed. Only Tane rose above the melee. His right hand was gone; his wrist a bloodied, ragged stump. He held his khukuri in his good hand and hacked at the horde that was grabbing to pull him down. He dodged back and put some space between him and them.

Sylfe stood, ready to fight her way out. Her wasps pulled close, their buzz rising in warning.

Behind her, Rachik had wheeled the crated annulus as far as the exit. Tane had reached Fontaneau, and Beltran was cowering at his feet. They were about to make their escape.

Sylfe realised the mob had fallen silent. She looked to the doorway and saw Hugo Denantes standing there, flanked by armed guards and holding a weapon that was definitely compensating for something. He was stripped to the waist, his eyes ludicrously wide, pupils massively dilated. Sylfe thought he looked completely drug-fucked. Either that or high on the chaos he'd longed to visit on everyone he'd despised for so long.

As he entered, those of the augment-locked that could, stood and moved aside for him. Clearly Denantes had complete control of their augments. He could make them see whatever he wanted them to see. Feel whatever he wanted them to feel. Knowing him as she did, Sylfe thought this must be his very own wet dream.

"You shouldn't have tried to fuck me over, Ernes," he said, red-faced and sweating.

"I did exactly what you would do in my situation," Fontaneau said. "Except for the fact you didn't have the wits to see this coming. Your father had it right: you were never a credible heir. Your peccadilloes distract you from seeing the obvious. It was always going to end this way."

Sylfe saw the words land exactly as they were intended. Denantes's lips curled in rage and he levelled his weapon at Fontaneau.

Then the wall behind him disintegrated.

Just before Sylfe dropped behind the platform again, she saw Denantes and his henchmen blasted apart in the first volley. Then the smoke rolled over her and she was blinded for an instant.

Her wasps buzzed louder, switching to livefire mode, but she stilled them as she recognised a silhouette through the haze. Markusz. And he wasn't alone.

34

As the smoke cleared, Sylfe saw Elly step forward and level her rifle at Fontaneau and his small group, now frozen in tableau: Tane, eyes narrowed and blade held high, ready to take no prisoners; Leeuwin, eyes wide and clearly petrified, leaning as far away from the presumed centre of fire as he possibly could without moving his feet; Beltran, eyes closed in terror, a crumpled mass on the floor; and Rachik, who had prised open the annulus housing and was fiddling about inside.

"Don't move or you're all as dead as this shit," Elly snarled, kicking the steaming pile of meat that used to be Denantes. Sylfe would have liked to deliver that coup de grâce herself, but on the whole she couldn't complain about the result.

More of the Garian freedom fighters fanned out to either side of Elly, weapons ready.

As for the augment-locked, those that weren't actively bleeding out sat on the floor looking completely bewildered.

"And stop fucking about with the annulus, Rachik," Markusz snapped.

As he spoke, a bluish-coloured barrier bisected the room. Elly and her group opened fire, but it was useless. All that happened was the barrier sparked wherever it was hit.

Fontaneau turned to Rachik. "Quick thinking, my boy. Very well done indeed."

"Don't do this, Rachik," Markusz said. "You don't understand the forces you're playing with."

"Oh, fuck off, Markusz. Whatever happens I'll at least have

the pleasure of watching you blink into nothingness. Enjoy what's left of your shitty life." Rachik closed the housing and trundled the annulus towards the waiting transport.

Fontaneau smiled again at Sylfe. "I've already said my goodbyes." Then he looked towards Markusz. "You are a difficult man to pin down, Ind Zielinski." He bowed deeply and swept along the platform to the waiting ship.

"Tane!" Sylfe said as the Opitauan made to follow. He hesitated and she scoured her brain to think of something that would resonate with him. "Look at where he's led you. There's no honour in this."

Tane's face may as well have been carved in granite for all the effect her words had.

Then she said, "I'm not done yet," and the corner of his mouth ticked upward in a half-smile. He saluted her with his blade, and then he and Leeuwin were gone.

Beltran was still cowering on the floor by the exit. He opened his eyes, realised he was still alive and picked himself up to follow the others to the ship, safe it seemed by dint of being on the right side of the force barrier. Unless they threw him out an airlock on the way up, Sylfe thought.

"That could have gone better," Elly said, her rifle slung over one shoulder.

Sylfe looked at the young woman. She didn't seem at all fazed by what she'd done to Denantes, his henchmen and any augment-locked unlucky enough to get in the way. Sylfe remembered the holo-statues in Firmin's office. The times made the person, she supposed.

"Yes, it could," Markusz said. "But I prefer to look on the bright side."

Sylfe struggled to find one. They'd lost the annulus, and a lot of people were dead or dying. The control centre resembled a bombed-out bunker with bodies and parts of bodies lying among upturned crates and broken instruments left behind in the rush.

She heard the engines of the transport roar to life, ready to take Fontaneau to his new kingdom on the highliner where he truly would be lord of all he surveyed. The blue force barrier dissipated as the ship rose out of sight.

"What was all that about with the Opitauan?" Markusz asked.

Sylfe sniffed. "The battle between the Great Families of Fontaneau and Cachand. I put Tane on notice that it's not over yet."

"Which means?"

"I may still count on his help if I can deal an irreversible blow to Fontaneau's plans. But right now I have no idea what that could be. He'll be on his highliner soon and heading into what's left of open space."

Markusz squatted beside a large instrument case marked with the CSTO emblem and a row of numbers and letters.

"Intact, I think," he said. "Elly, can you have some of the lads take this to the ship?"

"Sure," Elly said. "Brak. Guys."

Four muscular Garians wrestled the case out of the surrounding debris and hauled it from the room.

"Come on," Markusz said to Sylfe. "We've still got a couple of problems to solve."

She barked a laugh. "Just a couple?"

He smiled. "Well, maybe more than that, but there's no point worrying about what we haven't done."

She walked with him out onto the now very crowded landing apron and followed the Garians to a medium-sized mover parked between her own and Beltran's.

"What happened to the M-Def vessels protecting the pad?" she asked.

"Weird thing. They all fell out of the sky when we were still on approach, and then these Fabrika SA transports flew in and dropped a heap of people. It was all quite convenient really."

"Denantes must have disabled them," Sylfe said. "The poor pilots."

Inside the mover, they found a spot between the cargo and Elly and the other armoured Garians where they could cling onto the webbing as the ship took off.

"So what now?" Sylfe asked.

Markusz grimaced. "Well, I do have a Plan B. Or F or G by this stage. And it involves getting back to the alien ship."

"Oh?" Sylfe said.

"Yes, we've found out quite a bit more with Eleven's hel– Oh, shit."

Markusz was staring off into the middle distance. Sylfe strained to see what he saw. Below them the city was burning. The scarlet sky was still aflame with debris. The sun was getting low.

He shared an augment window with her. "We've had another shrinkage. It looks like we're being punished for holding it back for so long. Or maybe Rachik is making good on his threat."

Sylfe took the window and expanded the view, adding in realtime data from her own satellite network in solar orbit. Or what was left of it. The curve of the sun was somewhat flattened against the larger curve of the Effect wall. It didn't look bad. The solar prominences were always energetic. HD68745 burned hot and hard. But …

"Everyone on this planet is fucked," she said.

"What do you mean?" Elly said.

"The last shrinkage shaved off part of the sun. Not a huge amount, but the electromagnetic field's showing a pronounced twisting where it interacts with the Effect. X-ray emissions are rising."

"And that means?" Elly prompted.

"It's down to saving what we can. For as long as we can," Markusz said.

Sylfe appreciated his ability to maintain focus regardless of what the universe threw at them. Under the circumstances, she could do no less.

Elly hadn't been sure what to expect when they got back to the refugee camp. But on the way they'd seen masses of people crossing the barren plain heading for the sprawling city. The augment-locked had woken up, realised they were living in a shithole and gotten the fuck out in double-quick time.

As soon as they landed, Brak and the others hustled Markusz's CSTO crate and other supplies down the ramp, heading for the larger "goods" elevator sequestered in a nearby tent. She, Markusz and Cachand followed. The car was waiting for them, but it was a little cramped with all the gear.

As soon as the doors closed and they were underway, Cachand asked Markusz, "Do you still have augment access? Mine's blocked."

Markusz at least had the sense to look a little guilty. "Elly, could you, uh … you know," he said.

"This is getting to be a habit," Elly said, but she linked her access to Cachand's augments.

After a moment, Cachand opened a shared window. They were looking at the sun, but with a false colour overlay of different zones twisting around each other. Elly didn't know if this was normal, good or bad.

Cachand flicked through different views. "It's definitely more unstable," she said.

"Which means Fontaneau will want to do something about it," Markusz said. "A nova going off now will scour every single scrap of matter in what's left of space. They'll have to do a 'controlled' shrinkage to get rid of the sun."

"Then what?" Elly asked.

"We'll be stuck in a starless void lit solely by Teel-Attar radiation," Markusz said. "Light from a dead universe named after two dead scientists. How apt."

"And everyone on the planet will quickly freeze to death," Cachand added. "So I doubt they'll care much what colour the sky is."

A bleak mood seemed to grab hold of everyone in the car.

Finally they made it to the lift lobby. While most of her crew went to find their families, Brak stayed to help Elly manoeuvre Markusz's crate into the control hub elevator. They left Markusz and Cachand to wait for the elevator's return.

Brak looked at Elly as soon as the doors closed. "What do you think?"

"I think he might still come through for us."

"The incomer?" Brak said and spat.

"They're not *all* useless."

Brak grunted.

The elevator doors opened, and they pushed and pulled the crate into the empty control hub.

A moment later, Markusz and Cachand arrived.

"Where did you get to?" Markusz said to thin air, then a moment later, "Not this again, please."

Brak caught Elly's eye and tapped at his head. "We're all fucked," he said and left.

Elly was forced to admit things didn't look good.

"Where's Eleven?" Markusz said, turning to Elly. "We need her to get the engines up and running."

"What do you mean 'engines'?"

Elly turned to see Mamie standing in the open doorway.

"What do you think you're doing, Zielinski?" Elly's grandmother said. She was clearly pissed off.

Markusz didn't seem too far behind. "I'm trying to *save* us all. I thought that would be obvious by now," he said. "Look, we don't have time for this. The sun's about to explode or disappear."

"If it explodes, we're dead anyway," her grandmother said in a tone that brooked no argument. "If it disappears, it won't make much difference to us. So again, why do you need engines?"

Markusz looked to one side where Elly suspected Helena was standing. "Alright, alright." He raised his hands, palms out, then turned back to her grandmother and sighed. "I'm sorry. I got a little carried away. Fontaneau's on a highliner with the annulus, and whether by design or just bad luck the latest shrinkage has destabilised the sun. It's either going to go nova" – he looked to Cachand, who nodded agreement – "or Fontaneau will shrink the annulus barrier to disappear the sun, meaning everyone on the planet will die."

"But not down here," Mamie said. "We'll be safe in the asthenosphere."

"Well, yes ..." Markusz said.

Elly thought he looked puzzled, but this was what her grandmother had been planning for, just not in these exact circumstances. At some point she was going to cut the base off from the outside world. Whether the outside world was liveable or not was a side issue. For her anyway, if not for Elly. But if Elly was going to accept a life here with no possibility of venturing outside ever again, she wanted to be sure they'd exhausted every other chance for something better first.

"I take it this base doesn't have environments suits?" Markusz asked.

"None that we've found," Elly said.

"So we'll be trapped here. Forever," Markusz said, echoing Elly's thoughts. "Fontaneau will be in his ship. He'll be able to send scouts down to the surface to gather whatever remaining resources might be useful."

"I don't care about Fontaneau," her grandmother said.

Elly knew all Mamie cared about was the safety of her people. Even if they were imprisoned here, they were still alive.

"He probably won't find you," Markusz continued. "But he'll still control the annulus. He can blink this planet out of existence whenever he wants to. When it's no more use to him, or just on a whim."

"You said there was still something you could try," Elly cut in.

"Yes." Markusz crossed to the CSTO crate. He cantilevered the lid open and started taking out components and placing them on the control hub's central table. "I'm going to build another annulus."

It was Elly's turn to be confused. "But didn't you say the universe can only hold one annulus at a time?"

"I did."

"So what happens to the other one?"

Markusz smiled but there was little humour in it, Elly thought. "As soon as we create this annulus, the other one will disappear. If we don't do it exactly right, we'll all die, because we won't be able to hold the Effect back. But if we succeed, we'll be able to maintain the current annulus field. There's also a possibility that the annulus we create will be in the original stable form, not the fucked-up product of delinquent tinkering by my ex-boss and his dickhead lackey –"

He paused. Elly had noticed Helena often spoke up when he got overexcited.

"And if it *is* that, we'll have more control," he finished.

"And if it isn't?" Elly asked.

"At least *we'll* be in charge of it. *Not* Fontaneau." He turned to her grandmother. "But if we're going to replace the annulus, we need to be a hell of a lot closer to it than we are now. So you have a choice, Mayor Firmin, between safety, albeit illusory, or –"

"Or hope," Elly said. "It's your decision, Mamie."

Her grandmother looked at her and Elly wondered if perhaps she was also seeing her daughter – Elly's mother, Octavie. She'd always told Elly never to settle for second best. And Elly suspected Mamie had told her daughter the same thing.

"You're sure you can do what you say?" her grandmother asked Markusz.

"I've never been surer of anything in my life."

Her grandmother gave Elly the briefest of nods and she felt her heart swell.

"Brak," her grandmother said into a comm window, "bring the Haibeu here. And spread the word to make everything secure. We'll be on the move soon."

35

As soon as Eleven caught sight of Sylfe she pulled away from the big Garian escorting her and covered the short distance between them. "You're safe!" she cried, throwing her arms around Sylfe.

More than a little disarmed by the warmth of Eleven's greeting, Sylfe hugged the woman back, feeling her eyes prick with incipient tears. But when she drew back, Eleven's smile warmed her again.

"Come on," she said, placing an arm around Eleven's shoulders. "We've got work to do."

She sat beside Eleven on the strange but comfortable chairs and watched as the woman's fingers played across the alien control station.

"It seems you've made quite a bit of progress in understanding things," Sylfe said.

"A solid translation helps. The controls themselves are fairly intuitive once you know what they are."

She shared a window with Sylfe, who integrated it into her augments and the alien characters suddenly made sense. These were standard ship navigation and propulsion controls. Whoever made this ship was highly advanced in some respects but not completely beyond Sylfe's frame of reference.

"Yes, I see," she said. "But we need to find an exit. Roche?"

A comm window opened and Roche was there. "I've lost location for you, Ind," he said.

"We're underground but shielded. I need you to send imaging for the asthenosphere directly underneath Refugee Holding Facility RMHL12-9G. We have to plot a way out."

It was a testament to Roche's experience and long service with the Cachand Family that he simply did what he was told, and after a moment Sylfe and Eleven were looking at the magma chamber where the ship was located alongside a window Eleven had shared showing the immediate externals around the ship.

A simple visible spectrum image would have been useless. It was pitch black outside. Instead the image used false colour to indicate temperature differences between the magma and the more solid surrounding rock and plot flow patterns. Garia was a big planet, massing 3.85 times bigger than ancient Earth, but it was also far less dense, a mere 0.66 standards. This accounted for the fact the surface gravity was only a little less than 1.2g. But it also meant the mantle was far less solid. The image from Roche showed a network of magma chambers and channels modelled in 3D extending out around them.

"We need to find an ocean floor ridge with volcanic activity," Sylfe said. "The asthenosphere is much closer to the oceanic crust than under a continental plate."

She reached into the window and turned the model this way and that, looking for a way that was wide enough for their ship and headed in the right direction. A couple of promising pathways petered out.

Firmin came to stand behind them and Sylfe felt the pressure of her disapproval. Still, she was at least onside with Markusz's plan now – thanks in no small part to Elly, who Sylfe surmised from her use of the term "Mamie", was Firmin's granddaughter. Nice to know the mayor had a human side.

"How about this?" Firmin said, reaching into the window and pointing to a channel that extended downwards before angling up again.

Sylfe looked. Turned the model. Looked again. "Yes," she said.

"I suggest everybody that can, straps in," Eleven said. She merged the forward view of the ship with Roche's scan. "All elevators are now locked and disengaged."

Firmin activated the comms unit at the board near the entrance. "Attention. Attention," she said. "We're about to move."

The floor started to vibrate accompanied by a growling reverberation from above. Markusz checked his feeds but it wasn't the Effect or the annulus. It was just the engines.

"Are we going to make it?" Helena asked.

Markusz regarded her. She looked worried. Which meant he was worried. "I really don't know," he said.

The CSTO crate they'd stolen was completely empty now and everything Markusz needed was laid out in order. The floor lurched and he grabbed onto the edge of the table, then pulled himself onto one of the gimballed chairs and strapped in.

"Sorry," Eleven said. "But we're getting somewhere."

"Somewhere is good," Markusz said.

"You know the odds of succeeding in what you're planning?" Helena said.

"I haven't calculated them."

"Well, that's not true; you just don't want to acknowledge them."

"Because it's not helping," he said, and Helena frowned and looked away.

Elly sat at the table opposite him. "Do you need a hand?"

He smiled at her. "Actually, yes. We're going to build the annulus generation unit. You take the same components I do and just follow me. We're making two halves then putting them together. Oh, and I'll need a standard power supply when we're done."

"Alright," the girl said, already mirroring his moves.

"Now that *is* helping."

"Fine," Helena said, still not looking at him. "But like you said, there's no do-over here."

He glanced at Firmin, who was intent on Eleven's navigation through the asthenosphere. "The time for second thoughts is long past," he said under his breath.

The feeling of down shifted, and the chairs and the room shifted with it as if the whole control hub was mounted on gyros. Perhaps it was. Markusz concentrated on building the generator and slowly he and Elly cleared the table of parts.

When they were ready, they brought the two halves of the apparatus together to click neatly in place and smiled at each other.

"I'll hook up the power supply," Elly said.

Markusz glanced again at the navigation window between Eleven and Sylfe. Against all the odds they were nearing their destination. Then the engine sound dropped.

"I think we're going to have to use the atomics before we get much closer," Sylfe said.

"Bad news?" Markusz asked.

"Not too bad. The magma channel to the ocean ridge we've identified is blocked ahead. Roche will clear the way with a low-yield atomic. Should do the trick."

"No-one around up there?"

"There's a power harvester making use of the hydrothermal vents, but from the records I have it's completely automated. But even if there was …"

True. Everyone on the surface would be dead soon anyway.

"Ten seconds," Sylfe said.

The feed from Roche showed the warhead leaving his sunbarque and spearing past the orbital debris into atmosphere. Christ knows what Fontaneau would make of it if he was watching.

There was a small chance their ship would be destroyed in the blast. But the news from space was actually worse. As the highliner moved away from Garia, the annulus shield moved with it, which meant more and more of the sun was disappearing, making it more and more unstable. Sylfe didn't really feel like sharing this news because there was nothing they could do about it. If they blew up in Roche's atomics it would all be over very quickly. That may actually be preferable.

Clouds whipped by and she was looking down on the planet. Far off to the east, the city was already deep in night. She could see sporadic fires burning. Big ones. Beyond the terminator lay the coast and the ocean pontoons, though it was hard to pick out where one ended and the other began. But even the pontoon city gave way to plankton farms after a couple of thousand kilometres.

"Two seconds."

The ocean leaped at the missile, and then it was under the waves and the window abruptly closed. The whole ship shook and the room tipped, then righted itself.

Markusz and Elly grabbed the annulus device they were working on and Firmin helped steady it.

The shaking increased and there was a not-too-encouraging creaking noise.

"We're in the channel. And accelerating," Eleven said.

Sylfe watched as the solider walls surrounding their magma flow streaked past. "A little like a cork in a bottle," she said.

"Coming up on the crust," Eleven said.

The noise and vibration ramped up to a previously unimagined level of incipient doom. And then they were through and out.

Another window from Roche and this time Sylfe saw their ship – a bulbous teardrop – boiling out of the water, surrounded by steam. It shot into the air, not even slowing for a quick look around, leaping skyward and leaving the doomed world of Garia/ Redout behind for an equally doomed volume of space that was on the verge of collapsing.

But not yet. Not if they could help it.

The sound of the engines dropped to a dull roar as they reached the upper atmosphere, and the room stopped vibrating so much. She saw Markusz, Elly and Firmin relax their grip on the annulus device.

Eleven's hands played quickly across the control interfaces as she concentrated on flight data from shared augment windows.

"You're good at this," Sylfe said. Eleven really was a bit of a revelation in more ways than one.

She opened another window in front of them and she and Sylfe watched together as the last tinges of atmosphere fell away. Space was a strange and deadly place now. The orbital rings had completely disintegrated. This hemisphere's beanstalk terminus was nowhere to be seen, but the window identified the counterweight far higher up and receding quickly, towing what was left of the tether with it.

The window focused on a magnified view of the highliner, much closer in but moving away. Not too quickly though. Those things weren't built for speed. The torus-shaped traffic control station that had been closer to the counterweight than the orbitals before the beanstalk broke was following it. Presumably they'd surmised correctly that the highliner was a better bet than the planet. But there was another problem as the window highlighted two ships keeping pace either side of Fontaneau's ship.

"Those are M-Def gunboats," Eleven said.

"Just two?" Sylfe asked.

"A lot of their ships were grounded or docked at the station and orbital rings, otherwise I suspect there'd be more."

"I don't see any weapon system controls," Sylfe said, looking at the control surfaces.

"Possibly because there aren't any," Markusz said. "This ship wasn't here to start a fight."

Looking at a tactical view, Sylfe saw Roche's ship moving up to join them, and alongside it the transport with Eleven's fellow Fukei onboard. Further back, approaching Garia orbit from sunward, was the rest of her sunbarque fleet.

"We need to get a lot closer to the highliner," Markusz said. "When I generate a new annulus I don't want the epicentre of the field to shift too much. We can't afford to lose what little of the universe we still have."

"They shouldn't be difficult to catch," Eleven said.

"Go get 'em," Sylfe said and Eleven smiled.

"Roche?" Sylfe asked.

"Still here, Ind. Sensors are reporting what's left of the sun is showing definite signs of distress."

"There's nothing we can do about that now. Follow us. We're chasing down the highliner. And have the other sunbarques vector in for a rendezvous."

"The Haibeu transport will stay alongside," Eleven said.

"They'll be safe with Roche," Sylfe said. She watched as they gained on the highliner. "Where the hell does Fontaneau think he's going?"

"I suspect he planned to get far enough away from Redout so no-one could bother him," Eleven said.

"Live out his life in his own highliner fiefdom," Sylfe said, nodding. "Not sorry to fuck up that particular fantasy."

"The Effect–" Eleven said and stopped.

Sylfe saw it. The sphere of the universe leaped towards them and suddenly the light outside was a lot dimmer and far more red. "Oh, Jesus," she said.

"Well, that's one problem solved," Markusz said. "The sun's gone."

"Everyone on the surface of Garia is going to freeze," Sylfe said.

"If it's any consolation, I don't think the planet or the people will be around long enough for that to happen," Markusz said. "That last controlled shrinkage has really fucked things up."

Sylfe turned as Markusz opened a shared window showing two energy graphs.

"Once we solved the maths for the Effect we were able to plot it against the annulus's energy output," he said. "They've been in complete lockstep. But that last transform is changing the annulus output again."

Sylfe looked at both graphs and how the annulus was trending. "The graphs are starting to overlap," she said.

"I need to do some calculations for the generator. But every time there's a shrinkage I have to start again," Markusz said. "Eleven, can you help?"

"I can fly this thing," Sylfe said to Eleven. "Go do some maths."

Sylfe increased the power output and they leaped towards the highliner. "I'm coming for you, Ernes," she whispered.

Three tiny flashes of light flared at the rear of one of the gunboats and her window refocused. Missiles. Incoming. No time to veer off.

Her window flared with explosions but that was all. No sound. No hull breach or decompression alarms. The missiles had detonated a hundred metres off their bow. Another three inbound did the same. And another.

"This ship has held back the molten heart of Garia for centuries," Firmin said over her shoulder. "A few pissy explosions aren't going to make much of a dent."

Even so, Sylfe thought. "Roche, can you dissuade that gunboat, please?"

Roche's ship fired another of the atomics. The gunboat tried to dodge but the missile was too fast. The explosion was blinding, and the highliner heeled over as the remains of the blast washed over it.

"Let's maybe not shoot explosives too close to the highliner until we have the annulus up and running," Markusz said.

"Point taken," Sylfe said. Still, the other gunboat wasn't firing at them and she had five more sunbarques on the way.

"Fuck!" Markusz shouted in frustration.

The tactical window shuddered, the image blanking and then rebuilding to take account of the new universal topography.

Fontaneau had engineered another shrinkage, possibly to remove the threat of the incoming sunbarques, or maybe he really hated the people on Redout and had decided to do to them what he'd done to the sun. But it hadn't worked.

Instead of a perfectly sphere-shaped universe, or one that was squashing into an ovoid as the highliner moved away from the limit of the annulus shield behind them and the Effect ate the space that was left, things had gone very strange indeed. Ahead of them and above them, the Effect wall curved in a hemisphere as before, but behind them that sphere had deformed to create a lengthening tunnel preserving a planet-wide pathway back to Redout, along which Sylfe's sunbarques were currently travelling.

The highliner had stopped and was turning slowly to face them, its remaining gunboat still at its side. The traffic control station had slowed too and was currently closer to their ship than to the highliner, perhaps wondering which was the better bet for survival.

"Markusz, can you ..." Sylfe wasn't quite sure how to ask what she wanted to ask.

Markusz looked up from the window he was sharing with Eleven.

"Oh, yes. We expected as much. Redout is the siphon point for the Effect energy. It can't be destroyed until there's no universe left to siphon."

"You didn't think to mention that before?" Sylfe said, more than a little annoyed.

"It was only theoretical until a moment ago. And I've had a bit on my mind of late."

"So as long as we stay between Redout and the annulus ...?"

"We should continue to exist," he said.

36

"How does this look to you?" Markusz asked Eleven.

She scanned the rows of equations while the expected energy transformations played out in an adjacent window.

"Yes," she said. "Ready for the next set."

Markusz began inputting another group of derivations. They were getting close. He just had to hope Rachik didn't trigger another shrinkage before they were ready.

"You know," Eleven said, "if you do succeed and the new annulus inherits the current settings, it won't be the end of the world."

"Damn close to it."

"A poor choice of words. And I know you don't share my views, but I believe the mathematical end point will not be null. It can't be."

"Because it doesn't fit your aesthetic?" He bit down on the note of exasperated scorn he couldn't help feeling in the face of Eleven's blind faith.

"Because it doesn't fit the universe's aesthetic."

"Isn't it better to live in hope than in fear?" Helena said.

"Not you too," Markusz said, but he had to admit she was right. He wanted to believe. He just couldn't.

"I sincerely hope you're right, Eleven," he said. Another set of equations displayed. "How does this look?"

"Yes," Eleven said. "Next set."

Elly – freed from generator-building duties – had moved over to the comm station. "We're being hailed," she said. "It's Fontaneau."

Markusz couldn't afford to break concentration. Someone else would have to deal with that madman.

Firmin, still standing behind Sylfe, said, "I have nothing to say to that man."

"I do, if you don't mind," Sylfe said, craning her neck to look up at Firmin.

The mayor nodded and a comm window opened above Sylfe's control station.

It showed Fontaneau, looking ridiculously imperious, with Leeuwin standing at one side, master of his ship in name only, and Tane at Fontaneau's other side, the stump of his ruined arm bandaged and strapped across his chest. Rachik was visible in the background, mothering the annulus.

"It's good to see you, Tane," Sylfe said.

Fontaneau's glower darkened by an order of magnitude. "What do you think you're doing, Sylfe?"

"It's *Matri* Cachand to you," Sylfe said. "And I should think it's obvious what I'm doing – I'm fucking up your little power trip. Your annulus tricks aren't going to help you any more."

The corners of Fontaneau's eyes crinkled and his lips parted in a poor facsimile of good humour. "Well, I certainly must commend your perseverance. This ship of yours was wholly unexpected." His face darkened again. "But the time for games is over. You may have atomics, but you can't exactly fire on us while I have the annulus *and* a ship full of hostages. You are ordered to dock unarmed with the highliner and surrender to Tane or I'll start the executions."

Sylfe laughed. "Is that the best you've got? For someone who prides themselves on being three steps ahead of everyone else, how does it feel to be blindsided?"

Fontaneau's lips curled into an expression of utter hatred. Sylfe thought it was probably the first genuine emotion she'd seen him display since she'd met him.

But the majority of her attention was on Tane. The Opitauan

was unwaveringly stolid with a face not disposed to giving away his thoughts. But perhaps there was something there – not just wishful thinking on her part – that registered a certain disappointment in the usually unassailable head of the Fontaneau Family.

"Fine," Fontaneau spat. "Then I suggest you float where you are and we'll float where we are. We'll see whose supplies last the longest. I suspect mine."

"How are your calculations coming along, Markusz?" Sylfe said, her gaze remaining fixed on Fontaneau.

"Ready," came the reply.

"Well, the universe might be nearing its end, but at least we've all lived long enough to see the day when the great Ernes Fontaneau is confounded not once but twice," she said. "Let's get started."

Behind her there was a rising hum of energy. The device Markusz and Elly had built was a webwork of hexagonal components twisting in to create a three-dimensional cradle for a very familiar shape. As Sylfe turned to watch, flickers of light danced between the components like candle flames, there then gone. The hum grew in pitch and intensity, sounding like a tone played on a flute, then a human voice, then a choir – a resonant frequency she could feel on her skin.

The flames were dancing now within the framework, twisting together, gaining form and glowing with more and more colours: green becoming yellow to orange, red, violet. The knotwork of colour lengthened, thickened, became more persistent, bending around itself, its two ends flickering like tiny fountains of stars, seeking each other out, closer, closer, closer, then melting into one another.

In the comm window there was a scream. Sylfe saw Rachik staring at an absence where a moment ago there had been an annulus.

And in the control hub, a dazzling brightness as the annulus shone forth, bathing every upturned face in its warm glow.

Everyone was smiling. Caught in rapture at its beauty.

"Get it back!" This from Fontaneau.

"I can't!" Rachik howled. "We left the equipment on the planet."

"That doesn't exactly look right," Helena said.

"I know," Markusz said. "The reset didn't work. The annulus is operating under the same parameters as Rachik's fucked-up version."

He looked at Eleven. "I suppose you take this as a good sign?"

Eleven smiled. "I prefer the figures to speak for themselves."

She wiped the current window and showed the new transform that was building.

Markusz watched the equations scroll past. Helena leaned in beside him.

"Well," she said. "That is …"

"Unusual," he said. "The topography is becoming …"

In the comm window, Fontaneau was red-faced and screaming. "Leeuwin, ram their ship! Order the gunboat to attack!"

Sylfe watched as Tane rested his remaining hand on Fontaneau's shoulder. Fontaneau was so startled by the contact he halted his tirade.

"It's over, Patri," Tane said. "The Matri has won. We can't attack the annulus. And it is on her good grace we must now rely for survival."

"About that," Markusz piped up from behind Sylfe, "we need to get all the ships back to Redout as quickly as possible."

"You heard that?" Sylfe said. But she wasn't talking to Fontaneau.

Leeuwin nodded. "Course plotted and making best speed. Mr Samson, contact the gunboat and the orbital to follow on. Tane?"

"Yes, Captain?" the Opitauan said, his voice and face unfazed by the shift in power that had just occurred.

"Take Patri Fontaneau to his quarters where he'll be safe."

And just like that, it was over. Sylfe would have liked to take a moment to celebrate but she didn't think the universe was inclined to wait.

She started the vessel back the way they'd come, then swivelled in her seat to face Markusz, Eleven, Elly and Firmin.

"Care to enlighten me?" she said.

"Still theoretical," Markusz said, looking pointedly at Eleven, who was as sublimely calm as always. "But the annulus and the Effect have been acting on each other ever since the first shrinkage. The operating parameters of both and the underlying mathematics have undergone … Well, phase changes is how you might describe it. But it was impossible to calculate what each change would be. Personally, that fact alone scared the living shit out of me, but others were a little more sanguine about it."

"Or hopeful," Elly said. "Like Eleven here."

"*I'm* hoping you'll get to an actual point," Sylfe said.

"He does this," Elly said. "He's not very good at explaining things."

"Well, it's a little hard to explain," Markusz snapped. "To a teenage layperson that is."

"I think I can help," Eleven said, and Markusz threw up his hands. "The Effect siphons energy out of this universe. The annulus was a barrier, but now it's becoming a –"

"A bridge!" Markusz finished, clearly unwilling to be upstaged.

"To where?" Firmin asked.

"Does it matter?" Markusz said. "Out of here, though I have my own theories about where it might lead."

"Spare us," Elly said.

"The important thing is we need to get back to Redout orbit. There's another shrinkage coming and I think this will be the last one."

"Alright. We'll be there in a matter of minutes," Sylfe said. "Then what?"

"Then it should be obvious," Markusz said.

37

Markusz looked again at the transform window Eleven had shared and opened another, mapping the local spacetime substrate. Yes. Things were definitely occurring around the siphon point.

"They don't need to hear your other universe theory," Helena said. "Or what you think this ship does with the Effect energy. But do you really think it can go home?"

"We're going to find out," he said under his breath. Then, louder, "Look!"

Sylfe had shared a window tracking their progress down the tunnel of safe space towards Redout. They were in convoy now: this ship, the Haibeu transport and all Sylfe's sunbarques, followed by the traffic control station, the highliner and the remaining M-Def gunboat. Redout was close, its face lit only by the glow of Teel-Attar radiation, so it was easy to miss what was happening, but Markusz could see it building in the substrate view so he knew where to look.

He pointed at the image. "There."

At the dead centre of Redout, something wasn't quite right, as if the visual relays for the window were malfunctioning. The planet was bleeding around a dark hole that brightened as it continued to grow. Three-dimensional space bent around it and started to fall inward as the hole deepened, the centre becoming brighter and glowing with a multitude of colours as the planet melted into it.

"We're going to make it," Markusz said.

"You've saved them," Helena said. She smiled and he smiled back. "You don't need me any more."

"What? No! If you're just my memory, you'll do what I say.

You'll stay because I want you to."

"Do you?" she said and vanished.

"No, no, no! I do. I want you. Come back!" He slammed his hands on the central table, shaking the annulus in its cradle, and looked wildly around the room for a glimpse of her.

A hand on his shoulder. "Are you alright?"

It was Sylfe who had spoken, but everyone in the control hub was looking at him as if he'd lost it and they really couldn't afford for him to fall apart right now.

He shook his head. She'd be back. She'd gone before. But he felt deep down that he was lying to himself.

He tried a smile, but from the reactions he got he could probably have tried a little harder.

"It's Helena," he said. "She's gone."

"I'm sorry," Sylfe said.

"There will be a reason," Eleven said.

But Markusz didn't know what that might be.

He shook himself and focused on the window. "We're going in there," he said, pointing at the now blinding portal ahead. "Keep away from the sides."

Behind them, the last vestiges of space collapsed.

Whether they were traversing a bridge, tunnel or n-dimensional polytope, the landscape was giving Markusz a headache. It kept unfolding in unnatural ways. And they had to keep moving because everything behind them was folding into itself, or possibly extruding into another form of non-contiguous space that was no longer accessible. The maths would look interesting if he had time to ponder it.

It was all very pretty though: the walls glowed with a million colours like a constantly shifting kaleidoscope. And the annulus was protecting them still. Reality inside their ship – and presumably the others in their convoy – remained strictly three-dimensional. It was his and Helena's greatest achievement. All he had left of her now.

The others in the control hub watched the exterior display in silence. Only Sylfe was busy, keeping their flight steady. Which was a feat in itself.

"I presume – with no actual foundation to do so – that we're going somewhere?" she asked.

"There's a couple of possibilities," Markusz said. "The Effect harvests energy from universes to feed what you might think of as the overversal engine – whatever that actually is – to create new universes. If we're unlucky, we'll end up at whatever the entry point for that process is and be ... recycled."

"New birthed stars will be made of us," Eleven said.

"Well, yes," Markusz said. "From a romantic point of view, pretty cool. But probably not so cool in real life."

"And if we're lucky?" Sylfe asked.

Markusz paused, recalling Helena's warning not to appear too insane to the others. But there wasn't much they could do about it now.

"This ship was created to divert the Effect energy for its own purposes. If we're lucky, we'll end up wherever that diversion leads."

"Another revelation you didn't share," Sylfe said. "How did you work this out?"

"It's more of a conjecture than an actual finding."

"Not exactly filling us with hope," Elly said.

"We're still alive," Firmin said. "We wouldn't be if we'd stayed on Garia." She placed an arm around Elly, drawing her close.

It was only looking at them together now that Markusz thought they might be related. Somewhere Helena was no doubt shaking her head at how dim he was about human relationships.

The room tipped as the tunnel twisted in what Markusz thought of as a left-up-in-through direction that made him queasy. But after that, things levelled out. Up ahead, he thought he caught sight of a sliver of black among all the colour. He blinked, but it was still there.

"We may be about to reach our natural or unnatural conclusion," he said.

The darkness became clearer and, unlike the shifting colours of this space, persistent. He saw now that its edges glowed blue as with an electrical discharge.

"Maybe don't get too close to the side if you can avoid it," he added.

Markusz reached into the window and pulled the image so the glowing rim was magnified. The light came from something attached to the walls of a perfectly black tunnel. Something material and engineered and extending into the dark as far as he could see. The space near it appeared dimmed by comparison.

"I think I might actually be right about this," he said.

"About what?" Firmin asked.

The structure thickened as they moved closer, taking up more and more of the tunnel, leaching the colour out of everything.

"There must be a safe exit point," he said. "The ship came this way. It had to."

Of course it didn't have to at all, but that would mean they were about to die, and they'd come too far and survived too much for that to happen. Not that the universe – any universe – gave a shit.

"We're going in," Sylfe said.

The superstructure of what Markusz thought of as the universal energy harvester pressed in all around them. But there was still space to squeeze through, and up ahead – did he imagine it? – were pinpoints of stars.

The ship started to accelerate.

"Not my doing," Sylfe said, startled. "We're caught in something."

Their speed increased again. Glowing blue superstructure crowded in closer and became speed-blurred, the starry darkness swelling. Markusz grabbed the table, feeling sick.

The engines were suddenly roaring and the whole room vibrated. And then they were through.

Space opened up all around and Markusz saw that they, the sunbarques, the highliner and everyone else were safe in a universe full of stars so beautiful his throat almost closed up.

Beneath them, some kind of macrostructure tethered to their exit point, stretching out to all sides. An energy collector or transformer or maybe something else entirely. Markusz would find out. They all would. Because they were going to live.

He sank back in his chair, feeling disoriented, exultant, exhausted, stunned. Exactly how everyone else in the room looked.

Then Firmin spoke, her voice drenched in disbelief. "We're being hailed."

She opened the channel. A voice spoke but the language was gibberish.

"If we're in the land of the shipmakers," Eleven said, "our translation program may help. Repeating message."

The voice spoke again. "Harvest Base to Ship UI791. Come in. Can you hear us?"

"Are there any visuals with the signal?" Markusz said. He couldn't believe what he'd heard.

Eleven opened a comm window to show a woman who spoke the words again.

It was Helena. She looked exactly like … Actually, her hair was different. Shorter. But she was there. Living and breathing. Markusz's heart felt like it was plummeting off a cliff and jumping out of his chest at the same time.

"Open a channel," he said.

"Ready," Eleven said.

"It's you," Markusz said.

Sylfe looked at the awestruck expression on Markusz's face, then back at the woman in the comm window. "Is that —"

Markusz cut her off. "It's Helena. Parallel-universe Helena, I mean. Not my Helena."

In the window, Helena's eyes narrowed. "Who the hell are you?"

"Okay, parallel-ish," Markusz said. "No 'me' in this universe, maybe?"

"Your mother probably strangled you at birth," Elly said.

Sylfe felt this wasn't the most auspicious start to inter-universal communications. It was time for an adult to take over.

"I imagine this is something of a shock," she said. "It certainly is for us. But our universe just collapsed and we only just made it out alive and found ourselves here."

"That ship is one of ours," parallel Helena said. "But none have ever returned."

"Ah," Markusz said, "I suspect that's because none of them has ever had an annulus onboard." He turned to indicate the shining band of colour behind them.

"We're bringing you in," parallel Helena said and the window closed.

The floor shifted under them and Sylfe saw from the flight control that they were moving on a path directly for a tall tower-like station floating above the massive construct that spread out before them.

She opened windows to Roche and Leeuwin.

"The natives are friendly so far," she said. "Stick with us."

EPILOGUE

"How much longer do you think this is going to take?" Markusz asked Sylfe.

"You don't exactly have any place else to be, do you," she said under her breath. "Besides, we need you here in case there are more annulus questions. Just sit back and look non-threatening."

Well, that wouldn't be difficult, Markusz thought. But this was the third day of talks and he was beginning to get restless. He'd rather be out inspecting the extraversal energy collector they'd seen on arrival and working out what made it tick.

Still, things could be a lot worse. They might have found themselves in a universe of alien cannibals or something equally dire. But there were, it seemed, more social, ethical and moral parallels between his universe and this one than there were differences. The Sovranty – which was what they called their government – was more cohesive and monolithic than the Thousand Worlds had been, perhaps in response to the threat of universal collapse they'd overcome. But it afforded Markusz and the others legal status as refugees, which meant there was a framework for dealings between them – once Markusz and Eleven had upgraded the arrivals' augments for instant translation.

Apart from Markusz, Sylfe, Firmin and Eleven, there were several desks worth of bureaucratic functionaries and administrative personnel involved in the talks. Markusz had had plenty of time to ponder what on earth they all did, without much success. It seemed the Sovranty was deeply in love with bureaucracy.

"All stand."

There was a rumble as chairs were pushed back and people got to their feet.

The woman in charge – Adjudicator Taisa Maas – entered the chamber and took her seat behind the raised bench.

"Please be seated," she said.

There was another rumble and scraping of chairs, and Adjudicator Maas began as she'd begun every session, with a recap of discussions.

Markusz quickly tuned out. The annulus represented a huge bargaining point for his fellow refugees and he was happy for them to capitalise on that to push for whatever they could. But that didn't mean he wanted to sit through all the tedious details. He'd done his bit on day one by explaining the workings of the annulus, which was something of a sensation among the scientists of this universe as it suggested new avenues to engage with and possibly even manipulate the Effect, as well as allowing their extraversal crews a means to return to their own universe.

The other Helena had been there for his presentation and had asked a number of very salient questions. While her presence had been a major distraction – he was sure he'd rambled on a bit more than usual – it did give him the opportunity to observe her more closely and to see the differences between her and his Helena.

For a start, her name was Aliona. Her manner was a little different too. Far more formal, though that was perhaps because of the situation they were in. But she looked a little older as well. More careworn. Of course, she hadn't had a Markusz in her life – perhaps that's what she was missing? He knew that Helena had changed him a lot from the self-absorbed and socially awkward boy who had first joined her on the CSTO team. Still, he did see a lot of Helena in Aliona and it wasn't something he could ignore. There just wasn't anything he could do about it. This woman was her own person. It wasn't fair – and a little creepy – to want to turn her into someone else.

"With respect, Adjudicator Maas …"

Firmin's voice broke into Markusz's thoughts and he saw she'd risen to address their arbiter.

"Your offer is, as we have already indicated, most gracious. But we want – we need – more than simple Sovranty citizenship and the right to live in your cities. Ask any of your own citizens where they are from and they will tell you planet, city, suburb, street. All with a certain pride, because that is part of who they are and how they came to be that person.

"We are unlike any refugees your system has had to deal with before because where we come from – our place – no longer exists. There's not even a part of visible space we can point to and say 'this was ours'. Any sentient being needs that if they are to truly know who they are. Our communities need that if they are to thrive. To suggest anything less is to consign us to oblivion. Within a generation there will be no Garian, no Paradisan, no Haibeu. We cannot allow that. And we hope you can understand and agree with us."

"So, you want a planet?" Maas asked.

"The shared history of our communities is a troubled one," Sylfe said, also standing.

That was putting it mildly, Markusz thought. There was no way the Garians would settle a world alongside Paradisans.

"The Garians need their own world," Firmin said.

Maas's finely sculpted eyebrows headed north. "You want two worlds then?" she said. "Or perhaps three?"

Eleven got to her feet beside Firmin and Sylfe. "The Haibeu are happy to live alongside the Paradisans and Garians," she said. "As long as we can have our own space."

Markusz saw Sylfe's smile broaden. He'd been observing her and Eleven over the past couple of days and it was clear they were growing closer. He knew the signs: he'd lived through just this sort of thing with Helena. He was glad for both of them. Helena notwithstanding, he hadn't seriously considered a relationship with Sylfe. He didn't want a romance with someone else.

"Two planets," Maas repeated. "And the resources to settle them."

"The planets of the Thousand Worlds numbered eight hundred and sixty-seven," Sylfe said. "The energy of all those worlds now sustains your universe. Two worlds doesn't seem all that much to ask for."

Maas's countenance darkened and Markusz thought Sylfe might have pushed things a little too far. After all, the Sovranty had little choice in doing what they'd done. And Markusz's universe was doomed anyway. Still, Maas and others may feel some measure of guilt about it, and if so perhaps they could afford to be generous.

"If that is all, we will consider your statements and adjourn to deliberate," Maas said finally.

"What do you think?" Markusz asked once the meeting had broken up.

"I don't know," Sylfe said. "But if Fontaneau was calling the shots, they'd probably have fired us all into the sun."

Markusz grunted agreement. Fontaneau was still confined to quarters where he could do no harm. Markusz found he didn't even have the energy to despise the man any more. Without his wealth and position, he was nothing.

Sylfe and Eleven went to find something to eat, and Firmin set off to find Elly, leaving Markusz to wander down to the observation lounge that spun slowly above the extraversal collector.

He supposed the others would be leaving for good soon. He, however, was to remain here to pass on his annulus knowledge. It was only then it struck him how alone he was going to be when everyone else was gone. The wonder he'd felt looking at the massive superstructure was replaced with a feeling of insignificance.

"I'm not interrupting, am I?"

Markusz turned from the observation window to see Aliona. "No, not at all," he said, standing quickly. "I was just wool-gathering."

Her brow crinkled in just the way Helena's used to and he realised the translator was perhaps not so good on idiom.

"I was thinking about nothing in particular is what I mean."

She smiled. "I wanted to tell you that I've been reassigned. I'll be the lead engineer on the annulus project. And I'm looking forward to working with you."

She held out a hand. Markusz took it for just a moment, because any longer than that and he felt his heart might explode.

He swallowed and said, "That's very good news. I'm very much looking forward to working with you."

She smiled again. "I'll see you in the project lab tomorrow morning then."

"Until then," Markusz said.

Aliona left and Markusz felt … He didn't know what he felt.

"Have you told her she's a duplicate of your dead wife?"

It was Elly.

"That's a bit of a conversation killer," he said. "We'll probably have to work up to that. What are you doing here anyway?"

"We've got our two worlds."

"Just like that?"

"Just like that. So I wanted to say goodbye. You know, before all the formal goodbyes and stuff."

"You're going with your grandmother?" he asked.

"For a while. Then I think I'll join Sylfe and Eleven on their world. And after that … there's a whole universe to explore." She flashed him a smile before turning more serious. "I've got you to thank for that. We all have."

Finally, the recognition I deserve, Markusz thought. But he didn't say it out loud. His Helena would be proud of how far he'd come.

"And what about you?" Elly asked.

Markusz looked in the direction Aliona had gone. "I don't know. Not many people get a second chance at something. But I think I'm going to take it. And that makes me feel …"

"Hopeful?" Elly said.

Markusz smiled. "Yes. I think maybe it does."

THANK YOU

After spending so many years working on and refining the Lenticular Series, the first half of *The End Times of Markusz Zielinski* flowed out of my subconscious and onto the page in a little under a year. I didn't have a specific ending in mind at the time, but I knew I wanted the back half of End Times to go in unexpected directions. I had to set the manuscript aside to focus on publishing the Lenticular books and during that hiatus, I read Katie Mack's excellent *The End of Everything (Astrophysically Speaking)*. As well as providing a refresher in astrophysics and cosmology it presents five possible scenarios for how the universe might end. It inspired me to think up another way that the universe might cease to exist and I hope it's been as much fun for you to read as it has been for me to write.

As always I'd like to thank my own 'Helena': editor Nicola O'Shea, who pushed me to write better than I could on my own. Thanks also to fellow Serapeum writers' group member Peter Hickman, for valuable input on an early draft of Markusz's and Sylfe's adventures, and to real-life scientist and friend Susanna Guatelli. Talking with her about the work she does for the European Space Agency, CERN and other incredible projects is a regular source of inspiration for me.

If you've enjoyed *The End Times of Markusz Zielinski* please consider leaving a rating or review on Goodreads, Amazon or your website of choice. It really makes a difference. Thank you for reading!

ABOUT THE AUTHOR

Keith Stevenson is the author of the science fiction thriller *Horizon* and The Lenticular Series. His short fiction has appeared in *Andromeda Spaceways Inflight Magazine*, *Aurealis Magazine*, *Oceans of the Mind* and the Agog! Press anthology *Agog! Fantastic Fiction*. He's a past editor of *Aurealis – Australian Science Fiction and Fantasy Magazine*, hosted the Terra Incognita Speculative Fiction Podcast, and edited and published *Dimension6*, the free Australian speculative fiction electronic magazine.

Subscribe to *Beyond Newsletter* for news on current and future projects, discounts and freebies, including 'Traitor's Gathering' a Lenticular Series prequel story. Scan the QR code:

WWW.KEITHSTEVENSON.COM

GLOSSARY

atmosphere reprocessors	Devices used by the Garian settlers to make the atmosphere breathable.
augments	Hardware that enables M-World citizens to access and interface with ubiquitous electronic database, information and control systems. The hardware is generally grown into the foetus while it is still developing.
augment window	An information space which can be private or shared between citizens.
beanstalk	Redout space elevators. Redout has two beanstalks servicing the western and eastern hemispheres of the planet.
Common	The *lingua franca* of M-Worlds.
Consource	The trading hub and clearing house for M-Worlds, where planets and companies trade goods and services.
Corps d'Ingénieurs	A Paradisan Guild contracted by the Great Families to undertake any and all engineering work.
Council Tower	One of the tallest buildings on Redout, it houses the Redout Council Chambers and ancillary offices. Sub-levels also provide accommodation for council members and functionaries.
CSTO Task Force	Congress of the Thousand Worlds Cooperative Sciences and Technology Organisation (CSTO) Task Force on the Effect.
Destruction sur Commande SA	A company wholly owned by the Great Paradisan Family of Fontaneau, specialising in complete planetary destruction, remodelling and terraforming.

Fabrika SA	A company owned by the Great Paradisan Family of Denantes that provides equipment and equipment maintenance to all forms of industry including mining and planetary and space construction.
Fordana	Providers of management control systems and infrastructure to M-Worlds. The Fordana are consummate bureaucrats able to deliver whatever project is required and interact seamlessly with other contracting agencies or governments.
Fukei	Home system of The Haibeu.
Galactische Handelsonderneming (GH)	The pre-eminent trading company for M-Worlds providing carriage and logistics for all goods and services between M-World members.
Garia	Former name of Redout.
Great Paradisan Families	The powerful founding Families of Paradis who comprise that planet's oligarchy and include Fontaneau, Cachand, Denantes, Depharian, Archambault, Normand and Savatier.
Haibeu	Cybernetically enhanced group that provide information technology systems design, support and maintenance to the Fordana. The Haibeu cyberocracy lives on the planet Fukei IV.
Herku Depharian	Paradisan Oligarch who funded and led the original settlement of Garia by Paradisan refugees.
highliner	GH mass transport vessel, normally used for carrying goods between M-Worlds, but pressed into service as refugee transports.
Hiver	Derogatory term for Haibeu.
ident	Information encoded in an M-World citizen's augments identifying them in the system.
Ind	Non-gendered honorific, contraction of 'individual'.
justacorps	A knee-length fitted coat with wide turned back cuffs, often decorated with brocade at collar, lapels and cuff. Fashionable amongst the citizens of Wiszenti.

Kaito	Opitauan honorific given to a leader among warriors.
Khukuri	Traditional Opitauan knife – as large as a short sword with an inwardly curved cutting edge.
lumen	Portable light capable of autonomous operation.
M-Def	Short name of the Thousand World Congress Defence Force.
mover	Ubiquitous term for planetary transport units which can be dedicated to single, small group or mass use.
M-Worlds	Short name for the collection of worlds that make up the Thousand World Congress.
Palisades	A suburb of Redout Central built along the original barrier wall constructed by the first Garian settlers. The Palisades overlooks a river plateau although the Redout Project has completely urbanised the land. The apartment towers of the Palisades are inhabited by wealthier Redout residents.
Paradis	Planet of a Plutocractic Oligarchy
Paradisan	Inhabitant of Paradis
Paradisan Combine	A group of Paradisan companies that together provide bespoke planetary, solar and system engineering solutions for the Thousand Worlds.
Patri/ Matri	Formal title for the de facto head of each Paradisan Great Family.
Redout/ Redout Project	A project commissioned by M-Worlds Congress to create a last refuge for humanity on the planet of Garia.
Redout Central	Primary city of Redout and location of the Redout Confederation Council and various headquarters of the Redout Project.
Redout Charter	The legal document passed by M-World Congress providing for the legal powers and authorities of the Redout Project, the Redout Confederation Council and the various project bodies and organisations listed therein.

Redout Confederation	A group formed to manage the Redout Project. The Confederation includes the government of Garia and a number of other governments and organisations who have resources and expertise necessary for the Redout Project and who were proximate enough to move operations to Redout as the emergency unfolded.
Redout Confederation Council	The group of senior representatives that oversee the project.
Redout Refugee Management	Administrative body overseeing intake assessment and resettlement of refugee arrivals on Redout.
Respaxon	Home of the M-World Mathematical Seminary and adoptive home planet of Markusz Zielinski who was taken there as part of the M-World Screenings at the age of thirteen. Coincidentally, Respaxon is the homeworld of Kelan Teel and Wasim Rachik.
retasker	A device capable of breaking down physical objects and using the raw material to build anything required.
SolEng SA	A company specialising in all forms of solar engineering, majority held by the Great Paradisan Family of Cachand.
Standards (shortened from Earth Standard)	Baseline planetary measure - where the baseline is Earth and all measures are proportional to the Earth measurement.
sub-mover	Underground mass transport.
substrate	The dimensions above, below and between four-dimensional spacetime.
sunbarque	Specialised vessel owned and operated by SolEng SA for survey and engineering operations on solar bodies.
tat-têtes	Garian slang for Opitauan security. Literally 'tattoo-head'.
Teel-Attar radiation	Visible radiation that resembles a slowly blooming flower seen after a region of space is destroyed by the Effect.

Thousand Worlds	Name for the collection of human-colonised worlds existing under the Thousand World Congress.
Thousand Worlds Congress	The overarching governmental body of the Thousand Worlds.
windowwall	Smart, glass-like barrier used in contemporary building.
Wiszenti	Planet of Markusz Zielinski's birth. A member of M-Worlds but with a constantly changing political system that suffered regular upheaval, revolution and replacement.

The Lenticular Series

Two outcasts. One goal. Stop Earth.

Available in print and ebook

Available as an ebook

Coeur de Lion

Thirty-four light years from Earth, the explorer ship *Magellan* is nearing its objective – the Iota Persei system. But when ship commander Cait Dyson wakes from deepsleep, she finds her co-pilot dead and the ship's AI unresponsive. Cait works with the rest of her crew to regain control of the ship, until they learn that Earth is facing total environmental collapse and their mission must change if humanity is to survive.

As tensions rise and personal and political agendas play out in the ship's cramped confines, the crew finally reach the planet Horizon, where everything they know will be challenged.

"Refreshingly plausible, politically savvy, and full of surprises, *Horizon* takes you on a harrowing thrill-ride through the depths of space and the darkness of the human heart." – **Sean Williams**, New York Times bestselling author of the Astropolis and Twinmaker series

"Crackling science fiction with gorgeous trans-human and cybernetic trimmings. Keith Stevenson's debut novel soars." – **Marianne De Pierres**, award-winning author of the Parrish Plessis, Sentients of Orion and Peacemaker series

Available as a print book and ebook